Paint Me True

Paint Me True

A NOVEL

E.M. TIPPETTS

Paint Me True is a work of fiction. Names, characters, places, and incidents are either the product of the author's imagination or are used fictitiously. Any resemblance to actual persons, living or dead, events, business establishments or locales is entirely coincidental.

No part of this book may be reproduced, scanned, or distributed in any printed or electronic form without permission. All rights reserved.

Cover design © 2011 Tiger Bright Studios

Copyright © 2011 by Emily Mah Tippetts

ISBN-13: 978-1468002515
ISBN-10: 1468002511

*for Trevor,
I know you must love me
because you read
my rough drafts*

Big Night Out

Six months isn't a long relationship for normal people, but Len and I weren't normal people. We were Mormons. For our kind, it was a courtship long enough to be respectable, but not so long that it looked hopeless. Six months was a terrible oversight on my part. One minute I'd agreed to go with the guy on a pity date, and now here I was, being taken on a Big Night Out by the nerdiest loser I'd ever met. What was even worse? I let him take me out on this date. Whether this was out of pity for him or myself, I couldn't say.

Said date was at a steakhouse. As we walked in, Len held open the heavy, wooden door for me, which had been stained dark and shellacked with a layer of varnish. Odd the details I noticed as I tried to avert my attention from him. His worn slacks, with threads that brushed the tops of his not exactly formal shoes cut a sharp contrast with the warm and luxurious interior of the restaurant. His shirt was threadbare, but he'd ironed it, at least, which meant he'd made a real effort, and he vibrated with nervousness. His gaze darted here then there, not resting anywhere for more than a second, and his fingers drummed against his leg. I'd never seen him do that before.

"Reservation for two, Leonard Hodge," he told the hostess.

She ran a perfectly manicured nail down the seating chart and blinked in surprise. "Table outside? Under the awning?"

"With the outdoor heaters." Len nodded. It wasn't raining at the moment, but clouds hid the late evening sun. And this was Portland, Oregon, so an awning and heaters were no doubt a permanent feature of the outdoor table.

I didn't even know this place had an outdoor table. It was the most expensive steakhouse in the neighborhood, not a place I dined often, but Len had said he wanted to make this evening, "Something special."

I'd spent almost as much time on my makeup that evening as I had on the last painting I'd done on commission. Nothing looked or felt right, so I'd washed my face and started over again and again. I didn't want to look overdone, but I had to hide the puffiness under my gray-green eyes and my sunken cheeks from a sleepless night, and I had to draw attention away from my mouth, as I knew I'd scowl no matter how hard I tried not to. My hair was a mouse brown that wasn't dark enough to be dramatic or light enough to be notable, but it curled just right and was easy to style. I'd pinned it up in an elegant twist.

The waitress picked up two padded leather menus from her podium and led us through the restaurant and out the back door onto a covered porch, decorated with some potted plants and fruit trees, and a table with two chairs and two long candles burning away, shedding their muted gold light on the dark tablecloth and white china dishes.

Len pulled out my chair for me, and I did my best to compose myself as I sat down. I smoothed my hands down my blouse and skirt, crossed my ankles, and tucked my feet under my chair.

The hostess laid the menus in front of us and slipped back into the restaurant.

"Sooo," said Len. He took the seat opposite me. From the determined look in his eyes, I could see that he wasn't going to wait until after the meal.

I squared my shoulders. I could do this. I'd turned down proposals before from guys way better looking and more enthusiastic than Len.

"I- look, you know how I feel about you. These last six months have been unreal, just... yeah, unreal." Eloquent he wasn't. "So, I think we should stop seeing each other."

That was a new twist. He was going to pretend to break up with me and then pop the question? I was supposed to look devastated and then really happy? I'd been planning to look uncomfortable and politely upset, but he'd thrown me off. I laid my wrists on the table and waited for him to continue.

"That's all," he said. "Figured we could have one last meal together and make it a nice one. I mean, thank you for the last six months. That was cool, but it's time to put you out of your misery, you know?"

In the silence that followed, I heard one of the outdoor heaters go tick-tick-tick, as the metal expanded with the heat. A soft breeze stirred the leaves of the plants.

Len covered his face with his hands for a moment, then pumped his fist in the air. "Yes! I did it. I mean... sorry, I don't mean to be a jerk. Really, I know it's gotta hurt your pride to be dumped by me, but better than the alternative, right? Look, order whatever you want. You deserve it. You just got broken up with. If you need a filet mignon to deal with it, be my guest." He gestured at my menu.

All of his nervousness had evaporated and now he grinned a goofy grin. "It's okay to look happy," he said. "I mean, come on. You and me? That never made sense, though it was cool to be that guy for a while, you know? The guy who got to date you." He flipped open his menu and perused the contents.

I looked down at my hands and saw they were shaking. A lump rose in my throat.

"Whoa, what's wrong?" he said. "You didn't want this to go another way, did you?"

I shook my head, which wasn't the nicest thing to do, but he was being honest with me, so I returned the favor. "No," I said. I dabbed my eyes with the corner of my napkin. "Sorry. You just surprised me."

"I surprised me too." He grinned again. "I mean, not that I didn't plan this. I just wondered if I'd chicken out at the last minute. But look, I am sorry, okay? What do you need? Prime rib? Top sirloin? Extra chocolate on your dessert? Or are you meeting up with your friends for dessert so that you can all gossip about how you almost bit the bullet?"

"What?" That came out before I could think.

"Hey, it's nice of you to look all surprised, like you don't know what I'm talking about, but gimme a break. An hour from now you'll be in the ice cream parlor gossiping with Hattie about this whole evening."

"No," I spluttered. Len was a *guy*. He wasn't supposed to intuit things like that. He was supposed to be clueless and loyal and enamored with me.

"Don't lie," said Len.

"It's in ninety minutes," I confessed.

"Wow, you must've thought I was gonna hire some musicians or something-"

"No." That idea now felt absurd, that he'd make some extra effort.

"It'll give you time to eat dessert here and there, though. I think you're entitled."

A tear spotted the tablecloth in front of me. I dabbed at my eyes again with my napkin.

Len stopped smirking and stared. "I'm sorry. You all right? I know this is a real low point for you. I wasn't sure how to do it. I mean, over the phone is too mean and I knew I'd never get the nerve up to do it on a date unless I prepared so... I did this." He had the palest blue eyes. Those and his sandy blond hair made him a pretty decent looking guy, if only he'd get a haircut now and then. It wasn't scruffy kind of long – even that might've worked on him. It was "I'm-too-cheap-to-get-regular-haircuts" kind of long, and his shirt was even more worn than I'd noted before. There were holes in the breast pocket. I wondered how many years he'd had it. "E-li-za," he singsonged my name. "You know you're happy about this. It's okay. The waterworks were real nice of you, but enough. I'm flattered. Let's eat steak."

Now he was teasing me? I covered my face with my hands.

Len fell silent.

I did my best to compose myself. For a moment I toyed with the idea of making a beeline for the bathroom, but if I did that, everyone inside the restaurant would know I'd been humiliated. I didn't need to make this moment public. I wondered what was over the fence behind the ornamental fruit trees, and for an insane moment I pictured myself trying to vault it. In a skirt.

Len still stared at me. It was mortifying. "So... did I at least make this date memorable for you?"

How to answer such a stupid question? "Yeah," I whispered.

"Score." He said it tentatively. No laughter. "Do you want me to take you home?"

"Can we not go through the restaurant?"

"Liza, I'm really sorry. I thought you'd be happy and relieved. Seriously, that's what I wanted. But I guess I screwed this up too."

I made myself take a deep breath, then another, the cool air flushing all of the quivering sadness out of my chest. I could look him in the eye now.

He really did look contrite, and he began to fidget, moving the silverware around on his side of the table as if it wasn't laid out perfectly to begin with.

I considered my options. We could leave. I could ask him to drive me home and say goodbye to him and have that be that. We could stay, and eat steak in an uneasy silence and I could make him pay, financially, for all this nonsense. The former option seemed like the obvious one. I ought to storm out of this situation and rake him over the coals. It's what I always did when a guy treated me badly.

But even just the prospect of having a fight wore me out. I wasn't sure I could sustain the drama for the entire drive home, and if I could, then what? I'd have to be huffy to him at church, maybe? Whisper about him to my friends? Ten years ago, that would've been easy. I'd have done it without thinking. Now though...

"Look," he said, "you sure you don't just want to have some steak and that can be that?"

"Yeah," I said. "All right."

The List

"He did what?" Hattie still stood, her light jacket half off and half on. The ice cream parlor was empty except for us. Most people weren't crazy enough to eat ice cream on a chill night like this. It had begun to rain, not heavily, but enough to make the air that gusted in the door smell sweet.

"Look, that's not the worse part," I said.

"You got dumped by *Len,* and that's not the worst part? What did you do? Propose to him?"

"No, I-"

"Did you beg him to take you back?"

"No. Um-"

"Did you run into the restaurant with your eye makeup all smudged from crying?"

"*No-*"

"Did you-"

"Stop. Let me talk, okay? It's not anything that happened tonight. The worst part is..."

Hattie tugged her jacket the rest of the way off, sat down across from me, and leaned in as if drawn by a magnet.

The words were stuck in my throat. I couldn't look my friend in the eye.

"Do you have cancer?"

7

"No."
"Pre-cancerous-"
"No."
"Did another relative die?"
"No."
"Is your dad getting divorced and your step mom about to throw you out of her old house?"
I shook my head.
"She going to charge you rent?"
"No."
"Your last painting got rejected?"
"No."
"The Church is going to ex-communicate you for your subversive art?"
"No."
"You're pregnant with Len's baby?"
"No."
"You're pregnant with someone else's baby?"
"No."
"You registered as a Democrat?"
"No-"
"You've decided you're a lesbian?"
"No, just-"
"You voted for Obama?"
"Stop!"
"Look, I love you, but if you join the liberals, our friendship is over."
"I did not join 'the liberals'." I made air quotes. "So spare me the lecture about Obama being the antichrist."
"An antichrist, not *the* antichrist. The scriptures say-"
"I'm thirty." There. I'd said it. "And nine months." Three months away from the dreaded age of thirty-one, when I would be too old to go to church in the singles ward. My records would be sent to a regular old family ward full of married couples and children.

Paint Me True

Hattie sat back, then grinned as if she'd won a bet. "I knew it!"

"You did?"

"Well, I knew there was some reason you were dating my loser cousin."

Yes, that was another detail. Hattie and Len's mothers were sisters. She had his same pale blue eyes, though there the aesthetic similarity ended. While he was rail thin and all angles, Hattie was all contours. Full cheeks, a graceful curve to the neck, hands with short fingers that always rested closed, little fists even when she was relaxed. Her hair was light brown and cascaded down her back in gleaming waves.

I raked my hair back from my face with my nails and then stared miserably down at my hands.

"It's not too late," said Hattie.

"I'm not gonna find my soulmate in three months, and please-" I held up one hand "-don't tell me some story from the pioneer days about an ancestor of yours who met someone and got married in five days or something."

Hattie smirked at me. That was something else she and Len had in common, the ability to laugh without making a sound. A dimpled cheek and twinkling eyes said it all. "You can still date even when you're out of the Church's young single adult program. It's allowed, you know? And so what if you can't come to the singles ward? You'll be that exotic girl the guys don't see every Sunday. You can totally make this work for you."

"Hey," said the guy behind the counter. "Your sundaes are ready."

Hattie made a pushing gesture to keep me in my seat and went to get them. Once she'd returned, she slid mine and a spoon across the table and said, "Your age isn't why you're single. It's the fact that you settled. You have to stop doing that."

The truth was the last thing I needed to hear at the moment. I wanted more sympathy first. My first spoonful of ice cream was the perfect grace note to a symphony of good eating that night. Sweet strawberries and the non-low fat ice cream.

"Seriously," said Hattie, "you're gorgeous. I bet you've been proposed to at least three times."

I swallowed. "Five. But I lived in Utah before. People propose on the first date there."

"How many non-first date proposals, then?"

"Well, five." I hadn't counted the time Ryan had proposed on April Fool's day, or Andrew's proposal at the airport when I arrived home from a trip. I'd assumed that one was a joke too, since he was dating my friend, but he never did speak to me again after I cracked up laughing, pranced around with the ring on my finger, and then pretended to punch him in the face with my left hand.

"So see? You're in demand. You need to remember that."

"You're one to talk," I said.

"What do you mean?"

"You agreed to go out with Mike when his friend asked you out on his behalf, and then had to go convince him to follow through. Talk about undervaluing yourself. You shouldn't date a guy who isn't clearly interested in you."

"Mike was interested. He likes me."

"Not interested enough to ask you out himself." I knew I was being cruel. Hattie had been infatuated with Mike for years and had leapt at the chance to date him. Still, truth was truth. "Listen, you don't date a guy who doesn't ask you out himself, and who can take no for an answer. You want a guy who adores you. Who thinks you're the most amazing person ever."

"So, what, a guy who keeps asking you out even when you say no?"

"Yes. He needs to show commitment. I used to require that guys ask me out at least three times before I'd consider saying yes."

"Fine," said Hattie. She reached into her purse and pulled out a little notebook and pen. "Rule One, guy has to ask you out three times and still act interested. Len wouldn't have passed that test."

"What are you doing?"

"I'm writing you a list of things you need to remember for next time."

"I don't need a list."

"You were dating *Len*. What's Rule Two, then?"

"I don't do rules."

"Guidelines, then. Suggested practices."

I shook my head and focused on my ice cream.

"He has to be in your same political party," said Hattie.

"No," I snapped. "Maybe for you they do, but not everyone's even into politics."

"Then name another Rule. What's something else my cousin did wrong?"

I ignored that prompt and instead thought about her and Mike. "Remember how Mike forgot your birthday?"

"He didn't forget-"

"He did. And when someone reminded him, he got you a gift certificate to McDonald's?"

"It was a gag gift."

"I don't see how that's even funny. You need a guy who can give good gifts, who stops to think about it, who really wants to make you happy. I mean, even if he can't think of something creative, he can at least buy you flowers."

"He gave me flowers."

"He gave you a half wilted bouquet from the grocery store. I'm talking real flowers, from a florist. The kind that can run fifty bucks or more."

"Well, I'm not into flowers."

"Yeah, but at least by spending real money, he shows he cares. Would you get a bouquet like he got you for a friend in the hospital? I don't think so."

"Okay, Rule Two, has to give good gifts, e.g. fifty bucks worth of flowers or more. What's the next Rule?"

"No, I'm not helping you draft rules. I'm just saying-"

"Did Len ever get you flowers?"

"No. But we weren't dating over my birthday-"

"Valentine's Day, what did he do?"

"He sent me an e-card."

"Ah-*ha*, so you do need to follow some Rules."

"It's not about rules, it's about standards."

"Which is what I said before. What's the next Rule?"

I scraped my spoon around the edge of my sundae to get all the drips of melting ice cream.

"Hmmm?" prompted Hattie.

I wasn't going to play this game.

"I think politics really is important," she said. "I mean, the Church leaders are clear, this is the End of Days and as the world refuses to repent, we find ourselves in enemy territory."

I glanced around. Hattie didn't have much grasp of nuance when it came to politics or taking spiritual guidance from church leaders. I always worried that her comments would provoke a fight when she aired them in public like this, but the parlor was still empty, and the guy behind the counter was busy tooling around with the milkshake blender.

"Seriously," she went on, "I dated this one guy whose sister was gay-"

"Your brother's gay."

"And look what happened to him and my whole family!" Her voice rose to a crescendo.

This wasn't a discussion I wanted to have again. Her brother and the rest of her family had left the Church and I didn't want to hear Hattie's theory that liberals had conspired with Satan to make this happen. "Okay, fine, Rule Three... um... howabout the first date Mike took you on? Took you to a movie he wanted to see with a bunch of his friends. He basically just let you tag along."

"I like action movies."

"You so don't. Besides, even if you did, tagging along with his friends? You need to only date guys who put thought into dates. I mean, he should figure out the perfect date for the two of you. Like I had one guy take me on a 'hot chocolate date' once-"

"How is that a good date?"

"We didn't really know each other and he..." I quickly amended what I was going to say. The guy had pointed out that the rest of society did coffee dates, where people who didn't know each other well met in a casual setting to drink coffee. The date could be as short as the time it took to finish the coffee, or could go longer if they really hit it off. Since we Latter-day Saints didn't drink coffee, he proposed a hot chocolate date instead, and it had worked well. I didn't want to get Hattie started on her anti-coffee rant, though. "Okay, so it made sense for us. It turned out to be a really casual, low stress date, and afterward I wasn't interested in going out again, but he picked up on that while we drank our hot chocolate and it was just perfect. I wouldn't have known how I felt without it, and if he'd taken me somewhere more expensive, then he'd probably have been way more disappointed."

"So a guy should do a cheap, no strings attached date?"

"No, the guy should really think about the first date. Put some real planning into it. I mean, I knew a guy at BYU who did the same first date, same second date, same third date – no matter who he was dating. It became a joke. We'd be like, 'Oh, you made it to the frisbee golf date? Wow, you were serious about him. I only made it to the bowling date.' He put no thought into it. Planning a date should be like planning a-a diplomatic event. Guys need to engineer a date that shows they get you and where you're at. They need to ask you out at least three days in advance and demonstrate that they are willing to do what you want and they need to put work into the whole thing, not just the planning, but the execution too. I mean, a date's like a job interview, and they need to act accordingly. It's their proposal to get you to spend more time with them, so they better make it a good one."

"I don't know how to write that as a Rule."

"Well, don't bother writing it down-"

"Rule Three, treat first date like a job interview and work very hard to impress. No generic dates, and no doing whatever it is he wants to do. It has to be about you. 'Kay, how's that?" Her pen scrawled the words across the page.

"Whatever. Sure."

She tore off the notebook page and pushed it across the table to me.

"What? Why?" I said.

"Because you need to remember. You made the Rules. You have to follow them."

"I was trying to help *you*."

"You know the scripture about the mote and the beam. Thank you for noticing the mote in my eye, but you've gotta take the beam out of your own." She pushed the paper at me.

I snatched it off the table and stuck it in my pocket.

She grinned at me as if she'd won this whole exchange.

While I'd been trying to be helpful, not start a game of one-upsmanship. It was time to finish my ice cream and go home.

Three

Phone Call

The sight of my two story house bathed in the light from my headlights gave me another wave of discomfort. I activated the garage door and pulled my car in from the slanting rain.

This house was why I'd moved to Portland.

The car pinged as got out, reminding me to shut off the headlights before I gathered my clutch purse and went through the creaking back door to the kitchen area with its giant print of the Last Supper on the wall. Not DaVinci's version, mine. I'd been working for almost ten years as a painter, and I did make money this way. Some, at least. I sold prints through LDS bookstores and gift shops, and had a somewhat steady stream of private commissions.

I tossed my keys on the counter where they landed with a dull crash. My shoes hit the floor with two hollow clacks and I tiptoed in my nylons to the carpeted hallway, which featured more of my art on the walls and propped up on the entryway table. Carrie, my stepmother, had bought a lot of my work while she dated my dad. Then, when they'd married and she'd moved to Utah to be with him, she'd asked me to house sit for her. The housing market was so bad, she had no hope of selling the place and I made just enough money to cover utilities.

One year later here I was, dumped by Len Hodge, living on my stepmother's charity, and without a plan to move forward.

That, in a nutshell, was my life.

The phone rang when I was halfway up the stairs. I peered down at the entryway table, at the caller ID box and noted with a start that the phone number began with 44. I bounded back down and lifted the receiver. "Hello? Aunt Nora?" I glanced at the clock. It was nine thirty, which meant it was five thirty a.m. in the UK. Something was wrong.

"Hello sweetie."

"Hi! How are you? Everything okay?"

"Well, I broke my arm. Silly thing for me to call you about, I know."

"No it's not. What happened?"

"I slipped and fell in the kitchen. Thing is, they're not letting me out of the hospital. They want to do extra tests to see why I fell, even though I told them. I dropped a bowl of frozen peas, stepped on a few, and went down. They want to scan my brain. Me, I think they're just trying to run up fees to make some money. I guess my private insurance pays way better than their National Health Service."

"That's ridiculous."

"That it is. Listen, honey, is there any way at all I could get you out here?"

"Absolutely. When?"

"Well, I'm trying to talk sense to the doctors, but they won't listen. Maybe if you and I gang up on them? Or maybe you can just think more clearly than I can. I'm so tired, honey. And I hate hospitals. They remind me of watching my mother die."

"I know the feeling."

"And my sister, and my other sister."

Paint Me True

"And my sisters and my cousin." Our family had the BRCA 1 mutation, a gene that put the women at risk for cancer. On top of that, we had hideous luck. My grandmother, great aunts, mother, aunts, and sisters had all died before the age of forty. None of the technological advances in cancer treatment over the course of the last century made the slightest bit of difference; the cancers spread like wildfire once they showed up and they bounced right back no matter how many times doctors removed tumors or hit them with radiation and chemo. Nora and I were a rare breed, adult women in the family, survivors of a silent war. I'd sobbed when I got the results of the tests back that showed I didn't have the mutation. "I will be there as fast as I can. I'll go book a flight."

"Thank you, sweetheart."

"Anytime. You get some rest. I'm on my way." Even as I said this, I ran up the stairs to the office, where the computer was on standby. I had Nora's credit card number written backwards on a sheet of paper in the drawer.

I'd first met my aunt at a family reunion. My mother was from a tiny town outside Tooele (pronounced "Tu-willa"), Utah. The place had one gas station, one diner, a tiny cluster of houses, and a church. I was fourteen and the family had taken over the church and had filled the cultural hall with tables for a potluck. A huge spread of casseroles, mashed potatoes, and jello salads took up one wall.

My oldest sister had just died half a year earlier and my next older one was sick, not with the cancer that killed her, but with the one before. People were waiting on her like a princess as her bald head turned this way and that to receive the plates piled high with her favorite flavor of red jello.

The place was a madhouse. I could barely hear myself think, there were so many voices jabbering away, punctuated with loud "He*loooo*"s as cousins and siblings happened upon each other in the crowd. But when Nora's figure appeared as a silhouette in the doorway, the place went quiet.

She was slim and wore a tulip skirt and a translucent, short sleeved blouse that seemed as insubstantial as smoke when backlit by the sun. When she stepped forward, the blouse shifted to a more substantial cream color and I beheld her jet black hair and gray blue eyes. She was twenty-nine and moved gracefully in her pumps, like a doe stepping out from a copse of trees.

Her gaze fell on me, and I smiled. The smile that I got in return was all relief and she came right over to me. "Are you one of Sarah's daughters?"

"Sara Dunmar's, yeah." There were at least four Sarahs at the reunion.

"I'm your aunt, then. Nora."

"Eliza," I replied. I'd heard of my Aunt Nora. I knew she lived in England and was married to a wealthy man with a mansion, but all the stories of her were static. There were never any new ones. No one had spoken to her in years, except to mutter with disapproval that she'd stopped going to church.

She leaned in and whispered, "Do you think they'd notice if we went to the diner and got malts? I've got the most desperate craving for a malt."

I glanced around and saw that both my parents were staring at me from two tables over. I pointed in the direction of the door and they both nodded and waved their consent.

"Excellent," said Nora, "let's go."

We'd gone to the diner for malts. She'd paid, and just laughed off my attempt to pitch in. We got them to go and spent the rest of the afternoon walking around the town. I'd been there dozens of times to see family, but through Nora's eyes, the place ceased to be just a boring collection of houses, and instead became rich with history. "The woman who used to live here had a crush on Uncle Ron," she said as we passed one of the smaller woodframe houses. This one had a heart motif cut out of the faux shutters nailed on either side of each window. "She used to feed him, basically. She'd leave him dinner on his front doorstep every evening."

"So did they ever get married?"

"Uncle Ron wasn't the sharpest knife in the drawer. He assumed it was charity and by the time Cousin Shayla set him straight, the woman had moved on. She kept cooking him dinner, though. That was the funny thing. I guess her new husband didn't mind."

When we walked past a cow pasture, she paused and rested a hand on the barbed wire. I pulled out my sketchbook and set about trying to capture the brightness of the sun, and the lazy expressions of the cows, laying with their feet tucked under them. They looked content, as if they were all having their backs scratched.

"Are you an artist?" Nora asked.

"I just draw."

"Let's see. These are *wonderful*." She leafed through my sketchbook. "You've got real talent. Are you going to become an artist?"

"No. It's not practical."

"Oh, pffft. You only live once, who's got time for practical? Let me ask you this, what makes you happy, a day when you get three square meals and a lot of homework you don't like, or a day when you draw and don't even remember to eat dinner?"

That was easy to answer. "I love to draw."

"Choose to be happy, then, even if it means you go hungry sometimes. You and I both know how short life can be."

That evening I'd drawn a picture of the little house with the hearts on the shutters. I drew it as a longing house, its windows like eyes turned upwards, its porch steps like a sad frown. I found that if I made these subtle enough, the casual observer would only see the house and get a sense of sadness. That was the night I began to call myself an artist.

And even though my parents were not in favor of this career, by the time I was eighteen I had a trust fund filled with life insurance payouts from my mother and one of my aunts. It covered the fees for my degree in fine art. I then turned down jobs as a graphic designer, which paid well but wasn't what I loved, and instead went into painting gospel subjects. I chose to be happy, as if by living one full life, I might make up for the lack I felt in the absence of my sisters, whose lives had come to such abrupt, decisive ends. I wanted to feel enough joy for the three of us.

My father was indifferent, at best, to my choice of career. My brother was a jerk about it, saying I clearly just wanted a cute hobby for when I was married with kids. Only Nora was unreservedly delighted.

Years later, when her children had both left home, she flew me over for a visit, and I'd gone again every year since. Her husband had long since died in a car accident, so it was just her and me.

A knock on my front door pulled me out of these memories. I looked at my watch. It was nearly ten o'clock.

Blessing

I flipped on the porch light and hauled open the door. A whoosh of damp, sweet smelling air blew in, and there on the stoop were Hattie's loser semi-boyfriend, Mike, and Len's housemate, Chris. Chris, who was medium height with ash blond hair, had his hands shoved deep into the pockets of his khaki pants. "Hey," he said. "Um... so... I couldn't find Ben tonight but I wanted to come see how you were." Chris and Ben were my home teachers, two priesthood holders in the ward assigned to visit me every month and look out for me in any crisis.

"I'm fine, guys, but thanks for coming by." I shrugged at Chris. "It was an amicable breakup, you can tell the media that we intend to remain friends. Why, is he upset?"

"I dunno. He's in the middle of a *Bioshock* marathon."

Len was an obsessive video gamer, yet another trait that made him all wrong for me.

It was chilly out here on my porch. "You guys want to come in, or..."

They exchanged a look. "Yeah," said Chris. "Sure."

Not what I'd expected, but I knew it would be rude to show my surprise, so instead I stepped back and ushered them in. With the front door closed, the air inside was still once more. I flipped on the lights to the living room and went to close the curtains as the guys plopped themselves down on the couch.

"Would you like a blessing?" Chris asked me.

Chris wasn't a very intuitive person, and he wasn't hyper religious, so I must've looked like I was in bad shape. Some guys offered blessings with the same frequency they offered handshakes. Chris didn't even bother to visit me most months. Usually when I saw him, he'd be on his couch at home eating an Evol burrito and watching reality television. If he even noticed I was there, all I got was a wave of the burrito. Now that Len and I were over, odds were, I'd never see him at all outside of church.

"No, I'm okay. I mean, I just got a call from my aunt and she broke her arm, so I've gotta go fly out to help her."

"Oh, she all right?" Mike asked. He had dark hair and very green eyes that were slightly almond shaped. They gave him a kind of weasley quality as he gazed directly at me. He was a youngster, too. Twenty-two, barely back from his mission, still living at home. He still seemed like a teenager to me, self absorbed and clueless about making his own way in the world.

"I think so. I just have to pack. I'm flying out in eight hours."

"You need a ride to the airport?" Mike asked.

"Um, no, don't worry about it. I'll manage."

"No, I'll do it. I'll come by at what time?"

"It's an international flight. Three hour check in. Really, I'll be okay."

"Three a.m.? Okay, I'll be here."

Chris palmed his hair forward – an odd habit he'd developed since he'd started buzzing it himself. He claimed it stuck straight up and he wanted to train it to lie flat. "You sure you don't want a blessing?"

"Um... okay, sure." There was no harm in a blessing. If they were willing to go through all this trouble on a Saturday night, I might as well oblige them.

"You need a blessing for the sick or one of comfort and counsel?" Mike asked. He got up from the couch.

"Just comfort and counsel," I said. I hauled the piano bench out and sat on it as the guys stood on either side of me.

The two of them put their hands on my head. I felt a little silly, doing this. It was yet another reminder of how, as a Mormon, I couldn't ever really aspire to be a normal person, but I shut my eyes and bowed my head and resolved to listen.

Mike began by invoking his priesthood authority and pronouncing a blessing.

Then Chris took over. First he invoked his priesthood authority, and then it was time for him to give some additional counsel.

This is where I pricked up my ears. Not that the other words were unimportant to me, but this part of the blessing was the part that was personal. Chris would do his best to clear his mind and speak as he felt moved to speak by the Holy Ghost.

I waited.

He shifted his weight from one foot to the other. After what felt like minutes, he spoke. "Your Heavenly Father would have you know," he said, "that He has a very special lesson for you to learn." Then he paused.

I tried to sit up straight despite the gentle pressure of their palms upon my head.

The pause stretched into a prolonged silence. Then Chris closed the ordinance in the names of the Godhead and lifted his hands. I looked up at him and he just shrugged in reply.

"Thanks," I said.

"That's gotta be a record for shortest blessing ever," said Mike.

"I appreciate it," I said, and I did. My heart wasn't on fire with the Spirit right then, but what mattered was that these two guys had cared enough to make an effort.

I saw them to the door and thanked them again as they stepped out into the chill night.

"I'm sorry," Chris said, but I waved that away and shut the door.

One thing about being older than most of the ward, I felt more settled in my faith. I wasn't trying out religion as an adult to see whether or not it was something I could sustain. My testimony was burned in deep. If it weren't for God, I knew I'd be a very different person. How else could I survive the deaths of all my close, female relatives and still get through the day? Adages like "time heals all wounds", are lies. Let me be clear on that. Each death hurts just as bad today as it did the day it happened. The people I've lost were ripped from me and took pieces of my soul with them, and I can feel the wounds every second of every day. Like a Hollywood actress I can call up tears on demand. They're always there, tickling the back of my throat. There isn't a moment that I don't miss my mother, or wish I could pick up a phone and call my sisters.

But I've had holes in my heart for as long as I can remember. One of my earliest memories is my last visit to my Aunt Claire, before she died later that night. All through elementary, junior high, and high school I'd taken breaks for funerals with the kind of regularity other kids got the flu. Still, people were always surprised whenever they heard the family medical history. Many asked how I got through the day.

Step by step, I guess. The Lord has never given me a major miracle. None of my relatives had a spontaneous remission from cancer. I've never seen great white lights or angelic figures. But the Lord gives me small blessings every moment. Turmoil that I can't purge by whining to a friend disappears when I pour my heart out in prayer. Nights when I wondered how I'd endure, I'd get a full and deep sleep and wake up just strong enough to put one foot in front of the other again. And then there were moments like tonight, when two guys from my ward felt impressed to come check on me. Even though they'd stayed less than twenty minutes, I felt better knowing they cared.

Nora

Twenty-four hours later I was in London, Heathrow, another face in the hordes on the move. I'd cleared customs and immigration and now tried to stuff my passport into my pocket with one hand, hold onto my bag with the other, and follow signs to the trains all at the same time. I'd done this before, and just like before it gave me a thrill to know how far I'd traveled. The glimpses of sky I caught through the windows showed gray clouds, but it wasn't even six a.m. Given how far north I was, and the fact that it was the middle of the summer, the sun was already up and with luck it'd burn off that layer of cloudcover. Right now, though, I imagined the landscape as watercolor material, the pale gray concrete of the buildings overlain with all shades of greenery.

I got some pounds sterling out of the first cash machine I found – using a debit card Aunt Nora had given me. We'd fought about that, years ago, and suffice it to say, she'd won. My bank and credit card company charged fees for every foreign currency transaction I made, and Aunt Nora had showed me her checking account balance. It was six figures. That, and she'd broken down in tears and told me neither of her children ever came to visit, so she wanted me to come as often as I liked. Since she doted on me like a mother, I decided to think of myself as a daughter to her, even if there was only a fifteen year age gap between us.

The train to Oxford was already in the station, its silver gray cars stretching off down the platform like an articulated metal snake. I selected a car about halfway down its length, stashed my luggage in the metal rack and sank into a seat facing forwards. I fished out a can of Dr. Pepper that I'd bought on my way through the airport and drank it as fast as I could. I needed to stay awake, or else I might sleep through my stop.

As the engine spun up and the train began to move, I took out my British cell phone – one I'd bought a couple of visits ago – and switched it on. The UK had pay-as-you-go phones that never expired. I could keep my number and prepaid minutes for as long as I wanted, a deal I wished I could get in the US. The phone chimed to let me know I had a message.

"Hello, my name's Colin Radcliffe. I'm a nurse at St. John's private hospital. We've received your aunt into care and she asked one of us to call you. We're located in Summertown. I'm sending you a text with directions from the train station."

Sure enough, there was a text with the directions. I loved modern technology.

The train pulled into Oxford at 7:48, and I stumbled off with my luggage. I needed to sleep, but more than that, I needed to help Aunt Nora. I bought another Dr. Pepper in the station and downed it fast, then went out to the taxi stand and explained I needed to get to St. John's hospital in Summertown. For a few confused minutes the cabbie at the front of the line argued with me about the location, then said, "Oh, right, you mean the private ward in the general hospital." I knew nothing about the hospital system in Oxford, so I just had to take his word for it. He claimed, looking at the directions on my phone, that this was the right place.

He helped me load my bags into the car and then we were off. I tried not to look. Walking around Oxford was pretty easy. The roads twisted and turned and changed names sometimes, but you could pick a direction and work your way to where you wanted to end up. Driving, though, required knowledge of the one way streets and weird intersections. I ignored how often the driver turned in what seemed like the exact wrong direction as we darted down the narrow lanes, dodging bikes and pedestrians.

Yet at the same time, I willed myself to be alert. If the hospital was giving my aunt a hard time, then I needed to be ready for a fight. I *hated* hospitals, but I had enough experience to know that it never paid to be easygoing. You had to demand what you wanted and make sure you didn't let the staff rest until you got it.

When I opened my eyes again, we were in Summertown, a part of North Oxford known for its beautiful Victorian homes. The cabbie took us down what looked like a residential street, only a large parking lot opened up on our left and there was a hospital set back from the road. He went around the side to a smaller building with a sign that read, "St. John's Oncology Centre". My heart just about stopped. My aunt was being treated for cancer?

I got out of the cab, paid the fare plus tip, and thanked the cabbie when he hauled my bag out of the trunk and left it on the curb where I directed him. The car pulled away in a cloud of gray, oily fumes as I hefted my suitcase and went through the sliding glass doors. Ahead of me was a reception desk, and behind it was a woman with a scowl.

"Hi," I said, making no effort to hide my accent. "I'm here to see Nora Chesterton? I got here as fast as I could."

The scowl melted and the woman sat up straighter. "You came all the way from the States?"

"Yes, I just landed in Heathrow at six."

"You didn't? Oh my, you must be shattered."

"I'd really like to see my aunt."

"I'll ring the ward."

While the woman chatted to whomever was on the other end of the line, I did my best to stay upright. The room seemed to sway slightly and my eyelids felt like they had lead weights attached to them.

"Right." The woman looked uncertainly at my baggage.

"I didn't have time to drop it off," I said.

"Why don't you just pop it back here? They're quite eager to see you. Go round the corner and through the fire doors."

"Thank you." I hauled my bag around behind the partition and desk.

"That's all right then. Nurse Radcliffe will meet you once you go in."

I went down the hall and pulled open the fire doors, doors that every public building in Britain seemed to have. They were just plain doors that swung shut automatically and which always had instructions on them insisting they stay closed. I was ready to demand information from whomever stood on the other side. Only, no one did. I stepped through onto clean industrial tile in a broad hallway that was lit with a mix of fluorescent lights and skylights. The natural sunlight made everything seem so much more alive than the usual artificial lights. The nurses' station was just ahead and to the left. A guy stepped out from it and I stifled the urge to gasp audibly.

He was gorgeous. Light brown hair and liquid brown eyes. His scrubs fit well on his tall frame and revealed well defined biceps. I tried to see his hands, where they grasped a folder of records, which he scanned. Was it too much to hope that he'd not have a wedding ring? That he'd maybe wear a CTR ring as well? That last wish was ridiculous, I knew. If he was a Latter-day Saint, I'd have met him at church during my last visit. Unless he was new...

His eyes scanned down the page he was reading, then paused. He looked up at me. "Oh, hello," said the familiar voice. He'd been the one who left the message on my cellphone. "You Eliza Dunmar?" Those calf eyes gazed at me through thick lashes.

"Ah..." I said.

He put down the records he'd been reading held out his hand.

I shook it. His skin was warm, or mine was cold. I didn't know which. "Yes," I said, "I am."

"Right, so your aunt is in room-"

"Why is she in an oncology ward?"

He gave me a wry smile. "Excellent question. Not normally the place a person with a broken arm gets sent. The public hospital thought that she might need her brain scanned for a tumor."

"A tumor?" Alarm bells went off in my head.

"Well, her behavior's been a bit erratic. She won't let anyone x-ray her arm."

"What?"

"Simple break, should be easy enough to set, but she won't allow an x-ray. That plus the mystery of how she fell-"

"What mystery?" I said. "I thought she slipped."

"Mmm..." He picked up another set of records, flipped it open, and scanned down the page. "Arrived unconscious, first was disoriented and accused the hospital staff of kidnapping her, then yes, she did say she'd slipped and fell. So it's really just the x-ray she needs."

"Did she say why she didn't want one?"

"Says she thinks it's unnecessary and just an attempt to inflate fees. This from a woman who's stayed two days in two different hospitals for a broken arm. She needs to go back to the other hospital, get her arm x-rayed and have it set. It's that simple." He closed the folder.

"Okay, let me talk to her."

He gestured for me to follow him down the hall.

When I stepped into Nora's room, shock hit like a punch in the chest. She looked so much older than when I'd seen her, eight months ago. She'd lost weight and her skin had a papery texture to it that made it seem like it could part with just a touch. In reaction to our shadows darkening the door, she lifted her head. "Eliza?"

"Yeah, it's me." I went to take her hand, which felt bony and fragile. "How are you feeling?"

"Been better. That nurse there's been cutting back on my painkillers."

I glanced back over my shoulder, but the nurse had already left. "So how did you end up in this place?" I asked.

"Just trying to get to people who will talk sense. All these ridiculous tests they want to run."

"Okay, so they say you need an x-ray and that's all. Did anyone else tell you different?"

"They say I'm acting crazy."

"They're probably not used to anyone refusing an x-ray."

"You can set a bone without an x-ray."

"Well, what's wrong with getting an x-ray?"

She sighed. "I hate medical equipment and tests and all that garbage."

"Okay, but if you keep refusing treatment, they'll start requesting more scans and stuff."

"I'm not refusing treatment. I'm refusing an x-ray. X-rays don't treat anything." Her hand had tensed up to the point that her bones dug into my flesh.

I didn't want to fight with her. "Okay, well, how about this. You get an x-ray and I'll paint you a picture of anything you want."

Her hand relaxed and a light appeared in her eyes. "You bribing me?"

"Yes."

"Anything?"

"Anything."

"We-ell, maybe I should've broken my arm sooner."

"And maybe now is not the time to admit that I'd paint you a custom painting anytime you asked."

She laughed then and patted my hand. "I'm glad you're here, honey." She even talked like she was an old woman. "You really think I'm being that silly?"

"I think they're used to following their procedures. They don't do creative compromises."

"Well, I suppose you're right about that. I don't want an x-ray."

"But you'll get one?"

"I want it on the smallest possible area. The need to zoom in as much as they can."

"All right, I'll tell them."

"The less radiation they put into me, the better."

I wasn't sure that her idea would cut the radiation dose, but now wasn't the time to point that out. "I'll be right back," I said.

I found Nurse Radcliffe back out at the nurse's station with a manila folder in one hand and a pen in the other. "All right?" he said when I approached. He didn't look up.

"Yes."

"Mmmm?" Now he did look up with those soulful eyes of his.

I had to remind myself that "All right?" in Britspeak meant, "How are you?" He hadn't asked me about Aunt Nora at all.

"She'll have her arm x-rayed."

He arched an eyebrow. "You didn't twist her arm too hard, I trust? We're quite certain it is broken."

"No, no twisting."

He put the folder down and turned his whole attention to me. "Then what did you do?"

"Not that it's any of your business, but I bribed her." I tried to keep my tone flat, but it came out flirty anyway. I was tired. My inhibitions were low. Now that I could see both his hands, I saw no wedding band and no CTR ring.

33

"With what?" he asked.

"With art." The words should have shut the conversation down, but I said them in a way that invited him to ask.

"Art, eh? You're going to buy her-"

"Paint for her. I'm a professional artist."

He blinked with surprise, as most people did when I said that.

I clasped my hands behind my back and tried not to tilt my head and swing my shoulders just so, but my body wouldn't listen. I was being a fool.

Even worse, it seemed to affect him. He smiled. "You're quite useful to have around. You got her to switch just like that?"

"You're welcome. Can you book her x-rays?"

"I'll give the hospital a ring and we'll get this sorted."

I nodded and turned to go. A quick glance over my shoulder let me know he watched me leave. We exchanged another smile.

When I returned to Aunt Nora's room, she looked agitated again. "Eliza, have you been to my house yet?"

I shook my head.

"I'm worried about Pip."

Pip was her little Maltese. "I can go check on him, as long as you're okay?"

"I'll be fine, now that you're here."

I gave her a gentle half-hug, the best I could manage while she lay down. "I'll go look after him."

A Scared Little Dog

My anxiety level ratcheted up as the cab got closer to Nora's house. It wasn't far from the hospital, but it was far enough for me to have time to worry my stomach to shreds. What if the paramedics had broken the door down and her house had just been left open? What if Pip had run away? What if the thawed out peas on the floor had attracted in wildlife? Would I find an urban fox in residence?

As the cab turned the corner of Charlbury Road, though, I saw the house and there was no visible damage to the door. It was shut, which meant it was locked. She had one of those front doors, common in England, that had no knob. If it was latched, it was locked.

Many of the upper story windows were shuttered and only the ground floor had lace curtains that allowed light in, but no prying eyes. It was a grand house built of Cotswold stone that had been in the Chesterton family for a hundred years – according to Nora.

"Go ahead and pull into the driveway," I told the cab driver. The house had a semi-circular drive of gravel that crunched under the cab's tires.

I got out, paid the driver and thanked her as she helped me carry my bags to the doorstep.

It occurred to me that the paramedics might have used a back door instead, so that signs of their entry wouldn't be so obvious from the street. My aunt had given me a copy of her key years ago and I used that to let myself in. The lights in the foyer were off. "Pip?" I called out. "Hey boy!" My voice echoed hollowly.

Turning on lights didn't drive out the empty, abandoned feeling the house had. I made my way to the kitchen first, where I expected to see plates out on the counters and fragments of crockery on the floor, only the floor was clean.

"Pip!" I shouted. "Where are you? Pip!"

He was a shy dog, so I didn't expect him to come running. I did expect an answering jangle of tags, though. Maybe some barking. He was a dog, after all, and I was encroaching on his territory. "*Pip!*" I yelled.

The kitchen was next to the formal dining room, which had a pair of French doors that opened out into the back yard. No sign of forced entry there. I wondered if the paramedics had used a window, though there was no stirring of breeze in the house that would give that away. "Pip?"

The size of the house meant it had plenty of places for a tiny dog to hide. I decided to start from the top story, which meant I had to climb two flights of stairs. The corridor of the top floor had sea green carpet and slightly crooked doorways to each room. "Pip?"

Just silence.

At the far end of the corridor was my cousin, John's room, still decorated for a little boy, even though he was now in his twenties. Blue wallpaper and a ship's wheel on the wall gave it a nautical air. On the windowsill was a flashlight which seemed out of place. Other than that, the room was neat as a pin. I went over to the window and hefted the flashlight. It was an old one with a plastic sliding switch. The window looked out on the back yard. A glint of light on the garden wall caught my eye.

Of course. I was being foolish. Pip had a doggie door that couldn't be locked. If he didn't come when I entered the house, he was probably not in the house.

I jogged back downstairs and out the back door. "Pip!" I called out.

A jangle of tags answered me, and I immediately stepped down onto the grass and called his name again. "Where are you, boy?" The jangle had come from a cluster of bushes just to my right. I got down on my hands and knees in the damp grass to peer underneath.

Sure enough, there he was, his back hunched in a sad horseshoe, his tail tucked between his spindly back legs. He looked at me with his silky ears pressed to the sides of his head.

"Hi, Pip," I said. "I don't know if you remember me. I'm family. You're safe. You want to come out?" I held out my hands to invite him to come and sniff me. "Hey boy. Come here."

My aunt always kept him impeccably brushed, but now he had mud on his legs and belly and even some splashes of it on his back. He shook himself, tags jangling.

"Your fur's not thick enough to be out here," I told him. "Come on. Please."

He tilted his head one way, then the other, then shot forward with a burst of nervous energy. I had him in my arms now, his little body shaking like he'd just gotten out of a freezing river in December. I tucked him under one arm and went back inside.

His fur was dirty and had some snarls, but nothing that wasn't easy to put right. His paws were whole, no cuts or scratches that I could see. I held onto him as I searched the entire ground floor. There were no broken windows, no broken doors. The kitchen, I now noted, wasn't just devoid of a broken bowl and peas, it was clean. There was nothing on the counters, no dirty dishes in the sink, nothing on the stove or in the microwave.

I opened the cabinet under the sink and there, in the garbage can, I found the remains of the peas and broken shards of bowl. Well, I thought, there was no reason my aunt couldn't have swept that up and put things away before letting the paramedics in. But the nurse had told me she'd arrived at the hospital unconscious. Had she passed out on the way?

Pip eyed me curiously as I carried him out the front door and went to the third flowerpot along the driveway, the one that was shielded from view of the road and the other houses by a weeping willow that drooped its long, leaf laden branches all around three sides of the pot. I dug about three inches down in the soil and came up with nothing.

Someone had taken the spare key.

I carried Pip back into the house, shut the door behind me and threw the deadbolt. Unease warred with the rational voice in my head that pointed out that my aunt could have moved the spare key. Aunt Nora's laptop sat on the dining room table. The china in the glass cabinet still crowded those narrow shelves. The silver tea service was out on the sideboard and her plasma television hung, unmolested, over the fireplace in the sitting room, framed by the two paintings I'd done of pansies that went with the rest of the décor. Her e-reader sat next to a stack of mail on the table in the entryway.

I was jumping at shadows. Odds were, Nora had merely fallen asleep waiting in the emergency room for treatment and someone had put down that she was "unconscious" when she arrived.

I went out onto the service porch and filled the sink with warm water. Pip wriggled with excitement as I lowered him in. His dog shampoo was on the shelf, just as I'd remembered, and I scrubbed the mud out of his coat, which was mercifully short. He was patient as I ran the wire brush through his fur, cleaning away the last of the dirt, though it snarled enough that I had to pick the knots out with my fingers.

After I got him out of the water, I fluffed him with a towel and then blew his fur dry. This he also tolerated; he was accustomed to being spoiled and stood still as I dried his coat and ran the brush through it some more.

"Better?" I said.

He rewarded me with bright eyes and a wag of the tail. I noticed then that his food and water dishes were full. There was wet dog food in the dish that hadn't congealed too badly yet. It wasn't three days old. I put Pip down in the kitchen, got a change of clothes from Aunt Nora's room, and then set out for the hospital again. Since I didn't have my suitcase to lug, I could walk there.

By the time I arrived, Aunt Nora had been moved to the main hospital. I found her in the lobby with a splint on her arm. "There you are," she said. "They got my x-rays done and put this splint on, but when I asked for a phone, you'd think I'd asked them for a special referral to a holistic care clinic. They said they'd get back to me once they handled all the procedures for my request." She rolled her eyes as she got to her feet.

"Do you have a housecleaner?" I asked.

"Yes. You don't see her often, she's such a quiet little thing, but yes."

"Would she have come while you were here?"

"Mmmm, I'd have to check. I suppose so, yes. She comes on alternate Fridays."

"It looks like she fed Pip."

"Well that's good. Poor little guy."

"Also, did you move your spare key?"

"Olivia might not have put it back. I told her to use it to get a package of hers that had been left at my house. She called while I was out shopping a couple of weeks ago and I told her where it was."

"Oh, okay, because it's also gone."

"Well, I trust Olivia. She's a little forgetful is all. And she's in Tenerife at the moment, so I'll just remind her to give me the key back when she flies home."

I nodded. "Let me call a cab-"

"We're only eight blocks away. We can walk."

Normally we would have done so without me having a second thought, but she seemed so frail. But walking would be good for her. I held out my arm, which she took, and we set off.

"By the way, that cute nurse at the other hospital?" she said.

"Mmm hmm?"

"I gave him your phone number."

"Did he ask for it?"

"He was going to. I just helped him along."

I laughed. "You give out my number to random men often?"

"Did you see him? He's adorable."

"Yeah, I saw him."

"I bet he calls you."

"I won't hold my breath."

The Date Discrepency

When we got home, my aunt was a little winded, but otherwise fine. I let us into the house and found that day's mail had arrived. It was scattered on the floor, having been put through the mail slot. I stooped to pick it up as my aunt strode on over to the stack of mail on the table at the far end of the foyer. Pip darted out from the sitting room and stood up on his hind legs, tail wagging furiously.

"Junk, junk, junk," she said, tossing most of the envelopes in the nearby trash can. "Oh, so honey, do I really get a custom painting?"

I glanced through today's mail and noted most of the letters had been mailed yesterday. First class mail in Britain really was first class. "Sure," I said. "It'll give me an excuse to stay long enough to finish it."

"Sounds like a plan. You must think I'm ridiculous, calling you out here over just a broken arm."

I went over to put today's mail on the stack on the table. "You don't need an excuse. I'm always happy to visit."

She smiled at me. "Here, can you actually take these letters to the recycling bin? You know what I'd love? A

41

portrait of Paul." He had been her husband, and had died in a car accident before I ever got to meet him.

"Yeah, okay. Do you have a picture you want me to base it on, or do you have a moment that you'd like me to paint that you weren't able to get a picture of?" I dug the letters out of the wastebasket and saw that the date on the top one was Friday's. My steps slowed as my mind chewed that over.

"Ooh, I'll have to think about that."

"Your housecleaner comes Fridays?" I asked

"Mmm-hmm."

"There are letters here that would have arrived Saturday."

"Hmm?"

"Someone picked up the mail on Saturday. Would your friend who has the key do that?"

"She's in Tenerife, honey. I'm sure she's still gone."

I walked through to the kitchen, dumped the mail in the recycling bin, and checked the row of pegs by the back door where the car keys hung. There was no spare key. "Someone was in your house Saturday, but they didn't take anything. I mean, they left your laptop and stuff."

"That's... that's odd."

"Think, would anyone else have a key?"

"No, I got the locks changed when I married Paul, and I've been very careful about who gets keys. No one has one to keep, and I change the location of the one I hide out front every time I tell someone where it is – save for you, of course. You're the only person."

"What about your kids?"

"They live clear out in Bristol and up in Leeds. I don't think they'd be by."

"And your cleaning lady?"

"Right, yes, she has one. Maybe she stopped by again Saturday, or maybe she was late last week?"

I stepped back into the entryway. "Would it be an overreaction to call a locksmith and change your locks?"

"No. That's the easiest thing to do, isn't it? Yes, why don't we do that?"

I nodded and went to find the phone book. I heard Nora move into the sitting room and plop herself down.

"Sorry," I said, "we were talking about Paul. How did you guys meet?"

"I came over here for my junior year abroad. Did you know that?"

"Huh-uh."

"Yes, I came over here for my junior year abroad. I was studying English and the outfit that organized this put us up in a house off the High Street, but I did some of my tutorials at Balliol College. You know the one? It's on Broad Street."

"Right by the intersection of Cornmarket?" It was a fairly well known college, though I couldn't conjure up a picture of it just then. I joined her in the sitting room, the phone book tucked under my arm.

"Yes that's the one." She put her feet up and turned another page in the catalog she was perusing. "Paul was a student at Balliol."

"Oh, he studied here too?" I settled into one of the armchairs with its cushions so soft that it felt like I was being held in a plush embrace.

Nora nodded.

"But he lived here at the house?"

"He lived in the college."

"Do you remember the first time you ever saw him?"

"Oh yes." She smirked. "I was at the Porter's Lodge, you know the little front gate of the college? The porters are the ones who prevent just anyone from going in to wander, and that porter thought I had no business there at all. He kept saying that Balliol didn't take American study abroad students, though that's where my tutorial was." She shrugged. "Anyway, I was there arguing with this pompous man- you

43

have to remember, I'd never been on an airplane before I came here."

"Seriously?"

She shrugged, as if embarrassed to admit the fact. "I was so far out of my depth. You've seen the small town I'm from. I might as well have gone to a whole different planet."

"I can't imagine."

"Anyway, I was there arguing and trying not to cry. I felt so lost. Paul stepped into the lodge from the quad and took my breath away."

"Did he talk to the porter for you?"

"Oh no, didn't even look my way. Stood for a whole five seconds, reading a piece of paper, and then he walked on past and out onto the street."

"So what did you notice about him?"

"He had the most intense eyes. Blue-gray, like mine, and he carried himself with such confidence. He was tall and muscular, and even though he wore the same kind of sweater that every other guy seemed to be wearing, with brown corduroy trousers, on him they looked right. He could have been a model for that kind of clothing. And the way he looked at the paper was just so... I don't know. Brooding. He smoldered, if that makes sense. No, I guess that sounds silly."

"I get what you mean."

"I'll never forget the first time I saw him. You know that feeling when you really notice someone. They just stand out to you and you want to get to know them?"

I nodded.

"Well this was that, times a million. I mean, I was speechless after he walked through. I never thought in a thousand years that I'd meet him, let alone date him. It was love at first sight."

"I guess I've never felt that."

"Which is a pity. True love is all about those once in a lifetime moments when you don't just find yourself a good guy who's nice enough, but you find that man who's beyond your wildest dreams."

I cast my mind back to the first time I'd met Len. I'd joined the singles ward when I'd moved to Portland and my very first week there, I'd seen Len. He was already in his seat in the front row, wearing a tie that was coming apart. I didn't know that ties could be worn out like that, but his had been. The inner liner showed through several holes around the knot. He had a PDA in his hand and was poking away at it with his stylus – that's how old and out of date his PDA was. It had a stylus, and was covered in duct tape. His shoes were beat up old sneakers, also with holes in the leather, and his pants were so wrinkled, it looked like he'd slept in them.

I sat in the back row and Jenna Knight was the first person to find me. She was in one of her usual, sensible, straight skirts with a white blouse, and she sat down next to me with a businesslike air, her blond hair pinned back from her dainty, heart-shaped face. "You're new. I'm Jenna." She held out her hand.

"Eliza," I said. It felt a little odd to shake hands, but that, I'd soon learn, was Jenna's way.

"Welcome to the monkey house. Gah." She made a shooing motion at Len. He'd seen us and was smiling our direction. At her gesture, his eyes twinkled and he turned back around.

"Who's that?" I said.

"His name's Len. He's the clerk, so he'll come bother you about your records and all that."

"You don't like him?"

"He's annoying. Seriously, don't speak to him any more than you have to. He just talks about video games and stupid stuff like that, as if you're supposed to care. Oh, here he comes." She rolled her eyes.

Sure enough, he was advancing up the aisle. I waited until he was close enough to hear me. "You need my name and old ward?"

"Yup."

"Eliza Dunmar. Sa-"

"I'm Len," he cut me off.

"Yeah, hi. Eliza. I was in-"

"So what brings you to Portland?"

"Dork," said Jenna under her breath, which I know Len heard, but he didn't react.

I had no prepared answer to that one, and I realized this was a mistake. What was I supposed to say? I'm here because of free housing? "I'm an artist," I blurted, as if the connection between my art and living in Portland were somehow obvious.

Perhaps it was to a person like Len, because he just nodded and said, "Nice. So am I, more or less. You know. I'm a sysadmin for a law firm."

"Um... what?" said Jenna.

He smirked at her.

She gave him a look that would have made an oak tree wither.

But it didn't affect him. He turned back to me and said, "Give me your email and I'll send you the records transfer form-"

I realized then that I'd zoned out on Nora. My mind withdrew from Portland and returned to my body in Oxford with an almost audible thud. "Sorry."

"Good thoughts or bad?"

"Bad. Let's talk about Paul some more."

"Oh, all right." She winked.

This time I focused on her entirely and let the room melt away as she told her story.

I never let myself be caught in jeans and a sweatshirt again. The first thing I did when I got to my room was change into a skirt. I

shook my hair out of its ponytail and put on some lipgloss. The next time Paul saw me, I was determined to look more sophisticated. And I did see him around Balliol. I began to make a habit of passing by or through the college whenever I could and when I saw him, I'd duck behind the nearest wall and spy on him. Silly of me, I know.

A couple of weeks into my course, I was trying to get back home in time for dinner and I almost ran right into him on a street corner. He caught my arm and I just about fainted when I saw who it was.

"You all right?" he asked. He looked me straight in the eye as he spoke.

I just stared at him.

"I'm Paul."

"Nora."

"You American?"

"Yeah."

He looked me up and down. "What brings you to Oxford?"

"I'm majoring in English literature."

"Ah, right. Well, this is the place for that then." He chuckled. "I'm reading history."

"Reading?"

"It's what my degree is in. I'm a finalist. I graduate in the spring."

"Oh, okay." Since he still hadn't let go of my arm, I felt weak in the knees.

"You been to England before?"

"Never been outside of Utah before."

"Must be quite a change, then?"

I nodded.

"Sorry, you trying to get somewhere?"

"Just back to my house for dinner."

"What, you live out?"

"Um... I live in a boarding house with the other people on my exchange program."

"Oh, so do they feed you well or is it just rubbish food?"

"Um, I dunno." My mind wasn't working real well. I must've rehearsed a million conversations with him in my dreams, *but that didn't make the actual conversation any easier, you know? "Just, lots of boiled vegetables and stuff..."*

"Chippy is better than that."

My confusion must've shown in my face, because he started to laugh.

"You have chippies in America?"

"I... don't think so."

"Ah, no, you must have them."

I shrugged. "Maybe we call them something else?"

"A fish and chip shop?"

"Oh, sure, I guess."

"Real English culture, that. Tell you what. Come with me to the chippy. All right?"

"What, now?"

"What? You'd rather have potato and leek soup or some rubbish like that?"

"Um, okay."

He smiled, like he was proud he got me to change course. "All right, let's go."

"The chippy's over off the High Street," Nora explained. "Kind of down an alley, past where the Chaing Mai restaurant is, or was. I haven't been down there in ages."

"Was the food good?"

"Disgusting. Batter fried sausages and greasy fish and chips. Might as well just eat fried lard, not that I cared. He paid and put vinegar on my fries so that I could have them the 'real English' way. I thought I'd faint at any moment. It was like a dream. I wanted to pinch myself, literally."

"Was he just friendly like that?"

"No, I think he'd seen me skulking around." She smiled. "And apparently he didn't mind it."

"I've never had a date like that," I admitted.

"Well, sounds like you've been dating the wrong men."

Sketches

I woke up fully clothed on top of the covers of the bed in one of the guest rooms. I had a hazy memory of helping Aunt Nora to bed before I staggered here. Everything was dark, which meant it was after sundown. I glanced at my watch and saw that it was four in the morning. That was the problem with jet lag. I was now wide awake and would be tired again before bedtime.

Still, there was no point just lying there. There was a bathroom just across the hall from this room, so I took a quick shower in the antique, footed tub. The chrome was all gold tone, which gave it a luxurious look, and the shower curtain was heavy linen, lined with plastic. I dried off with one of the fluffy towels, dressed, and went back to the guest room. This was the one I usually stayed in, and the last time I'd been here I'd left acrylic paints in the closet. They were there, just as I'd left them.

There was also a set of colored pencils, and I grabbed those and got my sketchpad out of my luggage. A quick perusal of the walls along the hallway turned up several pictures of my Uncle Paul. I chose the youngest looking one and carried it back to my room. With the lamp on and me positioned right underneath it, I got more or less the kind of light I wanted. I'd had a lot of practice in this room.

The picture of Uncle Paul looked like it'd been taken when he was in his late twenties, maybe early thirties. I did a rough sketch of his face with softer lines. The photo did show his gray eyes that had had my aunt so entranced all those years ago.

While I sketched, my mind wandered to how things had progressed with Len after that first meeting. I saw him at every church activity, from Monday night Family Home Evenings (which those of us unmarrieds did in groups at each others houses) to Thursday night sports (usually volleyball at church) and Saturday picnics and temple trips. He showed up without fail, always in clothes that looked like they'd been stolen out of the discard pile of a thrift store, his hair threatening to become a mullet, his PDA in hand, and a smirk on his face like he knew what everyone thought of his appearance and could only laugh in response.

He always greeted me with a, "Hey, Eliza," then quickly looked away.

One Thursday night, about six months ago, the activities coordinators decided to make us play the Newlywed Game with partners we were to select at random. The only rule was that we couldn't have ever dated each other. Now, this was a really, really stupid idea and I said as much to Len, who was seated right behind me on the floor of the gym. "Half the girls are gonna get left out," I said. The gender ratio in the ward was way out of whack. "And what's the point of quizzing people about each other when they've never dated? They won't know anything."

"They could be friends," he pointed out.

"Well, right. Okay, look, I don't want to be left out. Partner with me?"

"I dunno..."

I turned all the way around. This felt very high school, sitting on the wooden floor of the gym, worried about

Paint Me True

whether or not I'd get left out as people chose teams. "What do you mean, you don't know? You got too many other girls lining up? You can't choose?"

"I'm the membership clerk. I know all kinds of random facts about people from their records. Doesn't seem fair."

"Oh come on. You know our parents' names, like that's gonna come up. Or our baptism dates? And you've memorized them? Quick, what's my birthday?"

He shrugged that off, but I felt mortified for a moment. He knew my birthday. He knew my age. Or if he didn't, he could easily find out. Moreover, if I played this game, I might have to reveal my age. I'd tried to hint that I was about twenty-eight. Old enough not to be interested in the young guys just fresh off their missions, but not too close to that dreaded age of thirty-one.

He looked over at me again and said, "Fine, okay. We'll team up, but unless you own an Xbox and know the difference between Evol burritos and every other kind of frozen burrito, we're gonna lose."

"How many great works of art can you name?"

"I was an art history major."

"What?"

"Just kidding. I didn't go to college."

"Oh okay."

"That was a joke too."

I folded my arms and waited.

"Computer science degree from the University of Oregon, in Eugene."

"That's hilarious. Ohmigosh, just the best joke *ever*."

That cracked him up. "You?"

"Fine art, University of Utah. Really. Truly. Totally serious. Don't laugh."

"That's cool. My middle name's Gareth. My astrological sign is Pisces, and my first car was a Ford Taurus. That'll get us through the first round. Trust me. I've been in this ward forever. Played this game a million times. What's your middle name?"

"Renee."

"Astrological sign?"

"They're not gonna ask that, are they? I don't even know."

"First car?"

"Honda Civic."

"Your astrological sign is Libra, if you care."

"You memorize that off everyone's membership records?"

He shrugged. "I have a good memory."

The sickening thing? He was right. We sailed right through the first round with those three questions. Three quarters of the couples got disqualified and joined the rest of the unattached girls on the floor to watch the rest of the game.

For round two, I and the other girls went to wait in the hall while the activities coordinator quizzed the guys. After she ushered us back in, I sat in the folding chair next to Len and hoped our impending crash and burn would at least be humorous.

"Where did you serve your mission?" was the first question.

"I didn't go on one."

"Five points!" I don't know why she did points in increments of five, but whatever. I never watched the show, *The Newlywed Game*. Maybe it was how they did it too. She moved on down the line and I ignored the results. This game was a pretty stupid way to spend a Thursday evening.

"What would be your ideal first date?"

I glanced up, surprised that they were back to us so soon. "Steakhouse."

"Five points!"

I looked at Len. People were usually surprised to find out I was so into red meat. I liked to think that it was because I looked like a health freak, all trim and toned. He lounged in his chair, one arm draped over the back, and returned my gaze evenly as the question was put to each other couple.

"What was your first boyfriend's name?" The activities coordinator stood over us again.

I kept my gaze on Len. "Greg."

"Five points!"

Len's expression didn't change.

"Why do you know that?"

"I listen, and I have a good memory."

"Are you stalking me?"

"Yeah... don't flatter yourself." He smiled.

"I never told you about my first boyfriend. I don't ever talk to you."

"I overheard it then. I don't know. I don't remember where I heard everything. I just have a good memory for random facts. Like that your mom's maiden name is Harris and your favorite flavor is vanilla."

"What's her favorite flavor?" I pointed to Jenna.

"She's my ex-girlfriend."

"Oh... well-"

"Just kidding."

"How is that funny?"

He laughed. "I don't know, it just is."

And then it was time for him to leave the room. I got all three questions about him wrong, and we got disqualified.

But he'd gotten my attention. I knew I had to be very careful about what I said around him.

When I returned to sit on the floor between Hattie and Jenna, they gave me sympathetic looks. "How did he get you to pair up with him?" Hattie wanted to know.

"He's got a photographic memory." That didn't precisely answer her question, but it nudged the conversation onto another topic.

"Yeah, he's smart," said Hattie. "But I felt so bad for you, having to sit next to him."

"Totally," agreed Jenna. "He's just gross. Dresses like a homeless guy."

"He just turned thirty." Hattie said this with satisfaction. "One more year and he's out of the ward."

"Does he ever even date?" I asked.

"Yeah, he had a girlfriend a couple of years ago," said Jenna. "But they broke up and she married someone else."

"My Aunt Shelly is always trying to set him up with friends' daughters from Utah and stuff." Hattie's Aunt Shelly was Len's mother.

Len didn't bother to return to the gym after we got disqualified. He often disappeared from church activities, usually to do some work in the clerk's office.

The next Sunday, after church, I went to the clerk's office, a boxy little room with a narrow window and an ancient computer. The keyboard had a layer of grime on it that turned my stomach. Len sat in the office chair with the keyboard in his lap and tapped away while his gaze flitted from the paper next to him to the screen, to the doorway. "Oh, hey," he said.

I folded my arms across my chest.

He lifted his eyebrows and the tap-tap-tap of the keyboard tapered off.

"Be honest," I said. "What else do you know about me?"

"Look, I'm sorry if I made you uncomfortable."

"Just promise me you're not a stalker."

"Guess that depends."

"On what?"

He raised his hands defensively. "Look, as far as I can tell, the only difference between a stalker and the most romantic guy ever is how the girl feels about him. If she's interested, the guy can sneak into her house and do her dishes or leave her love notes, and it's sooo sweet, but if she's not interested, it's freaky."

"Okay, what is that supposed to mean? You want to know if I'm interested in you?"

"Nah, I know the answer to that one." He turned his gaze back to the computer screen and resumed typing.

When I didn't leave, he looked up at me again. "What?"

"You know my birthday."

"Mmmm." He turned back to typing.

"Look... don't tell anyone how old I am."

"Why would I do that?"

"I don't know. Just don't."

"Of course not."

I should have turned to leave then, but I didn't. It had been so long since a guy had flirted with me, I couldn't shut down my one source of male attention, even if it was Len. "And you're wrong, okay?" I said.

"About?"

"I don't know you, so I don't know how I'd feel about you. It'd be better if you didn't go around gathering random facts about me, because yeah, that's a little freaky." Lies. Him collecting facts about me was more than "a little" freaky, and I did know how I felt about him. I felt he was a loser.

"I'm guessing you're not into nerds."

"Well, not really, no."

"Okay, and you and your artist intuition *have* picked up on the fact that I'm a nerd, right?"

That made me laugh.

He paused and looked at me again. "So it is possible to entertain you."

"Yeah, when you're being funny, not random."

"If I asked you out, would that be funny or random?"

"I don't know." I felt rooted to that spot. Logic dictated that I politely break off the conversation and leave, but I didn't. It'd been eleven months since I'd been on a date. Eleven months that I'd been invisible to all men.

"Well, let me know when you decide."

I lifted my chin. "Sounds like a purely hypothetical question, and I don't see the point in answering those."

"Fine, go out with me." He flicked his gaze in my direction, but kept his focus on his work. "There, not a hypothetical. You happy?"

"Hey, no reason to get mad at me."

He stopped typing and smoothed his hair back from his forehead. "Why are you dragging this out? Just say no and then you can go off and tell Hattie and Jenna how awful this was and I can go back to doing the tithing."

"I'm not like that. Really. I'm not that bad." I had no intention of telling my friends that he'd asked me out. They'd have been mortified.

"Okay. Sorry." He fidgeted with the stack of paper beside the keyboard.

I'd hurt his feelings, much to my surprise. He always seemed so aloof and amused by everyone and everything. This was the first time I'd seen him unhappy. "Um, okay, if you've got a specific idea for a date, let me know." It seemed nicer than just "No."

He still didn't look at me. "Okay."

"Okay... you know my phone number?"

"I can look it up. I don't have it memorized, if that makes you feel any better."

I left. At least I'd been nice to him, and it wasn't like he'd really call me. Only, by the time I reached the parking lot, I had a text. "I really like kids' movies. You want to see *Danger Dog* this Friday night?"

I was so shocked that I didn't reply then. I went home and fretted over it. A movie meant going to a public place. What were the odds that we'd be seen? I should have just said no, but the image of his downcast, hurt expression made that impossible. I couldn't be that cruel, so in the end I said yes, as long as we went to the six p.m. showing. That one wasn't likely to have anyone in the ward at it since it was too early to be convenient but still a full price evening show. And that's how it was I ended up going out with Len Hodge, the supernerd.

These thoughts ran their course as I finished off my sketch of Uncle Paul. I'd put a lot of effort into the eyes, making them stare off the page with real intensity. Aunt Nora had been so lucky. No guy that gorgeous had ever looked at me that way.

The sky outside was now light enough that I could move over to the window, only when I did, I saw a figure standing in the driveway, staring at the house, hands on hips. From this angle it looked like it was a woman. She moved and I saw that it was. She wore a long dark coat, not the sort of thing people wore in the summer. It was still six a.m., though. Not a normal time for someone to come by.

I went downstairs. Maybe it was Nora's friend, who'd come back to return the key.

The Figure

When I got downstairs, I peered through the window beside the front door. The figure was still there, but at the sight of me, she took her hands off her hips and retreated across the street. The trees in the front yard then obscured her from view.

I craned my neck and tried to get another glimpse of her, but it was no use.

Two hours later, when my aunt came downstairs, I told her about what I'd seen.

"Mmm, she really short?"

"I couldn't tell," I said.

"It's probably Louisa. Paul's sister. She stops to glare at the house whenever she walks by. I think she wishes that she'd inherited it."

"Oh."

"I don't like her. Horrible woman. Best to just leave her be."

"I drew a picture of Paul," I said. "A sketch. I need you to tell me what to keep and what to change for the final painting."

Her face lit up.

I went back upstairs, got the sketch from the bedroom, and went down to show her. Her gaze softened at the sight of it. "That's him," she said. "I'd make his nose a little broader and his eyebrows had a different slant, but you got the eyes perfectly." She blinked a few times and rested her head against her hand. "I'm so tired," she admitted.

"Go back to sleep, then. You've got healing to do."

Aunt Nora slept in until almost noon, or at least, she didn't come downstairs until then. I was working on different compositions for my sketch of Paul. This was the most time consuming part of the project, deciding on what to paint, what angle, what kind of lighting, and what sort of mood to create.

"Morning!" I said.

"Afternoon." She smiled.

"Are you hungry?"

"No, not really."

I got up from the couch. "You want a sandwich? Or something fancier?"

"I really am not hungry."

"Porridge? Or, cream of wheat?" I didn't know how to make porridge.

"Maybe something like that would be nice."

I followed her unsteady, rocking steps to the kitchen. The new keys were laid out on the counter and I handed her one. "The locksmith came by this morning."

"Oh, were you able to pay them?"

"Yeah." She had written out the check the day before.

The only cream of wheat she had was the microwave kind, so I made her a bowl while she sat at the table and rested her head against her hand once more. She really did look exhausted. I put her bowl of breakfast in front of her.

While she stirred her cream of wheat I dug out the slightly stale loaf I'd made toast from that morning and set about fixing myself a sandwich.

"I loved your sketch of Paul."

"Mmm, it was rough. It needs to look exactly like you remember him."

"You've got such skill. So much talent."

"Thanks. I-"

My celllphone rang. "Hello?"

"Hello, this Eliza?" The voice was male, and British.

"Yeah, hi."

"Hi, this is Colin."

Colin? As in Colin Radcliffe? The hot nurse? My pulse sped up. "How are you?"

"Sorry?"

I winced. Every time I came over here, I slipped and used that phrase, "How are you?" and many Brits either didn't understand, thought I was asking, "Who are you?", or thought it was funny to respond with a long litany of complaints. I never really understood the humor there. "Sorry, I should say, 'you all right?'"

"I'm good, yeah. Listen, would you fancy meeting up sometime?"

Aunt Nora looked at me expectantly, one eyebrow raised. I shook my finger at her.

"Sure," I said, trying to play it cool.

"We could go 'round to the pub-"

"I don't drink." I bit my lip and wondered if I'd even had to say that. I'd never "been 'round to the pub" in my life. Was the alcohol required?

"What? Not at all?"

"Nope."

"You're teetotal?"

"Um, I don't know what that means."

Aunt Nora spoke in a voice that was way too loud, "Would he like to take you to Carfax Chippy?"

I clapped my hand over my mouth to keep in the laughter that bubbled up.

"Carfax Chippy?" said Colin.

"She – ahem – sec." I took the phone from my ear and tried to shake my finger at my aunt again as I let all the giggles out, but she was most unrepentant. "Sorry, she was just telling me about her first date with her husband at Carfax Chippy."

"You've got to be joking."

"I take it the place still exists?"

"Ye-ah... why, do you want to go there?"

"No. It's just an inside joke. Ignore her."

"Why didn't he just take her to a kebab van? I mean, if you're going to set the standard low."

"Hey, it was a romantic moment for them. No mockery." To Nora I whispered, "What's a kebab van?"

Only Colin heard me. "They're the white vans you see parked around in the evenings. They sell chips and jacket potatoes and kebabs made from meat that's sort of congealed on an upright spit. There's one over on Broad Street that sells chips with cheese and curry sauce. Or even better, chips with cheese and mayonnaise-"

"You're kidding."

"I'm not taking you to one. A bloke's gotta have standards. If you want fish and chips, we could go to the chippy, though? They do a nice fish and chips."

"Sure, that sounds nice."

"You free Friday evening?"

"Yes, that'd work."

"Right, you know where Carfax Tower is?"

"Mmm-hmm."

"Shall we meet there at about seven?"

"Okay."

"All right. I'll see you then."

"See you then!"

Aunt Nora had her hands placed primly in front of her on the table and looked up at me with expectant, glowing eyes as I hung up.

"Um, kebab van, to eat chips with cheese and... I don't know. Sounded disgusting."

"Sorry if I ruined a romantic date."

"I'm joking. We're going to get fish and chips." I felt like I was sixteen all over again. I'd never dated a non-Mormon. I had no idea what I was doing.

Ten

Colin

Carfax Tower was square, built from stone, and always looked a little lopsided to me. It rose up from the corner of Cornmarket – a pedestrianized street with a lot of shops – and the High Street.

Because it was July, the sky was still light, and the tower cast a pale gray shadow, under which stood Colin. I was glad I caught sight of him from down the street, because my breath caught for a moment. He wore casual jeans and a shirt that was unbuttoned halfway down his chest. It suited him. Those warm brown eyes of his were fixed on his cellphone.

I composed myself as I threaded through the crowd of foot traffic and made my way to his side. "Hi," I said. "Hope I'm not late."

He glanced up and his expression brightened with recognition. "Hello. Nope, not at all." He slipped his phone into his pocket. We set off, weaving through the crowds. That's the thing about downtown Oxford, it's always crawling with tourists and locals doing their shopping. It was hard to have a conversation while we walked, but it wasn't far. The chippy was down a little, narrow alley off the High Street. The only problem was that it was closed. Our progress was brought up short by a heavy wooden door.

"Blimey, I've never seen them closed." Colin glanced at his watch. "Um, right, sooo, there's a nice sandwich shop over on Broad Street that we could try? I mean, I'm not sure what you'd like."

"That sounds fine, yeah," I agreed.

We cut across to the sandwich shop and I paused to look at the nearest college, which was across Broad Street from us and a little further down. It had a square tower over its front gate, complete with parapet at the top. Otherwise, the front of the college was flat sandstone. Narrow windows were spaced in vertical columns and each column was topped by a triangular gable that jutted up through the roofline. The building was old, though I didn't know enough about architecture to say what era it was from. "Is that Balliol?" I asked.

"I think so." Colin shrugged. "I don't know all the names of the colleges. Not from here originally."

It was in the right place to be Balliol.

"Why," asked Colin. "You want to go see it?"

"I'll see if I can get in some other time. My aunt was just telling me about it. It's where she met her husband and I'm trying to do a portrait for her."

"Oh, right. Well, the trick is to wave at the porters on your way in and act like you're a student."

We went into the sandwich shop and I paid for my meal. I couldn't tell if that was normal or if I'd breached the etiquette, or if Colin read anything in to my decision to pay. It was hard not to obsess over the details.

The shop, as it turned out, was about to close, so we got our food to go.

"Great," said Colin. "First I tell you that I'm taking you to a kebab van, then to a chippy, and then I take you to a place that's about to close."

Paint Me True

It was then that I noticed he was nervous. He did his best to act casual, but I recognized the darting gaze and self conscious posture.

That made it easier for me to relax. "My fault for saying no to the pub. I know nothing about pubs. I just assumed... I've barely ever been in a bar."

"You're joking."

I shook my head. "Just when you have to walk through one to get into a restaurant-"

"You've never just spent time there, talking to people?"

"No."

"None of your friends drink?"

"No, not really."

"Who are your friends, then?"

"A bunch of very dull people? No, I shouldn't say that. Um... I'm religious, and most of my friends are from the same religion." All of them were, to tell the truth. I'd had friendships with a more diverse group when I was in school, but I hadn't maintained any of those contacts. One thing about working as a gospel painter, it wasn't like I was forced to mix with others at the office. It hadn't occurred to me how one dimensional this made my social life, though.

He looked sidelong at me. "What religion is that?"

I had to tread carefully here. I wasn't going to lie, but I didn't want to make the situation more awkward than necessary. Even a religious person like me knows that this is one topic that makes most people squirm. "Is Christian non-threatening enough? And don't worry, I'm not preachy."

That earned me a smile as we stepped out of the shop.

"We could try to go see Balliol? I have no idea what's inside," he confided. "Maybe a nice place to sit."

"Sure."

We crossed the street, sauntered on in. The front gate was a stone arch and the porter sat on one side, behind what looked like a drive through bank teller's window. We both waved to him and he waved back, then looked past us. It worked. "Wow," I said. "Impressive."

"What did I tell you? Now, where did you want to see?" He and I stepped into the quad and stood to one side of the front gate so that we'd be out of sight and earshot of the porter.

"Well, actually, we've seen it." I pointed back over my shoulder.

"They met in the porter's lodge?"

"That's where she saw him first."

"Sooo, do you need a better look?"

"Let's look around inside first, before we get ourselves thrown out." The quad had a large oval of grass, surrounded by a walkway, and the college walled us in on all sides. Young people who could have been students milled around, though given it was summer, I wondered if any would be in residence.

Colin led me across the quad to another archway of stone, which we peered through. There was more grass and sunshine on the other side so we went through and found ourselves in a bigger quad, also surrounded by stone buildings and carpeted with manicured grass and walkways. We exchanged a look.

"I have no idea where I'm going," he said.

"Me neither. My aunt only came here for lessons. I don't know where those would even have been." There were other people sitting on the grass, though. "We can eat here, can't we?"

"Looks good to me."

We found a place to sit and opened up our sandwich bags. I took a bite of sandwich, which I barely tasted. I still felt anxious. This really felt like my first date ever. I didn't know how this was supposed to work. If I'd been out with another Mormon, we'd go miniature golfing or something and end things with a handshake or maybe a hug. "So you're not from Oxford?"

"Not originally, no. I'm from Reading. You know where that is?"

I shook my head.

"South of London. Not much else I can say about it really. I wouldn't recommend going there to sightsee. Where in the States are you from?"

"Utah."

"Oh... *oh*. So you don't drink because you're one of those... is Mormon the right word?"

"Yeah, that works."

"Or is that a slur?"

"No. It's not."

"But you're Christian?"

"Yeah. It's the Church of Jesus Christ of Latter-day Saints. We believe the Bible and all that." Plus some extra scriptures, I added in my mind. But again, I knew this wasn't a topic to linger on during a first date.

"What's Utah like?"

"Very pretty. Lots of mountains. Good skiing, but I kind of misspoke. I grew up in Utah. These days I live in Oregon. That's in the upper–"

"Northwest, just north of California. Yeah, that's the state that's got the same landmass as all of Great Britain."

"Really?"

"Without the sixty million people all packed in."

"Really? The island is that small?"

"You mean your state is that big, don't you?"

"Sure..."

He laughed. "Don't pick on countries smaller than yours, all right?"

"Sorry." This time I purposely lowered my gaze in a flirty way. "So when did you move out here?"

"For my job. Four years ago? How long you been a painter?"

"Ten years-ish?"

"Can I ask how old you are?"

"Thirty."

He didn't bat an eye. "Oh, right, well I'm twenty-seven. You've been working for a while, then."

"I guess. I kind of scrape by doing prints and commissions. It's not an easy way to make money, but it's flexible. I can come over here to look after my aunt on a moment's notice."

"How long are you here for?"

"My return flight's scheduled for a couple of weeks from now, but I really don't know. It's whenever Nora says she doesn't need me."

"How is she?"

"She's fine. Just her usual, stubborn self."

"That she is. Definitely a memorable case."

"I'm sorry if she made your life difficult."

He shook his head dismissively. "No, not really. The NHS staff treat people like sacks of potatoes sometimes, just toss them about and pay no attention to what they need. It was silly of them to send her to us, but I've seen odder cases. We had one little girl sent to us because the GP thought she had an eye tumor based on a photograph that someone took of her. I could look in the girl's eye and see there was nothing. Bloke didn't even know how to use an ophthalmoscope. Or we had a man once who had an upset stomach and the A&E told him he might have a tumor. No other symptoms, just nausea."

"Sounds weird."

"Yeah, it was." He shrugged.

I wadded up my sandwich bag.

"So, right, tell me about how your aunt met her fella."

"He walked through the porter's lodge when she was there and she fell for him and... well, that's pretty much all I know about what happened here. Later she saw him and he took her to Carfax Chippy."

"And she liked that?"

"Well, I mean, she ran into him and he flirted with her and talked her out of going to supper at her boarding house. She was totally infatuated."

"So if he'd taken her down a dark alley without a chippy at the end?"

"Don't say that."

"Sorry. Unromantic, I know. But I did work in an A&E for a while-"

"What is that? A&E?"

"I guess Americans call it the ER. Sorry to be morbid. I've just seen some spontaneous infatuations end badly."

"That is morbid."

"Eh, comes with the job."

"So, no, he fed her fish and chips."

"Well all right then. She was into that?"

"Sure. I mean, she'd only just seen him in the porter's lodge. They didn't talk or anything, and she thought he was the most gorgeous-"

"Okay, really? That really sounds like something that can end up in A&E. She'd never spoken to him before?"

"Please don't rain on my parade. I'm trying to learn what I can about the love story so I can paint her a portrait."

"Right, sorry. Besides, I shouldn't give you a hard time about going anywhere with a bloke you've barely ever spoken to before."

"Yeah," I said. "Good point." I wondered if Hattie would get after me if she could see me now for not testing Colin with a few rejections. The thing was, she'd get after me because he wasn't a member of the Church. Such people were beneath her notice, which was her prerogative. I just wished she wouldn't declare it so vociferously in public.

"They must've had other dates, other than at the chippy," said Colin.

"Yeah, I haven't gotten that far in the story yet. I just got here."

"Do you find that romantic? Seeing a guy and then having him be so... pushy? Would you like to be told where you should eat supper?"

"Well..."

He raised an eyebrow.

"Sorry, you just reminded me of something a, uh, friend of mine once said. He said the only difference between being a stalker and being the most romantic guy ever was whether or not the girl likes you."

"Wise words. I mean, there are other differences."

"Well, yeah."

"But there's something to that."

"Yeah. If my aunt had never seen Paul before, I'm pretty sure him trying to haul her off to a chippy would creep her out. But, I mean, he was being flirty, trying to see if she was interested by asking her to do something little like that with him."

Colin nodded. "If you say so. How old were they when they got married, then?"

"I don't know. I'm guessing she was about twenty-one-"

"Twenty-one? That's child marriage, that is."

"Yeah, another thing about Mormons, they – or we, I should say – marry young quite often."

"Are you looking to get married?"

"Eventually."

"But you're young. You're only thirty."

I suppressed the impulse to thank him profusely for saying that. He seemed sincere that I was too young to be worried about marriage, and if I showed him I felt otherwise, it'd probably push him away. Though, if he thought thirty was young, what did he think of his own twenty-seven years? Did he still consider himself to just be in the dating phase of his life? No commitments? It then occurred to me that he'd probably move in with a woman before marriage. That was a completely foreign concept to me.

He glanced at his watch.

I hauled my mind back from the tangents it'd raced down. "Think I can get some pictures of the porter's lodge?"

"Let's go see."

We hiked back and I snapped a bunch of pictures with my camera phone before we ducked out the little cutaway door in the front gate and stepped onto the pavement outside.

"I need to get to work in a few," said Colin.

"Oh, okay, well thanks for helping me get pictures."

"Yeah, this was nice. I can do better though. We should go punting some afternoon. You like punting?"

"I've never been."

"You know what it is, right?"

I had to shrug and shake my head.

"On the river. Wooden boats that you move by... well, punting is when you use a pole and push off the bottom of the river. Like what the gondoliers do in Venice, I think. I've never been there. You fancy going sometime? Punting... not to Venice."

"That sounds like fun."

"All right, I'll call you."

"Okay, great." That was the best I could do for a last line. The date wasn't Nora and Paul kind of fabulous, but it was fabulous enough to make me glow all the way home.

More Sketches

Later that night, as I checked my email, I saw Hattie log into her account. Nora's computer was in a little windowed office off the kitchen, though right then the windows were black as it was nighttime.

I opened a chat window and began to type.

Edunmar: Sooo, I had a date tonight.
HattieZ: With?!?!?!
Edunmar: Just some guy. Real nice. Very good looking.
HattieZ: I would hope so. Did you follow Rule One?
Edunmar: Did you? With Mike?
HattieZ: Yes!
Edunmar: What?
HattieZ: I told him that if he wanted to go out with me, he had to try harder. I wasn't going to just get up and go whenever he wanted, and the next time he asked me to go to the movies with him, I said no.
Edunmar: Then what happened?
HattieZ: He called again an hour later and asked if we could go to dinner, and I said no, so then he upped it to dinner at a fancy restaurant. I finally said yes, but only

if he promises to turn off his cellphone. No texting allowed.
Edunmar: Wow. Congratulations.
HattieZ: You were so right! So tell me about this guy.
Edunmar: Not much to tell, yet. Like I said, way good looking. Not sure how I feel about him.
HattieZ: Still, that's awesome! You want me to torment Len? I should totally tell him next time I see him.
Edunmar: Leave him alone. He's not worth it.
HattieZ: True. Well, wish me luck on my second first date with Mike!!!
Edunmar: Good luck

She logged off and I went back to my email. No new messages, so I shut down the computer and went upstairs to resume sketching. My aunt had already gone to bed, so the house was quiet as I settled into my usual spot under the lamp.

I hadn't told my friends about my first date with Len. I'd dressed casually for it in jeans and a plain cotton shirt and then spent the better part of an hour on my face. I didn't want to look like I had makeup on, but I wanted the benefits of makeup. I wanted to make my eyes look grayer and my lips fuller and my skin nice and smooth. Cosmetics is a difficult medium.

I tried to suppress the dread that welled up inside when his car pulled into my driveway. He was nonchalant when he came to the door, and his cargo pants and shirt looked relatively new. There were no dangling threads, no thin spots about to turn into holes, just a lot of wrinkles. One thing about working an office job and being a Saint, he wore his formal clothes a lot more than his informal clothes.

"Hi," was all he said.

"Hi."

And those were the only words we uttered to each other for the first two and a half hours of the date. We drove to the theater - which is an almost thirty minute drive from my house - in silence and once we were there and at the cash register to buy our tickets, I opened my purse to get my wallet and he dismissed the gesture with a wave. Even when the cashier asked if we wanted popcorn, Len told her he'd like some, then looked at me to see if I wanted some too. I nodded, reached for my wallet again, and he held out a hand to stop me. I was relieved when he got two tubs, rather than having us share one.

I barely remember the movie. I just remember munching popcorn while Len kept stealing glances at me. For whole long sequences, when the screen was bright enough to illuminate our faces, he'd stare at my profile, as if wondering why I was there. I wondered if the screen was bright enough for anyone else to see I was there with him.

On the ride home, I was the one to fold. "So, if you meant for this to be a one word date, sorry to break the streak here."

He flicked his gaze over at me and chuckled. His car was an old Ford Focus, well kept but showing its age. There were some water spots on the upholstery on my side and the top of the dashboard was faded. "Sorry," he said. "Just keep waiting for you to figure out that you really did go on a date with me."

"And do what about it?"

"Let me guess. You didn't tell Jenna and Hattie about this."

"Excuse me?"

"Sorry. Be honest, though. That... was your house I just passed." He turned left in order to go around the block.

"I'm not that awful," I said.

"I didn't use the word awful."

"Yeah, but everything you say about me-"

"You know, I do not think that you not wanting to date me makes you awful. I'm not that arrogant... and I just passed your house again... Sorry." Again he turned left.

"You think I'd never be interested in you?"

"I think you *aren't* interested in me. Quiet here for a min. I don't want to miss your house again."

I sat quietly while he made the last left turn, flipped on his turn signal, and stopped in front of my driveway.

"Okay," he said, as he turned in. "So, made it. Hope it wasn't too unbearable for you-"

"That doesn't really make a girl's heart melt, to be told that the date was 'unbearable'."

"For you. I don't mean me." He looked at me for a moment, then turned and let his forehead hit the steering wheel with a thud. "You want to go back to just being silent?" When I didn't reply, he hit his head against the steering wheel again.

"Could you please stop? I feel kinda bad whenever I drive a guy to self harm on a date."

He lifted his head and gave me a sheepish smile. "Sorry." He seemed to collect himself then. "Thanks for going out with me. It was fun."

Guys always said that on dates with me, but recently, it had begun to sound forced. Just a matter of politeness. I rarely got asked on a second date, and never a third. No one even tried to hold my hand anymore. It had been years since I'd sat through a movie with a guy who had his arm on the armrest, waiting for an opportune moment. The days when I'd kept my hands folded neatly in my lap, rejoicing at how frustrated a guy looked as a result, were an old and hazy memory.

Len pulled his parking brake, shut off the engine, and gave me a quizzical look.

I hadn't gotten out of his car. I just sat there. Worse, I didn't want to get out of his car just then. When I did, my last date in a long time would be over, and I'd have to face up to the fact that I'd had it with Len Hodge. Instead, I looked down at my hands.

Len shifted in his seat and touched my cheek with his thumb. "You okay?"

His touch startled me, and I felt my eyes grow hot with tears I didn't dare shed. I wasn't okay. I wanted to be ten years in the past, when I was one of the cutest girls in the ward and had just begun my career as a professional artist. People had been jealous of me. I had a cool job and trendy clothes and no shortage of guys lining up for dates. When anyone asked me out, I'd actually had to consult my calendar before I gave an answer.

How had I blown it this bad? Why hadn't I married one of those guys who'd fallen all over himself to get me on a date? I'd been proposed to five times – *five* times, and each time held out for better. None of them were quite perfect enough, and now all of them were settled with kids, while I lived off my stepmother's charity.

"Eliza?" His hand was on my shoulder now.

I looked up at him. He wanted to kiss me, I could tell, and I hadn't been kissed in years. Literally years.

Our gazes locked for a long moment, then I let mine drop to his mouth.

He didn't budge.

I shifted my weight, drawing a fraction of an inch closer to him.

Nothing. His hand stayed on my shoulder and his expression was all caring concern.

I chewed my lip, leaned in a little closer, employed every pathetic trick I knew, and he stayed put. But I could tell he wanted to kiss me. He was just being stoic about it.

So I grasped his shirt and pulled him in. For a moment, I felt despair as his hand on my shoulder pushed me away. Here I was, throwing myself at Len Hodge, and being rejected. Talk about desperation.

He let go of my shoulder, put his arm around my waist, and kissed me. His other hand took mine and he held it, palm to palm. I'd had a boyfriend who'd done that, once. A sweet guy whom I'd dated when I was nineteen. He'd left on his mission and I'd moved on within months.

The familiar gesture made me feel safe. Len's mouth was gentle and warm and his kisses were all closed mouthed and proper. One led to another, and each was a layer of balm on my lonely heart. He was the one to pull back, but even then he didn't push me away, but instead let go of my hand and held me. "You okay?" he whispered.

"No. Not really..." A tear slid down my cheek.

He wiped it away with his thumb.

More tears came. I hadn't been this stupid on a first date since I was sixteen and Rob Bilkins had pledged he'd marry me – in five years, after he got back from his mission. I'd bawled my eyes out in front of everyone. It was a group date, of course, three other couples. My dad didn't allow me to go on solo dates before I was eighteen, and given he was also my Bishop and I was proud of being righteous, I didn't push the boundaries there.

Len pulled a tissue out of an old faded box set in the console and handed it to me.

"Thanks."

"You want me to walk you to your door?"

"Sure."

We got out of his car. The night air was frigid. I pulled my coat tight around myself and he walked me with his arm around my shoulders. Before I went in, he kissed my forehead and said, "Have a good night, okay?"

"Okay. Night."

As soon as I stepped in the door, I wanted to flee to my room, curl up in fetal position, and never emerge again. I'd led him on, even though I hadn't wanted a date with him, let alone a relationship. At the time, though, it felt like he was the only person who cared about me. I hadn't just ignored Rule One, as Hattie called it. I'd done the opposite. I'd flung myself at a guy who was just being polite.

Paint Me True

A tear dropping from my cheek brought me back to myself in Nora's house. I looked at the assortment of sketches I'd done, and quite a few of them looked good. I chose one that was just a portrait of Paul staring out at the viewer. It was simple, but it had the most impact. I'd paint that one.

Twelve

At Church

That Sunday I went to church in the Oxford ward, which had its own building on Abingdon Road. It was all gray brick, with tall, two story windows that looked out onto the street like solemn, unblinking eyes.

A soft breeze pressed the hem of my dress to the backs of my calves and lifted my flounced short sleeves. I recognized some of the people filing in, but none were more than acquaintances. Several waved. When I got inside, I saw the chapel was about half full. A teenager with a shock of blond hair who moved with a dragging saunter came on over and gave me a program. "You new?" he asked.

"I'm visiting."

"Want a ward directory?" He tugged one loose from the bottom of the stack of programs.

"Yes, that'd be great."

He passed it over and sauntered on towards the door.

I resumed looking around. The Bishop was new. I didn't see the tall, imposing man who'd presided over the meeting last time. The man who sat on the stand now was shorter with gray hair and a hooked nose that was at odds with his kindly smile.

"Right," said a voice at my elbow. "Eliza is it?"

I looked and saw a whippet thin woman that I vaguely remembered from the last time I'd been to the ward. She was in a one piece red dress and had a pair of gloves folded in one hand, draped over a red clutch purse. "Oh, hi," I said to her. "I'm sorry, I don't remember your-"

"How long you here for this time?"

"We'll see. I'm looking after my aunt."

"What did the doctors say about her?"

"I'm... sorry?" One thing I never got about the English, they could look so prim and proper and yet be rude, nosy, and impolite, and they did it with such abandon, it was as if they didn't see the irony.

The woman clucked her tongue. "Never mind. She doesn't want me and my meddling. I know her answer. Never mind that we have an ambulance shrieking its way through the neighborhood at eleven o'clock at night. No one's business but her own, in her mind."

"Have we met?"

"Name's Louisa. I'm her sister-in-law."

"Oh." I looked at her again. She didn't have a dark trench coat, this time. Her hair was medium brown, straight as a pin, and a little bit stringy, probably because she kept stroking it back from her face. Her makeup was austere, but her eyes bright with curiosity. She glared at me as if I'd been the one to come up and ask the demanding questions. Her gaze slid over me, the judgment clear in the furrows of her brow.

"You've heard of me, I take it?" she said.

"Not really. Just that you were Paul's sister."

"Still am, right? Death doesn't dissolve a family bond."

"I didn't know you were Mormon."

She narrowed her eyes as if I'd said something rude and she was debating whether or not to call me on it, though I didn't understand how my comment could cause offense.

"Paul wasn't Mormon, was he?"

At that she barked a laugh. "No, no. Nothing of the sort."

"Oh, okay."

"You haven't told me how long you'll be here."

"Um, not sure, really. It'll depend."

"On?"

"How long Nora wants me to stay."

"And we're not to know anything about why she needs to fly you out from the States?"

"You know, it's not really any of your business, but she broke her arm."

"Don't you tell me what isn't my business. She's my sister-in-law. She's family. She owns the family *house*. Not that she thinks of it as such. Oh no, it's all hers."

"Sorry, um, even if you are a relative, I barely know you."

The woman rolled her eyes. "Typical. Can't say I expected any different. You're welcome 'round our place for supper anytime." She made it sound more like a challenge than an invitation. The words were barely out of her mouth before she'd turned on one spiky heel and stalked off. I saw her join a giant, bear of a man at the front of the chapel. There were thready blood vessels visible on his rather large nose, which met his forehead in a fold of skin that made him seem almost Neanderthal. His hands boasted fat fingers that had so much meat on them they appeared to curl, rather than have joints. The already diminutive Louisa looked like a child beside him.

I chose a seat towards the back. The more distance I could keep from these two, the better.

Aunt Nora was just getting up when I arrived at home. I found her in the kitchen in some jeans and a shirt that hung off her emaciated frame. At the sight of me coming in, she managed a thin smile. "Thought you'd be at church." There was the scent of toast browning in the air, and the electric kettle heated water with a whooshing crescendo.

"I was. It's over."

"Ah."

"You didn't tell me Louisa was Mormon."

My aunt grimaced at that. "Is she? Why am I not surprised?"

"How would she even find out about the Church?"

"By being a snoop. When I married into the family, she had to know everything about me. She didn't approve of the marriage. That's why I had the locks changed the moment Paul and I were man and wife."

"Still, it's kind of weird."

"No, it's not. She probably looked up 'Mormon' in the encyclopedia, contacted the Church, got some missionaries out to visit her, and then decided this was another way she could be superior to me, given I was inactive."

"It's worse, though. When she came up to me at church she..." My voice trailed off because all of the color had drained from Aunt Nora's face. "Are you okay?" Before I finished the sentence I had to dash into the kitchen and steady her.

She trembled, and gave a small cry of pain when I put my hand on her arm.

"What's wrong?"

"Just help me sit down." Her movements were jerky, like a marionette.

I slipped an arm around her, and noticed again how frail she was. Her shoulder blades bit deep into my bicep as I maneuvered her. "Are you all right?"

"I'm fine." The words came as a whisper and she squeezed her eyes shut in a prolonged wince. We made it halfway to the sitting room before she doubled over. I nearly dropped her, but managed to help her lower herself down to the floor. She curled up, shoulders pressed to her knees. The fingers of one hand clenched her clothes in a white knuckled grip. The other hand, with its arm still in the splint, was balled into a fist.

"Aunt Nora?"

"Just never you mind Louisa."

"Yeah, I wasn't thinking about her just now. What's the emergency number?"

"No, don't bother them with-"

"What is it, Aunt Nora?" I made my tone as firm as I could and cursed myself for not knowing the answer already. If I was going to look after her, I needed to be ready for things like this... whatever this was.

"Nine... nine... nine," she said between gasps.

I helped her lay down on her side on the carpet and scrambled for the phone. Seconds later I heard an almost bored voice say, "Emergency services?"

"Hi, my aunt's in severe pain. I'm not sure what's wrong, but she can't even walk."

"No x-rays," said my aunt.

I tried to keep my attention on the emergency operator, who double checked our address. "Now, are you certain you couldn't drive her?" he asked.

"I don't drive over here."

"Get a taxi?"

"Are you kidding me?"

"It's just that we don't like to send out ambulances if we can avoid it. They're quite costly-"

"She's got private insurance and is lying on the floor, unable to move. Get one out here now!"

"Right. One moment."

It was all I could do not to bash the phone against the counter top. My aunt looked so small and her shoulders were shaking. I didn't know if this was tears or tremors or convulsions of pain.

"One should be there shortly."

"Thank you."

Aunt Nora cried out again and I flew to her side. "Help's coming," I said. "Just try to relax." I cast about for something, anything to make her more comfortable and seized upon the throw pillows on the couch. I packed one underneath her back and tucked the other under her head.

"I just don't want x-rays," she whispered. "Or scans or-"

"Listen to me. First we're going to get you to an emergency room, and then we're going to talk to a doctor, and we're going to do whatever needs-"

She cried out again and tears ran from her eyes. One splashed off the tip of her nose and the other drew a line of mascara across her temple. I hadn't noticed that she'd put on makeup that morning. I moved to wring my hands and noticed that I still held the phone. For one hazy moment I wondered if I'd hung up or if the operator were still on the line, but the sound of the doorbell startled me into tossing it onto the couch and dashing out into the entry way.

The paramedics, two men built like linebackers with a rolling stretcher between them, followed my lead. At the sight of Nora, on the floor, they both knelt down. "Hello?" said one. "Can you hear us?"

My aunt nodded, but didn't open her eyes.

"Where do you hurt? Your belly there?"

Another nod.

"Can we feel?" He moved to straighten her legs away from her torso, but she screeched so loud that I clapped my hands over my ears.

"Right, I can't tell if the abdomen's distended-"

"Yeah, we just need to load her up."

The collapsed the stretcher so that it was low enough for them to hoist my aunt onto it without much effort. They raised it up again and I followed them as they rolled it down the hall.

"She's got private insurance," I babbled. "That affect which hospital she goes to?"

"Not when she's like this," said one. "We'll take her to the closest."

"Right," said the other one. "You want to ride in the ambulance, or you going to make your own way there?"

"I'll come with you if that's okay?" I was at my wits end, but I did remember to close and lock the door.

Thirteen

Back at the Hospital

The emergency room throbbed with noise and activity. Sounds ricocheted off the cheap industrial tile floor and plain white walls. The paramedics wheeled the stretcher in through two sets of sliding glass doors, exchanged a quick series of rapidly fired words with a clipboard wielding woman in scrubs and then carried on into the fray. Doctors and nurses bustled back and forth, yanking on clean rubber gloves with their teeth. Somewhere in the background, an alarm pinged and voices began to shout. The place reeked of antiseptic cleaner.

The paramedics deposited my aunt on a cot, drew the curtain shut around it, and were gone. I paced in that little curtained space, wondering if I'd need to fill out insurance paperwork or answer health history questions or what. Aunt Nora looked ashen, as if all the blood had leeched out of her face, leaving only thin, papery skin behind. She looked much older than forty-five, and I was terrified. I had no idea what was wrong, only that it was something bad. I felt at a loss, even though I'd spent hundreds of hours in hospitals, looking after my terminally ill mother and sisters.

"Eliza," my aunt whispered, "please don't let them take x-rays."

I had no idea how to respond. I felt like I was drowning, like all the noise and bustle on the other side of the curtain were tangible, palpable, able to displace the air in the room until I blacked out.

Get a grip, I thought.

"Eliza?" My aunt's thready voice was plaintive.

"Just give me a sec," I told her. I stepped through the curtain and into the insanity beyond. I had to leap back to get out of the way of a nurse pushing a man in a wheelchair who moaned about chest pains. Another team of personnel in scrubs dashed past in the other direction, talking what sounded like a code of letters and numbers.

My cellphone was warm from my pocket. I pressed it to one ear and covered the other with my hand.

"Hello?" Colin's voice answered after the third ring.

"Hi. It's Eliza." I tried to keep my voice steady, but I knew I probably sounded hysterical.

"You sound like you're calling from a warzone."

"I'm in the emergency room."

"So you are calling from a warzone."

"Look, I am so sorry. You were probably asleep. I mean, I know you work nights, and it's totally inappropriate for me to call you for help while you're not at work, but I just... I just..."

"Breathe," he said. "Deep breath. It's all right. You can call me. What's happened?"

"My aunt's in such severe pain that she can't even stand up, but she doesn't want x-rays."

"What do they want to x-ray?"

"Well, nothing yet. I don't know. She's just afraid-"

"Okay, slow down. Back up. Where does she hurt?"

"Her stomach."

"Like her belly area?"

"Yeah."

"That's soft tissue. You don't use x-rays for that. She'll need an MRI-"

"Which she'll hate too."

"Riiiight, or they can do an ultrasound. Ultrasound might be quicker."

Ultrasound? "Really?" No one had ever used an ultrasound on my mother or sisters, that I'd seen. For no logical reason, this made it seem like a much more humane and civilized tool. I'd always associated it with pregnancy and new babies and all that happiness.

"Yeah, but it's up to the doctors there, you know. They'll need to do a full examination and you're probably in quite a long queue. Anyone given her a pain pill?"

"No."

"Well grab the nearest nurse and ask her for a paracetamol or something. The doctor will want to prod her belly a little, and then they'll decide what kind of diagnostic equipment to use. It won't be x-rays, though."

"Thank you so much."

"It's no worries. You all right?"

"I'm just worried."

"Right, of course. Look, I'll call you tonight. If she's back in hospital, I'll make sure to ring and check on her."

"Okay. Thanks." Gray spots spun in my vision. I made myself breathe deeper and more slowly as I put my phone away. The antiseptic smells and the sounds of medical devices beeping were more than I could take. I *hated* hospitals.

You aren't the one who's sick, I reminded myself. This wasn't about me, and I'd left my aunt alone in her little curtained cubicle. "Excuse me." I stopped the next person in scrubs who went by, a young woman who gave me a startled look. "Sorry," I said. "My aunt is in extreme pain. Can she have a paracetamol?"

"What's she in for, then?"

"We don't know-"

"Can't give her drugs until we know."

"You're kidding, right? She can barely move."

"Right, look, I'll see what I can do," the woman said in that tone of voice that let me know she was going to forget all about me in thirty seconds, and she just wanted me to leave her alone.

"Well who can give me some pain reliever?" I demanded. "Something mild. I'm not asking for morphine. Ibuprofin will work."

The woman shook her head, so I jerked open the curtains. My aunt hadn't stirred. Her jaw was set and her forehead had permanent wrinkles as she withstood the agony. "Fine," I said. "Then you tell her you can't give her pain reliever." Being nice was a waste of time in a hospital. I'd learned that as a child. Healthcare workers looked after squeaky wheels first, to make the rest of their job more bearable. I folded my arms across my chest in a way that I hoped made it clear that I would not let this woman go if she didn't do something to help us.

She shut her eyes a moment as if willing me to disappear, then said, "All right, what's wrong here then?"

"Severe pain. That's all I know."

"She broke her arm there?"

"Yeah, a week ago. Got lightheaded and fell. This pain is in her stomach."

The woman picked up my aunt's chart and flipped through it. "Right. Let me feel your stomach."

Though I moved to protest, she arranged my aunt deftly so that she could prod her stomach with both hands. "Right, okay, no intestinal blockage. No ruptured appendix. This hurt?" She pressed hard and then let go fast.

My aunt didn't wince any more than she was already wincing.

"Right, we're going to need an MRI."

"What about an ultrasound?" I said.

"Or an ultrasound."

"Would that be... faster?"

"Could be. Right. I'll be right back."

I folded my arms and she gave me a longsuffering look. At least we understood each other. I was one of *those* kinds of relatives, the ones who took no prisoners when it came to getting healthcare for our loved ones. I didn't take my eyes off her until she'd rounded a corner and I had to jump back for another team of paramedics wheeling a stretcher.

"Honey, I don't want a scan," said Aunt Nora. Her voice was so soft, it was hard to hear over the hubbub.

"Ultrasound," I told her. "Fast and easy."

"Even that."

"They have to figure out what's wrong. Don't you want to know what's wrong?"

The woman who'd helped us before came back around the corner with a man in scrubs who pushed an ultrasound machine on a cart. They maneuvered over to Aunt Nora's cot and yanked the curtains shut behind them, closing the four of us in.

"I need to do a full pelvic exam," she said to me. "You might want to wait outside-"

"No," said my aunt.

"I'll just avert my eyes," I said. I turned to look at the wall.

"Right, need you to lay on your back," I heard her say.

If this hurt Nora, she at least didn't cry out.

"Okay... right... I'm feeling one ovary, but not the other. Have you ever had an ovary removed? I see you've got an incision scar here."

"No," said my aunt.

The realization hit like a slap in the face. A missing ovary meant the next thing to look for was a tumor, one that might have ruptured the organ. That event, I happened to know, was extremely painful. It had happened to my sister. I also knew that cancer of the ovaries could sneak up on a person. Its lack of early symptoms made it deadly.

"You know what this is, don't you?" I said. "That's why you don't want an ultrasound."

"Sweetie..."

I leaned one arm against the wall and pressed my forehead to it. This could not be happening. Aunt Nora was like me, one of the lucky ones, a survivor. But even if she'd been spared the family curse, that didn't mean she was immune to cancer. It attacked people without the BRCA mutation all the time. Moreover, I'd never asked her about the gene mutation. For all I knew, she might have it after all.

"Okay, this gel will feel cold," the woman said.

"Did you have any symptoms? Any at all?" I asked Nora.

"I'm seeing only one ovary... okay, right, we're going to need to book you in with an oncologist. This will probably need surgery."

"No..." My aunt's voice sounded weak and wrung out.

"She's got private insurance," I said. "Can you transfer us to St. John's?"

"Right. Let me just ring them and see. But first let's get your clothes back on."

I waited until they'd done that before I turned around to look at her.

Aunt Nora's eyes were still squeezed shut. Her pain hadn't been treated or dealt with, though I noticed the woman in scrubs was flicking the needle of a syringe full of something. "You'll feel a sharp scratch," she warned my aunt before she slid the needle into the flesh of her arm.

"It'll be okay," I said. "I've been down this road before. I'll take care of you."

"You've been through this too many times already," she whispered.

"There is no 'too many' for the people I love. I'll go through this again with you, no question. We are in this together." Her eyes were still shut, so she didn't see me lean against the wall and let the sounds and smells and lifedraining light of the ER wash over me.

"I can't believe this is happening again," I said to Colin that night as we stood out in the hallway. Aunt Nora was now at St. John's.

"You don't know that it's cancer."

"Sure, it might be a totally benign tumor that just busted her ovary. Come on, you don't believe that."

"I'm just saying, don't jump to conclusions. Just because that's how things played out last time someone in your family had this-"

"The last three times."

His eyes widened at that, as if he wasn't sure he'd heard me right. "Three times?"

"My family has the BRCA mutation, you heard of it?"

"Oh, right, yes."

"Even for a family with the mutation, our health history is bad. I think the woman who asked me all about it tonight thought I was lying."

"How bad?"

"Both my sisters, my mother, her sister, my grandmother and her two sisters-"

"Are you serious?"

"All diagnosed with cancer in their twenties, all dead before the age of forty. Three of them got cancer in the ovaries at some point."

"*Seriously?*"

"Yeah."

"So, if you don't mind my asking, have you ever been treated for cancer?"

"I don't have the mutation, and I didn't think my aunt had it either."

Those liquid brown eyes scanned my face for a moment as he let that sink in. "You must have seen a lot of hospitals."

"You have no idea."

"Well, anyhow, we've booked her for an MRI first thing tomorrow and we'll move quickly. I'll make sure everyone who needs to know, knows about how fast cancers tend to spread in your family."

"Thank you."

I went into my aunt's room and found her staring listlessly at the wall as if it were some dark, infinite, abyss. Her hand, when I took it in mine, was cool. "How are you?"

"Honey, I don't want surgery."

"MRI first."

Her mouth tensed slightly as if she had to fight the urge to say no.

"You can't just give up," I said. "You're a fighter. You're a survivor. You're like me."

That made her gaze flick back to my face. "I'm not as tough as you."

"Are you kidding? You're the strongest woman I know. I admire you. We're going to fight this, and we're going to win."

My aunt's eyes unfocused. It was as if I could feel her slipping away, out of her body into a nether space where I couldn't reach her.

"Please don't give up," I said.

Her hand in mine was too relaxed. Limp, almost.

"I'll paint you anything you want. Please."

The light returned to her eyes and she chuckled. "You've got my number, don't you?"

"It's all I know how to do. I mean, I know this has to be hard without Paul, and if I could bring him back for you, I would. But I can't. I can capture moments, though. Is there anything else you want immortalized and that you don't have a picture of? Some scene from your time with him that is vivid in your mind, but that no one else ever saw?"

"Oh, there are hundreds of those. Millions, even."

"Let's find one. And if you want to tell me long stories until we do, that's fine by me. I can listen."

Her hand tightened around mine. "I don't know what I'd do without you."

"I'll stay as long as you need me. My visa's good for six months, and then I can just take a trip over to Ireland or France and come back in for another six."

"You're sure this is okay? I don't want you to stop living your life for me."

"I do not miss my life back in Portland. No, this is good. Really."

Those stormy gray eyes scanned my face again and her lips parted, as if she would say something, but no words came.

I waited and gave her the space she needed to collect her thoughts.

But she gave my hand a squeeze and turned away. "I'm just so tired."

"Okay, well, I need to leave soon anyway, but I'll be back tomorrow."

When I arrived back at Nora's house, there was a tuna casserole on the front stoop. "Ah, there you are," said a voice behind me.

I turned slowly. Louisa was not whom I wanted to see at the moment, but there she was, striding up the driveway. I wondered if she'd been staked out across the street. "What's happening, then?" she asked. "Is Nora back in hospital?"

"Um, well..."

"I brought you a casserole. Why don't I take it inside for you, cut you a slice."

"No, that's okay."

"You're a painter, aren't you? That's what Sister Mason said when I was asking 'round about you during Relief Society." She peered up at me with narrowed eyes.

"I am a painter, yes."

"What kind?"

"Gospel art. The kind of stuff they sell in LDS bookstores."

"Riiight, I haven't been to Godstone in ages. That's where the LDS bookstore is here. Did you know that? Is painting very lucrative?"

"Excuse me?"

"I got the impression Nora flew you out here. Is that wrong? I know some artists make a lot of money, but I'd think for gospel art, you'd be just barely making ends meet. About how much do you make?"

This woman made annoyance a fine art. It was as if she could see every vulnerable spot and hit it with pinpoint accuracy. I felt like I was being pricked with a hatpin over and over. She had me backed up to the door. I nearly stepped in the stupid casserole.

"Look," I snapped. "Sorry to be rude, but I've had a rough day and unless you're offering to prepare my tax return, it's really none of your business how much money I make."

"Or don't make."

"Or don't make." I stood my ground.

Louisa looked me over. "Are you not going in?"

"No. I remembered I left something at the hospital." I stepped away from the door.

She rolled her eyes. "Fine then." And for the second time that day I saw her pivot on her heel and stalk off. This woman had issues.

I waited until she was around the corner before I let myself into the house. I scooped up a happy, wriggling Pip and went back to the computer, where I logged into Skype. My dad was on.

He was nearly always on, given he had an iPhone. I hit the icon to call him and Skype played its plinky notes, then the high pitched ringtone.

Fatherly Advice

"Eliza!" My dad's pixellated face smiled out at me. I couldn't tell where he was. The background was too washed out with light, but I guessed he was at home.

"Hey, Dad."

"How are you?"

"Um, I'm kind of in the UK."

"Oh?" He squinted out of the display at me. I saw his gaze take in the wallpapered wall behind me. "Is Nora okay?"

"No, she's not."

His smile faded. "Cancer?"

"Probably."

"Honey, I am so sorry. How bad is it?"

"I don't know. Her ovary ruptured-"

My dad winced in response to that.

"-and they're going to do scans and then surgery and we'll see."

"Well... drat, honey. I'd thought you'd call with different news."

"Hmm?"

"Never mind."

"Wait, what?"

"A young man called last week, asked what your favorite food was, introduced himself to me. His name was Len?"

"Oh... right."

"I take it you're dating him?"

"Um, yeah, I was. Not anymore, but we went out for a while."

"Not anymore?"

"It's all good."

"He was an interesting guy."

"Very diplomatic."

"I wasn't being diplomatic. I'm guessing you never went to that restaurant with him? Or did you go and break his heart?"

"No. Things are over, and no one's heart got broken."

"Okay. How does that work?"

I tapped my fingernails against the edge of the desk. "Len broke up with me."

"I'm sorry."

"Don't be. We were all wrong for each other. He took me to a steakhouse as a grand last date."

"I see."

"Yeah, it was weird, but that's Len."

"Kind of classy, I have to say. Though it's too bad. I liked the guy."

"How long did you talk to him?"

"Oh, I dunno. Twenty minutes? He introduced himself, asked about your favorite restaurant and he was real pleasant. Laughed when I asked him if I needed to get my shotgun and promised me he'd never dream of hurting you. We talked about you for a few minutes-"

"What about me?"

"Well... let me think. After the shotgun comment I asked him why he was taking you to a steakhouse and he just said... what did he say? He said you did a lot of things with him that weren't your style, like eating microwave burritos and going to children's movies, and that he couldn't get you to tell him what you'd really like to do, so he said he got up his courage and called me, and thanked me for getting through the gun threats early in the conversation. I didn't have the heart to press the guy, though I was burning up with curiosity, wondering if he was gonna propose to you. I didn't even have a restaurant to recommend him, and he already knew you liked steak. I tried to get a read on what he'd be like as a son-in-law, just in case."

"Dad, I'd never even told you I was dating him. Why did you think-"

"Two words. Jeremy Carlson."

"Dad! He was insane, okay? I'd been on three dates with him."

"Robert Oaks?"

"I told you I was dating him!"

"Before he proposed to you, what? The tenth time?"

"Dad..."

"Guys have been lining up for you since you turned eighteen."

"Rub it in."

"Rub what in?"

"That I'm thirty and unmarried and-"

"Whoa there. Guess I hit a nerve. Honey, relax. The right guy will be worth the wait."

I buried my face in my hands.

"You sure no one's heart got broken this last time around?"

"Yes!"

"All right."

"Can we talk about cancer again?"

"Sorry, honey. I didn't mean to upset you."

"No, it's okay. Thanks for letting me vent at you."

"Did you vent? I didn't notice. Does that make me compassionate, or just a clueless male?"

"Definitely compassionate."

"I'm relieved. Anything else you need?"

"Not really."

"So, I'll talk to you later?"

"Yeah. Love you."

"I love you too, honey."

The call cut off and I went to eat a slice of tuna casserole. Only, my hand shook. It was hard to get bites of casserole into my mouth without stabbing my lip. I tried to take a deep breath, but it went in shaky and came out like a sob. The fork hit the floor with a clang as my tear ducts began to burn. I can do this, I thought. I helped my mom and my sisters and my aunt. I can do this. I can do this...

I retrieved the fork, rinsed it, and choked down some more casserole before I gave up on that and went upstairs. I wanted to paint, but I hadn't really planned out the portrait as well as I'd have liked. I knew from experience that if I just painted without enough forethought, it'd make me irritable. I was very intellectual about my art. If I didn't know where I was going, I'd flounder and start touching up what I'd already done and mess around with it until I'd screwed it up past redemption and then I'd be in a really foul mood.

But right then I didn't care. I wanted painting to make me happy, even if I knew that it wouldn't. The bedroom next to the one I stayed in was set up as a studio. I busied myself arranging the lights and preparing my paints, then I put brush to canvas and dove right in.

Half an hour later, I was still painting and the tightness between my shoulderblades had eased. The brush moved easily over the canvass. I didn't *love* the portrait that was taking shape, but it was a decent start. I could touch it up into the painting I wanted it to be. This was going to work.

For the first time in my life, going with my instinct worked. *Finally* my formal training and my subconscious desires were coming together without hours of sketching and measuring and laying out gridlines and experimenting with color palettes that I always did to wrestle the subconscious beast of inspiration into something beautiful and comprehensible. My heart felt light enough to lift me off my stool.

I hadn't had a breakthrough like this in almost a decade.

Picnics in the Park

When I got to the hospital the next morning, my aunt was awake, her eyes bright. "Good morning," she chirped as I came in.

"Good morning." I hadn't slept much, but the hours I had gotten had been deep and refreshing. Now I felt I could put my game face on. The fact that my aunt looked so well made it easier than I'd feared.

"So, I've been thinking about what I'd like a picture of."

"And you decided?"

"Paul and I had a ritual. I'd like a picture of that."

"And I'd love to hear about it." I sat down in the molded plastic chair, smoothed my skirt, and got ready to listen.

Her eyes unfocused.

I had my first Oxford tutorial fourth day I was here, and it was awful. The tutor was a stuck up grad student who'd corrected all of the American spellings in my essay and made bucket loads of snide remarks about foreign students who bought their way into the

Oxford experience. I think he called us parasites, though since he also complained that colleges used us to fund their other activities, I don't think that's an apt term.

Anyway, he made me cry. I held it in until I was across the quad and in the Porter's Lodge, but then I lost control and the tears just streamed down. I felt so lost and inexperienced, like I'd been thrown in the deep end of the pool by people who just stood back and laughed while I flailed. I decided then and there that I was going home however I could. I'd pack and get a bus to Heathrow and just go. But then...

"Mi'lady?"

It was Paul's voice, and I was mortified. I couldn't let him see me like this, but I didn't want him to go away. He'd only taken me out that once and I hadn't hardly seen him since. If I didn't answer, he might disappear.

I looked at him, tears still streaming down my face.

"You all right?" he asked.

"Yeah."

"You don't seem all right."

I dabbed my face with my fingers. "I guess I don't feel well." I looked down at his brown leather shoes. He caught me under the chin with one finger and made me look up.

It was hard to meet his gaze. Those eyes were intent, focused. I couldn't hide from him.

"What happened?"

"Just a bad tutorial."

"Those are never worth crying over. Trust me. I don't cry over them."

"I don't feel like I fit in here."

"Also not a bad thing." He took me by the arm and pulled me through the gate and onto the sidewalk.

I was mortified. I couldn't go out, looking like this.

"Come on," he said. "I've just had a bad tute myself. Let's go." He put an arm around me.

"Go where?"

"Well, I can either go get a pint with my mates, or I can take a beautiful woman out for a picnic. I know which I'd prefer. Howabout you?"

My knees turned to mush at that. I started to walk and nearly ran into a girl. She gaped at Paul, then looked at me as if I were a mouse and she were a snake. Only, I was safe with Paul's arm around my waist. He didn't spare her a glance as he guided me past her and across the street.

We went to a sandwich shop where he ordered me a prawn cocktail sandwich. He barked orders to the people behind the counter like a lord ordering his serfs, and they hopped right to it and made the sandwich and packed it up in a bag with some slices of cake. Paul paid and then guided me out of the shop, past more jealous looking girls, and walked me to the park. We sat in view of the river and he laid out his sweater for me to sit on.

Even though there were the usual crowds of people milling around, eating, studying, and strolling, I felt like we were the only people in the world. Paul set out our lunch and then leaned back while I ate. I asked if he were hungry and he just chuckled and shook his head.

"Do you feel better?"

"Much."

"Good." He shut his eyes like a cat stretched out on a sunny windowsill.

We barely spoke. I just ate first the sandwich and then the slice of cake that he pushed into my hands. Then we lay on our backs and watched the clouds roll past. It was a sunny October day, and the shadows were lengthening. The clouds were distant and fluffy and watching them overhead made me feel like they took up my cares with them and carried them away for good.

Aunt Nora's eyes were shining. "I know it seems silly. Just an afternoon in the park, but..."

"No, it doesn't sound silly. I think I may know the sandwich shop, even."

"We went there a lot after that. It was on the way to the park. We'd go on walks or sit by the water and eat. I never took any pictures, though. Not sure what would capture that moment, really."

"Let me think about it and then we can figure out the composition."

The memory had restored the light to my aunt's countenance. I tried to think of a time I'd felt like I'd been rescued from my mundane life. There were countless memories when I wished I could feel that way. The hours I'd spent in the hospital waiting room as my mother fought to live and lost. The torrent of phone calls I'd gotten when Lindsay's cancer was diagnosed. I was in school and in the course of one class I'd feel my phone buzz over and over again as my family filled my inbox with message after message about cancer and treatments and options and last minute reunion plans.

The sound of my father overcome with tears when he called me to say that Rachel was gone. She'd been determined to have surgery, despite her weakened state. The doctors had warned us she might not make it, but nothing ever stopped Rachel. She was demanding and imperious and infuriating, and it made no sense that a mere operation could have ripped her from our world.

I squelched these memories, wadded them up like paper and threw them to the back of my mind. Now wasn't the time to see them, or to wonder if I'd soon have more to add.

If Nora noticed my clenched fists, though, she gave no sign. She sat up, her legs crossed, and fiddled with a fold in her sheet. For a moment, it was easy to forget she was sick. It was like I had the old Aunt Nora back.

I got out my sketchbook and got to work, blocking out possible poses and angles. Later, I'd make a trip to the park, but right now I wanted to find a good composition for the characters. I tried sketching the figures from above, but that didn't really pull the viewer into the picture. I tried several different angles, and finally decided on one with my aunt sitting with her back to the viewer, eating her sandwich. Paul lay propped up on one elbow, his attention entirely on her. Even with my aunt's back in the field of view, I still felt this drew a person into the picture. They would have some hint of what passed between Nora and Paul and would instinctively step closer, as if hoping to overhear what the two lovebirds said.

I shaded in Paul's hair and filled in more of his facial features. He was entirely focused on my aunt and looked at her as if the rest of the world didn't exist. It was easy to imagine him, his gray eyes intent. I'd find an open spot in the park, I decided. I wanted the painting to convey that these two people created their own space. They weren't hidden away somewhere, out of sight, but rather could make the rest of the world disappear no matter where they were, they were so enraptured with each other.

Someone behind me cleared their throat and I glanced at the time. An hour and a half had flown by. I sat bolt upright and turned to face the stern expression of the nurse who stood in the doorway. She had high cheekbones, skin as dark as undiluted coffee, and brown eyes that were narrowed in a way that said she would tolerate no misbehavior.

"Ms. Chesterton has an MRI over at the hospital."

"I don't want any scans," muttered Nora.

"Aunt Nora, please," I said. "You promised. No running away."

The nurse lifted her chin and looked down at me with approval.

"I'm not running away-"

"Get up. You're going," I said.

Her shoulders drooped as if she were a puppet and someone had just let her strings go slack. "Please honey, don't make me do this."

"You have to do this. I don't want to lose you, okay? It's not your time. Let's go." I put my hand on her arm but she pulled away from me like a sullen child.

"Ms. Chesterton," snapped the nurse.

I put up a hand to hold her back. I got the impression that, imposing as she was now, she could dial it up even further, and that wouldn't work on my aunt.

Nora looked up at me, tears in her eyes. "I hate all this." In that moment she wasn't my older, stylish aunt who breezed through the world with unstoppable confidence. She was just a woman, and she was scared. That was the worst part of cancer, the way it reduced people, casting them down to the depths of humility and fear.

"I'll come with you. It'll be okay. Just think about Paul and the painting I'm going to do for you-"

"Listen, I don't want anything but the smallest area possible scanned. No extra scans, no extra radiation, do you hear?"

"I've told them how you feel. Colin passed it all on." I took my aunt firmly by the arm and hauled her out of bed. This, I knew, was the loving thing to do, but my aunt looked at me as if I'd just betrayed her to her worst enemy.

There was a wheelchair waiting for her in the hall. The nurse and I loaded her on and we set off. My aunt sat rigid and stared straight ahead. The nurse was happy because she was getting her job done. I forced myself to be optimistic. We'd find a benign tumor, or a cyst. Yes, a cyst.

We went out the front doors, across the parking lot, and into the hospital. After a couple of turns, we rode the elevator down, then went down another hallway and into a room with a big, bulky MRI machine. It was an older model than the ones that had scanned my sister, I noted, as the nurse and a man in scrubs with tired looking eyes and a scruffy attempt at a goatee exchanged information and my aunt's records.

"Listen," Aunt Nora said, the moment the nurse left the room. "You scan here and only here." She blocked out a square on her abdomen with her hands.

"Aunt Nora, they may need-"

"Scan only here or I get up and walk out." Her eyes were like ice and her tone like steel.

The technician looked at me, as if she'd just slapped him in the face.

"Where do you need to scan?" I asked.

"I need to check for a tumor in her abdominal cavity. Probably not more than what she says." His eyes pleaded with me though. This was a man who spent his days taking pictures of peoples insides. It was likely that he went weeks without having a single real conversation with a patient, let alone a negotiation.

"I think it'll be okay," I said to my aunt.

She glared at him, then at me. I made sure not to let my irritation show. This entire moment seemed balanced on the tip of a pin, and I didn't know which way it'd drop. Would Nora get the scan and be angry? Run out and cause a scene? Curl up in a ball and cry?

Slowly, she got to her feet and faced the slablike table where she would have to lay. With another baleful glance at the technician, she shuffled over. I helped her up and the technician began to fuss with her gown in order to make sure she lay the right way and everything lined up as it should.

"You need to go outside, please," he said.

Nora didn't even acknowledge that.

"I'll see you soon," I said, and slipped away.

Out in the hallway I paced. These moments, the waiting, they always seemed to last an eternity.

That afternoon, when Nora fell asleep, I went to tour the park. It was somewhat difficult to pin down which park my aunt was thinking of. Along the river were several open spaces, some on college grounds, some not. Oxford had a fair amount of greenspace. I chose the most obvious location, a broad expanse of public park with gravel paths cutting pale lines through the lush grass.

There was plenty of open area away from trees, and I took dozens of pictures with my phone of what looked like the prettiest backgrounds. I wanted some dreaming spires in the distance, but all of my attempts to frame such a shot came to nothing, and I decided that I shouldn't let reality get in the way of a great picture. George Washington had probably not stood up and pointed as he crossed the Delaware, and Aunt Nora might not have been in line of sight of any dreaming spires the day she and Paul made the park their own place. The picture, I decided, was symbolic. I was putting in elements that filled out the rest of the story. My subjects weren't just falling madly in love, they were falling madly in love in Oxford, in autumn.

I looked wistfully at all the bicyclists who zipped past on the road. I wished I had the courage to join them, but not only did the cars all drive on the wrong side of the road, the roads were narrow and twisting, and the cars shot down them so fast that if I were to cross in front of one, there was no doubt who would live to tell the tale. It wouldn't be me.

When I got back to the hospital, the nurse on duty, a small man who spoke with such a low voice that I had to lean indecently close to hear him, told me, "The oncologist should be by today to discuss her scans."

"Okay. Well, I'll be here."

The doctor was busy for the rest of the day, though. I waited the long hours in Nora's room while she slept. It didn't seem right, her sleeping so much. No matter how hard I worked to compose my second painting for her, her sleeping figure was like an anchor that dragged on me. I couldn't cut loose and create.

Second Painting

That evening, my Dad answered Skype immediately. "What's wrong?" he asked. It was voice only, which meant he was walking around somewhere with his phone to his ear. Or maybe he was on his hands free device.

I turned off my video. "Dad, do you happen to have Keeley or John's phone numbers?"

"Your cousins?"

"Yeah."

He sighed into the phone with a blast of static. "I don't know, hon. Nora doesn't have them anywhere?"

"I don't know. I don't want to snoop, and I don't know whether to bring it up. She never talks about them. But..."

"What did the doctors find?"

"I don't know, but she's scared. Deep down, I can tell she's worried that this could kill her."

"She's like you, honey, a veteran. She's seen enough other people die this way that she knows too much about what's in store."

"Yeah."

"Eliza, are you okay out there? Do you need me to come join you, or we can get other family-"

"What other family? I don't think Mark would be able to take time off work, and he barely knows Nora." Mark was my brother.

"I know. I just don't like the idea of you facing this again, and alone this time."

"Thanks."

"I can come out-"

"I'll keep the offer in mind, but right now, I think that I'm best off not calling in the troops. It'll make things seem even worse to her. That's why I'd like to call her kids without having to ask her for their numbers. They should know, but-"

"Yeah... honey, why don't you think again about that? Either let Nora know what you're doing or leave it be. I don't know the details, but I gather Nora's estranged from everyone in her family but you. The fact that her kids either don't know she's ill, or know but haven't even called, means there's a situation there and you don't want to get in the middle of that."

"And if I find out she's terminal?"

"It's good to think ahead, but that's thinking too far ahead. You don't know any such thing yet."

That made sense. "Okay."

"Call me anytime, all right?"

"Thanks. Oh, and I should have said before, Hattie's house-sitting Carrie's house. You know, my friend-"

"With the really right wing political agenda? Yes."

"I don't know that it's an agenda. More like a dogma."

"Ah, I see. My mistake."

I giggled. "Dad, don't."

"I'm not doing anything."

"You're making me laugh at my friend."

"That is all you, honey."

"I hate how you do that!"

"Yes, I feel the anger." My dad could deliver irony with the most dead serious tone I'd ever heard.

"Night, Dad."

"I love you."

"Love you, too."

He waited for me to cut the connection.

I went upstairs. It was late, but I was in no mood to sleep. The first portrait of Paul rested against the easel in the studio. It had turned out all right. I moved it over to the wall, got out my paints, and started to work. I'd done even less pre-planning this time around. It'd been impossible at Nora's bedside, but I hoped some of the magic that had happened last night would happen again.

I let my mind wander to Nora's story about the park. She'd told me only that one, short story, but I surmised that there were hundreds more. The park, she told me, was their place. That second date hadn't really ended; it carried on every time they went back to the park.

Me and Len... our second date had been like that too, but in a different way.

"Um, hey," he had said on the phone a week after our first date. "You doing anything tonight?"

The casual ask out without even a whole day's notice. I was tempted to say I was busy, just on principle, but the truth was, it was Friday night and I didn't have anything to do. Hattie was on a date Jenna was at work. "Well..."

"I could rent a movie," he said. "Or I've got *Winnie the Pooh* from Netflix."

"I dunno. Is that one gospel appropriate?" I asked. "Those British can be kinda racy."

Stupid joke, but Len cracked up. His sense of humor was always a little... off. Or a lot off, actually. "That a yes?"

It wasn't, but since I could think of worse things to do than watch a children's movie, I said, "I guess so."

"Okay, I'll come by at... seven? I could bring dinner, but it'd be microwave burritos."

"No, that's all right." I'd slaved yesterday over a lasagna with white cheese and white asparagus – it was a gourmet lasagna, and the thought of eating it alone didn't exactly fill me with joy. "I've got dinner," I said. "You bring the scandalous European film."

"Disney is-"

"From Eastern Europe. That whole style of animation is. How uncultured are you?"

"I bet you can't take an animated character in *World of Warcraft* from level one to level eighty-five in a weekend."

An original response. That was about the only compliment I could think of for it. "Since that would involve trying-"

"I rest my case."

"Ye-ah. See you at seven."

"Okay, see you." He sounded cheery as he hung up.

At seven on the dot, he was at my door with a bottle of Martinelli's sparkling cider – not the alcoholic kind. The kind that's basically carbonated apple juice in what looks like a wine bottle. He presented it solemnly, and it sort of did go with the lasagna, which he regarded with open surprise when I produced it from the oven. "You do art in a lot of media," he said.

Talk about a stilted compliment. "Thanks."

I couldn't tell, as we sat down to eat, whether this was a serious date, with the gourmet food, us being alone at my house, and the movie to follow, or if this was some kind of light hearted, jokey date. Did Len think we were two lonely souls on a Friday night, or something more?

He didn't try to put his arm around me during the movie. Instead, he was asleep before the end of the opening credits, and he snored so loud that I couldn't hear the dialogue. Not that I needed to; it was the same *Winne the Pooh* I'd seen a million times as a child.

I turned off the movie and went upstairs to work on a painting.

Len's snoring stopped just as I'd begun laying down brushstrokes. I was working in watercolor, which I had to do all in one sitting. Otherwise, it was hard to get the colors to blend exactly how I wanted. I gritted my teeth and kept on working.

I was dimly aware of his footsteps on the stairs and braced myself to have to talk to him. I can't talk and paint at the same time, not very well at least. A lot of artists are like this, something about switching hemispheres of the brain to do our work. Even just paying attention to Len's approach was slowing me down.

He appeared in the doorway and I shut my eyes, ready to be ripped out of my zone.

He didn't say a word, but instead came into the room and stepped behind me.

That was even worse. No one came into my studio. It was my space, set up exactly as I wanted it. Since Len didn't speak, though, it was either break my concentration and tell him to get lost, or keep on working with him there. Neither was a good choice, and since I didn't know how bad the conversation with him might be, I endured having him there, like a rock in my shoe, intrusive and constantly irritating.

At least his silence let me slip back into deeper concentration. I layered on the colors, letting the water flow into the paper, its threadlike tendrils giving texture to the shapes I'd sketched out. As I worked, the pencil marks faded and the pair of hands, holding a smoke gray lamb came to life, with the blood vessels standing out just so, and the lamb's adoring eyes directed upward, at the benevolent face out of frame.

Hours could slip by while I did this. I often looked up from a painting to find that, much to my shock, I'd skipped lunch and it was past time for dinner. This time, when I came up for air, I saw that it was only ten. I'd worked fast and the painting was small. I put my brush down and turned to Len, who hadn't moved a muscle.

"So," he said, "when you look at something, do you see all those colors?"

"Do I see the colors?"

"To make flesh colored hands, you used dark blue and bright red and even a little green. I wouldn't have thought those colors had anything to do with flesh tone, but they blend right in to make the shadows and highlights. Do you see those colors whenever you look at human skin?"

"I don't know."

Len cocked his head, as if waiting to hear more.

"I don't look at people and see them as dark blue or green, but if someone asked me how to paint a person so that the light seemed to come in from one side, or directly behind the subject, I know what colors to start with to achieve that effect in the end. It's just watercolor technique."

"It's really interesting. When you look around a room, do you think that the light looks like it'd be best done in watercolor or... or oil paint or... I guess I don't even know what kinds of paint there are."

"Depends on the effect you want," I said. This moment, I thought, was an acrylics moment. Warm full spectrum light with the blackness of night visible through the window.

He glanced at his watch. "I should go. I'm really sorry I fell asleep. I've worked a lot of long hours this week. They're switching out the back office software at the firm, and it's a nightmare. Midnight last night I got a call that a new Windows patch broke all of our remote desktop capabilities."

He might as well have spoken Esperanto, that's how much sense he made to me.

"It's all right," I said. "Just try not to come in here, especially not with shoes on. Make sure there's no paint on them that you might track around the house."

"Oh, right. Sorry, didn't even think."

My doorbell rang.

Len looked at his watch again in confusion.

Dread poured into me. I darted to the doorway, slipped my feet into my slippers, and dashed down the stairs. Hattie stood on my doorstep, a baffled look on her face. "Whose car is-" Her mouth dropped open.

Len had slipped down the stairs behind me. He paused for a moment, looked from me to his cousin and back again. Warm air from my house spilled out into the chill night. "I'll see you later," he said. He put on his jacket and went out the door without a backwards glance.

Hattie watched after him, then looked at me. "Long story," I said. "You okay?"

"Not really. Mike spent more time on his cellphone than talking to me tonight. Can I come in?"

"Yeah, sure. Want ice cream?"

"I shouldn't."

"Two scoops or three?"

"I hate you."

"I have chocolate chocolate chip."

"You're evil."

The night was much better after that. Hattie and I ate ice cream while she recapped her non-relationship with Mike. "I felt like maybe he hadn't even asked me. Like I misunderstood and intruded on an evening with him."

"Then keep away from him, if you don't even know if he wants you around."

"I think I could really like him if he'd just not be so self-centered."

And so we'd talked about Mike. Len's name never came up.

Until two days later, at church. I could see Hattie standing toe to toe with him in the foyer as I approached the glass doors. Once I was through the doors, I had audio to go with the video.

"What is that supposed to mean? You were just hanging out at Eliza's house? At ten? She have computer problems or something?"

Normally, Len blew his cousin off. More than once I'd see him ignore her when she accosted him to find out the name of the newest guy in the ward. "I keep track of the membership for the Church, not to provide you with the latest news on who's available," he'd say, if he bothered to say anything.

She insulted him all the time in public. "Nerd!" she'd declare or, "Loser!" He'd smile as if he considered both compliments.

That morning, though, he looked like she had thumbscrews on him and was cranking them down as tight as they'd go. "Just mind your own business," he said.

"Just answer my question."

He looked over her shoulder, saw me, and jerked his gaze immediately back to his cousin. "I..." he began.

As I drew close, he shrank away and still didn't look at me. I could read his emotions clearly. He didn't want to hear my excuse for why he was over. It would confirm to him that I wasn't interested and had just used him a couple of weeks back. I'd been lonely, so I'd kissed him, and it had meant nothing to me. Clearly, it had meant something to him.

I couldn't be that awful. It was either be Len's girlfriend, or be a user. I chose the lesser of two evils. "He was over to watch a movie," I said. "Stop torturing him."

His expression shifted from guarded discomfort to surprise, then he smiled. The effect was like the sun coming out from behind a cloud.

Hattie turned to me. "What?"

"Leave him alone, all right?" I couldn't defend my decision to date him, but I could at least beat her at her own game. "Sorry if he doesn't measure up to your standards." I showed her my back and went into the chapel.

I made it to a pew about a third of the way from the back before she caught up with me. "Okay, okay," she said. "Sorry. I gotta ask, though, why?"

"He can be nice. He asked. I figured why not and..." I shrugged. "He's nice." Not exactly a valiant defense of the guy, but it was all I could muster. I remembered him snoring on my couch and winced. Well, I could figure out how to break up with him later. This didn't need to be a long term thing. I just didn't want to kiss him out of loneliness and dump him immediately thereafter. I wondered if two weeks later counted as "immediately".

Jenna strode in, then, smiling a sly smile like a cat who'd gotten the cream. Hattie pelted her with questions about what had her grinning, and she told us about her latest project at work... I think. I didn't really listen as my mind was still on Len. He entered the chapel with a smile and an easygoing stride. All throughout the meeting, he stole glances back at me.

"Oh," whispered Hattie at the end of the first hour, "when I turned on my phone this morning, I had a message."

"From Mike?" I said.

"Yep." She grinned. "He apologized about last night!" Her eyes sparkled like those of a little girl on Christmas morning, all eager anticipation. "I'm going over to his place after church for lunch." Mike's parents were both professional chefs. He could cook a souffle with one hand while playing his Nintendo Gameboy with the other.

"Just got a text from work," Jenna announced. "They want me to write the Motion to Dismiss." She wasn't pretending to be happy. She genuinely loved her job, and the prospect of more work on a weekend didn't dampen her spirits one bit.

So the moment church was over, one friend fled to her apologetic, maybe-boyfriend, and the other to her fast paced, lucrative career. I was by myself in the parking lot, facing a day of puttering around the house. I couldn't paint, as it was the Sabbath and, unlike Jenna, I didn't have any projects that just couldn't wait because some corporation was in danger of losing a big case. As all of the other cars pulled out and drove off, I felt this was a metaphor for my life. Everyone was moving on, except me. I was left behind, standing at the curb.

"You okay, Eliza?"

I turned to see Len coming out of the building, a notebook under one arm and a courier bag slung over his shoulder. As always, his PDA was in his hand. Just before the door swung shut behind him, his housemate, Chris, caught it and shouldered his way through. "*Frogger* marathon at our house," he said to me. "You should come." He kept on walking right past, though. It wasn't a real invitation.

Nerds had a weird sense of humor.

Len came over to stand next to me and looked as if he wasn't sure I'd let him stay there. Chris got in his car and zipped away out of the nearly empty parking lot. The day was dead quiet, not even much of a breeze.

"You really going to play *Frogger* all afternoon?" I asked.

"No. He's mad because I beat his high score."

"Here." I dug in my purse and produced the *Winnie the Pooh* DVD.

Len glanced at it. "Thanks." He reached out to take it.

I didn't let go. "Unless you still want to come over and watch it?"

"Okay."

And that began our ritual. Whenever I was lonely, I could call on Len and he'd be there with a DVD in hand. Or sometimes we went out to the movies, or occasionally I'd show up at his house and he'd microwave me a burrito. And then I'd kiss him and sign myself up for another couple of weeks of dating. His kisses were addictive, though, like hard candy out of a dish. Each one good enough that you kept going back for more and the next thing you know, the dish was empty, even though you hadn't planned to eat that many.

With Len, I emptied and refilled that dish over, and over, and over. I don't know what made me feel worse, the fact that I used the guy, or the fact that all those months of using him didn't cause me to miss a better option. There just wasn't a better option.

I blinked away these memories and stared at the painting I'd just done. The park looked drenched in sunshine. In the distance, dreaming spires jutted up from the trees, giving the merest suggestion of the ornate stone building beneath the canopy. My aunt sat with her knees to her chin and faced away from the viewer, so she was little more than an oval of shyness. Lounging opposite her was Paul. The expression on his face told the viewer that the woman he beheld was gorgeous beyond imagination. He saw her intelligence and her courage, and he was captivated. I could read a thousand emotions in that face, which acted as a mirror for my aunt.

This painting was good. It was better than good. It was better than I could normally do with a ton of pre-planning. For once, I'd just sat down and painted and the final product looked better than I'd envisioned.

I was definitely turning a corner! I was becoming a better painter. Or perhaps my aunt's stories were finally giving my work the spark it had always lacked. I'd worked for years on channeling my emotions into my art, but hadn't noticed that the well of emotion had gone dry. It was filling up again and this brought new color and life to my art.

I wanted to cling to these positive memories of love and Nora's youth. I hoped against hope that tomorrow or the next day wouldn't sour these for me.

Before I went to bed that night, I knelt for a long time in prayer. I begged the Lord to spare my aunt and to strengthen me to deal with whatever was to come, if sparing her wasn't in His plans. It was the kind of prayer that left me feeling wrung out, but at peace for the moment. It let me get myself to sleep.

Seventeen

Scans

I got to St. John's early the next morning. A woman with freckles across her nose and strawberry blond hair stood at the nurses' station, flipping through files with a cheery smile on her face.

"Hi," I said to her.

"Yes?" The smile widened and crinkled her button nose. Her eyes were hazel behind strawberry blond lashes.

"I'm Nora Chesterton's niece. Eliza."

"Hi. She's not awake yet."

"Has the doctor been by to discuss her scans with her?"

"Give me a second." She rummaged through the stack of files on the counter, then cast about until she spied another stack. A moment later she tugged my aunt's file loose and flipped it open. She frowned. "Right."

I braced myself. Was her cancer stage two? Three?

"The oncologist would like to speak with you."

"With me?"

"Yes. Hang on. I'll ring him."

"Well, I'm going to go see my aunt. He can find me in her room."

"She's still asleep, though."

I'd heard her before. With a nod, I moved on past the nurses' station to my aunt's room. Nora's eyelashes fluttered when I walked in, but otherwise she didn't stir. Her breathing was still slow and deep. Her throat just barely scraped a soft snore every time she inhaled.

Breakfast was set out next to her bed on the rolling table and her jeans were draped over the other chair in the room.

I tugged the clean clothes I'd brought her out of my bag and laid them down on the edge of the bed, then flipped open my sketchbook and started on a sketch of Christ's suffering in the Garden of Gethsemane. I needed to get back to the kind of work that paid the bills. This was a subject I sketched a lot, because it was so hard to convey. It was literally the worst suffering anyone had ever felt in all of human history.

So I never did a sketch of his face or his whole figure close up. I'd done a picture of his hands, gripping the rough surface of a boulder. One of his back, his head so far down it was out of sight and his hunched posture conveying all. I'd done one of a teardrop that showed the reflection of the sleeping Apostles who should have been there for the Savior, but had dozed off.

This time I sketched a rough outline of the garden at night, with Christ's figure down in the corner. Sort of like the *Fall of Icarus*, a momentous event that passed almost unseen. The Apostles were asleep and oblivious, and the nighttime sky was endless and eternal above it all.

Much about this event was shrouded even in the scriptures, given the only witnesses slept through it. There was, however, a passage in the *Doctrine and Covenants*, a revelation given to Joseph Smith by the Savior himself.

> For behold, I, God, have suffered these things for all, that they might not suffer if they would repent;
> But if they would not repent they must suffer even as I;

> Which suffering caused myself, even God, the greatest of all, to tremble because of pain, and to bleed at every pore, and to suffer both body and spirit—and would that I might not drink the bitter cup, and shrink—
>
> Nevertheless, glory be to the Father, and I partook and finished my preparations unto the children of men.

In that moment, the story went, Christ had felt all the pain any human had ever felt. He'd felt the pain of my mother's cancer, the heartbreak of my brothers-in-law and nieces and nephews when they lost their wives and mothers, the sensation of reality ripping to shreds I felt every time I lost someone I loved. And these pains were such a small fraction of the whole, they would be to His pain as a pinprick to being flayed alive.

I set up each part of the sketch with precision, making use of every space. The sky had to look endless and the stars distant in order to enlarge the world and make Christ even smaller in comparison. The Apostles were out cold, dead to the world and at peace, which was a stark contrast to the angles of pain that the Savior felt. The garden was quiet and contained dark shadows, corners where anything could lurk. This made Christ more vulnerable as he sat without guards, wracked with pain.

The over all picture wasn't coming together like I wanted. I planned to do the final version in acrylics, but even without the vivid colors, I could see that something wasn't right. The magic that had happened last night was not happening again like I hoped it would.

"Ahem."

I twisted around in my chair. A man with south Asian features and a white doctor's coat stood in the doorway. His hair was streaked with gray and his nose had a Roman kink in it. His eyes were a light honey brown that peered at me with curiosity.

A glance over my shoulder confirmed that my aunt was still asleep. "Should I wake her?"

"Are you..." He glanced at the file. "Eliza Dunmar?"

"Yeah."

"Why don't you and I talk?" He looked at my open sketchbook with interest. "You draw?"

"I'm a professional artist."

"Oh, right." He raised both eyebrows in that expression I knew all too well, a mix of "that's impressive" and "really? Do you actually make money doing that?"

I looked away from him to hide my irritation as I flipped my sketchbook shut. He stayed where he was in the doorway, which I took to mean that I needed to get up and follow him somewhere. Sure enough, when I got to my feet, he stepped back and gestured that I should precede him into the hallway.

"Just to the office down here," he said. He pointed to an open door near the nurses' station, which belonged to a small box of a room with a utilitarian metal desk with particleboard top. A dusty computer whirred away and displayed a screensaver of swimming tropical fish.

"I'm Dr. Singh, by the way." He pulled out a plastic chair for me and snagged a rolling stool for himself. The door swung shut with a nudge from his heel. "I wanted to go over what we found in the MRI." He extracted the silver disk of a CD from its cardboard sleeve and inserted it into the computer's drive.

I braced myself. MRIs always squicked me out. They looked like the person had been sliced thin, mounted on a slide, and photographed in black and white. This image was of my aunt's intestines, mostly.

"The womb is here." He indicated a black, hollow area with his finger. "One ovary there." That was a grayish bump that could've been anything. "No ovary here, but what looks like a tumor mass here." He pointed to another bump. "What concerns me is that I think this might be another tumor here, and I'd like a better image of this." He pointed to more gray lumps. "This is rather close to the lymph nodes. I take it you know what that means?"

"Um, yes." Lymph nodes formed a network throughout the body. If cancer got into them, it had a free ride throughout the system. "I've seen that happen before, multiple times."

"Yes, I saw the family history. I'd like to get more images," he said, "but I hear your aunt is being quite stubborn."

"I'll talk to her."

"How has she been lately? Does she complain about aches or anything of that sort?"

"She just sleeps all the time and barely eats."

At that the doctor frowned.

"What?" I asked.

"Those are symptoms of late stage cancer. Do you think that she knows this? That she's avoided treatment for that reason?"

"She's scared of hospitals. Negative associations."

"From her own past hospitalizations?"

"No, from family dying."

"That's interesting that you say that. If you look here-" he pointed to some squiggles on the MRI that meant nothing to me "-you'll see she's had surgery before. I'd like to know what that was, but it's not in her British medical history. Neither is the broken arm she had-"

"What? She just broke her arm."

"For at least the second time." He tipped an x-ray out of a large folder, snapped it open expertly, and tucked it into the top clamp of a light panel on the wall. It showed both bones in the forearm snapped in a clean break. "There," he said, pointing to a whitish line up towards the elbow. "An old break."

"How old?"

"As it isn't in her medical history either, I don't know. We don't have records that date back to her time in America."

I rubbed my temples.

"Are you sure her behavior isn't because she wants to avoid cancer treatment? Not medical treatment in general, but cancer treatment in particular?"

"Would an x-ray of her arm really show cancer?" I asked.

"Fair point. But maybe she's wanted to avoid all medical care once she developed cancer symptoms."

I didn't want that to be true. "I'll talk to her."

"All right, but I need to discuss one thing more with you. Just briefly. I'm able to show you her medical records because she authorized it."

"Right."

"In her living will. You are her agent, and if we determine she's incompetent to make her own decisions, you then make the decisions."

"Whoa, what?"

"I wasn't sure if you knew that or not. You should be aware of it."

"Okay..."

"This a first for you?"

"Yes."

"Well, right. You probably want to meet with her solicitor to discuss anything else that might be relevant. Her Will, perhaps?"

I had that feeling again, that all the air was being sucked out of the room and I was about to explode with stress. I did my best to relax.

"Would you like the solicitor's contact details?"

"Yes, please."

He jotted them down on a sheet of paper, which he passed to me, then flipped my aunt's file shut and got to his feet. I followed his white coat back out of the room and down the hall to Nora's room. She was still asleep, but this time, rather than be silent, I went up to her, put a hand on her shoulder and said, "Aunt Nora?"

Her eyelids fluttered. She wasn't in a deep sleep.

"Wake up," I said. "The doctor needs to talk to you."

She stretched and inhaled, then rolled onto her side and opened one eye.

"Hey," I said. "Morning." I went around to her breakfast tray, opened the little carton of milk, and sniffed it. The cardboard surface was still cool enough to bead with moisture and there was no sour smell, so I poured it over her cornflakes and peeled the lid off her juice.

"Ms. Chesterton," said Dr. Singh. He sat down in the chair beside her bed. "We need some more scans."

"No."

"I'm afraid I will have to insist."

"No." Her look was stubborn, not the set-jaw kind of stubborn, but the impassive "I can wait for eternity and never change" kind of stubborn.

I pushed her breakfast tray into place over her bed. "Aunt Nora, how long have you had cancer?"

"Excuse me?"

"Please."

"What makes you ask that?"

"Because you won't even let people x-ray your arm. Do you think it's spread that far?"

Her eyes popped wide with surprise, and then her chest shook with a breathless laugh. "Oh, honey. No. I just don't like x-rays or scans or any of that garbage."

"Why not?"

She sat up and dug her spoon into her cereal. Slowly she chewed, crunch, crunch, crunch.

"Aunt Nora. Why not?"

"Because I don't like the nasty machines and being in the hospital."

"But, you've been in the hospital before."

"Says who?"

"Says the surgical scar on your stomach," the doctor replied.

"Mind your own business! I'm not getting any more scans. Forget about it." Nora didn't even turn to look at him.

"Aunt Nora-"

"There is nothing you can paint that will make a difference. So don't even suggest it."

"Um okay."

"Get out. Get out now!"

I blinked in surprise.

"Ms. Chesterton," said the doctor.

"And you too. Get out!"

He didn't argue, just turned and left.

I took one last look at Nora, at her face crumpled with anger, and did the same. My hands shook so bad that I wrung them to try to massage the shakes away. Nora never shouted at me.

Eighteen

Legal Details

I dug the piece of paper with Nora's lawyer's details on it out of my pocket and dialed the number.

"Hello?" said a prim, female voice.

"Hi, my name's Eliza Dunmar. I'm-"

"Nora Chesterton's niece?"

"Yes. I was wondering if I could come in to speak with you?"

"How's your aunt?"

"She's in the hospital, so-"

"Is it serious?"

"We don't know yet. Maybe."

"You should come speak to me, yes. Sorry, my secretary's off at an appointment and I need to figure out how the calendar works." She laughed. "I look like a right fool here. Ah, there we go. I can fit you in tomorrow after five. Would you be able to come by then?"

"Is it possible to do it sooner?"

"What's happened?"

"I have some questions about her living will."

"Ah... well... right. Today at five?"

"Thank you so much."

"I'll see you then, Ms. Dunmar."

Helena Grayson, Solicitor, worked out of an office above a corner store, an Asian grocer. I pressed the gold tone buzzer and was admitted through a narrow door that opened on a flight of stairs. The door at the top was half open and indirect sunlight shone through the gap.

I jogged up the stairs and slipped through the door into a reception area. A heavyset woman with graying blonde hair stood by the front desk, dunking a teabag into a steaming mug. "Ah, hello," she said with a warm, but tired smile. "You must be Eliza."

"Yes. Thank you for meeting me at such short notice."

"Not at all, not at all. Would you like some tea?"

"No thank you."

"Coffee?"

"I'm all right."

"Come through then. She pushed open the door to her office, which had a wall of bookshelves that looked custom made to fit the burgundy, leather bound volumes that populated its entire length. Ms. Grayson's desk was a rich, deep mahogany, the kind of wood that only an oil painting could do justice to, in my opinion. Its polish reflected the sunlight in sharp, focused glares.

She gestured for me to sit down in a chair across from her, one made from dark brown leather with a comfortable seat and a u-bend of padding for the back and arm rests. I felt a little small for it, but I did my best to sit up straight and look like I belonged there.

"Right, then." She picked up a thick folder and flipped it open. "I'll be quick about this. I don't represent Nora. My partner in the practice, who died two years ago, was her lawyer and I declined to represent Ms. Chesterton upon his death."

"Sorry?"

"I did obtain permission from her to release her file to you. You may take it to another lawyer if Ms. Chesterton seeks new counsel."

"But... wait. I'm confused-"

"I chose not to take her on because of the way she put together her estate."

"What do you mean?"

"She elected to have one person as both her agent under all forms of power of attorney and as her sole heir. You, specifically. In putting you in this position, she disinherited two natural born children."

"She did what?"

Ms. Grayson's tension lined face relaxed into the barest hint of a smile. "I am relieved to see that this is news to you. All the same, this situation presents conflicts of interest I am not comfortable with. Conflicts for you, that is." She slipped the folder across the desk along with a sheet of paper. "This is a form acknowledging receipt of the file, nothing more. I just need it for my records."

My head spun so I had trouble reading the form. Luckily, it was short. It just said, "The undersigned hereby acknowledges the receipt of the file for Nora S. Chesterton." The date was written at the top and a line for me to sign below. I scrawled my signature and received the heavy file in my lap.

"So, wait-"

"I'm afraid I can't advise you further."

"You say there are conflicts of interest?"

"If you have the right to make end of life decisions for her, and are the heiress to all she owns-"

"But wait, I don't want to be her heir. I want to be taken out of her Will altogether."

"You must sort that out with Ms. Chesterton."

"But-"

"I'm afraid that's all I can do for you."

"I... um... okay." Assertiveness had never been my strong suit in a situation like this.

"I am very sorry about all of this, of course."

"Right."

"Good evening, Ms. Dunmar."

Not exactly a subtle hint. I tried to look dignified as I walked out.

I needed to call my father. This thought absorbed nearly all of my attention as I stepped out of the building. I say nearly all, because I still had just enough awareness of my surroundings to spot Louisa. She wore a floral print dress and sandals and was down the street. When she caught me looking at her, she got into a car that had been idling by the curb and zipped away, but not before I caught sight of the hulking silhouette of her husband at the wheel.

Both of them tailing me? I wondered when that had started. Had they caught sight of me going into the lawyer's office, or had they followed me from St. John's? All the way back home, I kept my eyes and ears open, but if they followed me, I didn't catch them.

Back at the house, I threw the deadbolt on the front door, then made a beeline for the computer. My dad's Skype icon was green. I double clicked and then lifted Pip onto my lap. His stubby tail thumped against my hip.

"Hello?" Audio only, no video.

"Hi, Dad."

"Everything okay, honey?"

"No. And I don't know what to do."

"What's going on?"

"Aunt Nora won't let the doctors do scans, and I just found out that I'm her agent on her living will and her sole heir and-"

"Slow down. Nora's doing what?"

"They did an MRI and found a tumor, maybe more than one. They want to do more scans, but she refuses."

"So she doesn't want to face having cancer?"

"She says she hates the machines and being in the hospital. She's got an old surgical scar that she refuses to talk about. When the doctor mentioned it, she threw him out of the room."

"Surgical scar from what?"

"Like I said, she won't talk about it, so I wouldn't know."

"Did she have a hysterectomy-"

"No, look, I've already thought about stuff like that." Women with the BCRA mutation did sometimes get preventative hysterectomies, but I'd seen her womb in the MRI, her ovaries hadn't been removed, and she had two children, which meant if she'd had a hysterectomy, it'd be after they were born, and thus in her British medical history. "She won't talk to me. So I went to her lawyer "

"You say you're her agent on her living will?"

"Yeah."

"I'm sorry. I wish she hadn't done that. Talk about stress."

"And I'm her sole heir."

"Well, sure. If you're the person she trusts."

"*Dad*, if it's my job to decide whether or not she gets treatment, that's kind of a problem because if she dies, I get all her money."

"Whoa, back up. Is her living will active?"

"Huh?"

"Or... go find it. Does it say it's effective now or only if she can't make her own decisions?"

"How do they usually work?"

145

"It depends on the local law and how it's drafted. Unfortunately, I would know. Check hers."

I tucked Pip under one arm and hauled Nora's legal file from the desk into my lap. It took a little digging. I couldn't find anything called a living will, but I did find a document titled, "Power of Attorney for Health and Welfare" that was written in such thick legalese that I had to re-read the first sentence five times before I gave up and moved on. "It says it stays effective if she is declared incompetent," I said. "Does that mean it's active now?"

"We-ell, I am guessing here but I would guess that this means that she still makes her decisions. Even if that thing is technically active, I don't think they'd let you overrule her. I mean, the doctors would have let you know if that was the case, and I've never heard of a situation like that. Let's assume it means you don't make decisions unless she's unable, so it isn't your responsibility right now."

"Her alternate agents are Great Uncle Morrie, who died last year and his ex-wife Cathy."

"She's got Alzheimer's, honey. She can't serve."

I leafed through the file more slowly as I said, "Okay, but here's the thing. If she's acting crazy, refusing treatment all the time, can't she be declared incompetent? I mean, she refused an x-ray on a broken arm."

"A stubborn person isn't incompetent. She'd have to be mentally ill – and the right kind of mentally ill, or unable to communicate."

"What do you mean, the right kind of mentally ill?"

"Well, a kleptomaniac can still make healthcare decisions–"

"Oh, right. Sure. But her weirdness is all about healthcare decisions. I know weirdness isn't a mental illness–"

"Lucky for all of us, eh?"

Against my will, I laughed. "Is it my job to get her declared incompetent or is it something the doctors or whoever just do?"

Paint Me True

"Good question. In the US, it requires a notarized statement from a couple of doctors. Over there, I've got no idea."

"Because here she is, refusing treatment, and I stand to inherit her fortune. If I don't try to get her declared incompetent so that she can be treated, will that look bad?"

"People don't normally dig into all of that, honey. Life isn't like what you see on the news."

"Dad, she's rich and she's got two estranged children. Why wouldn't they dig into this?"

"Ah... good point."

"And even if the doctors think she's all there, doesn't this look bad? I mean, I've been here looking after her. What if they think I scared her out of medical treatment or something?"

"I think that's a little extra paranoid, honey."

"I don't want to be her heir!"

"Well, look, don't worry about it then. Most places here in the US, if all the heirs agree on an alternate distribution of the estate, they can do that with a simple court filing."

"So what's that mean? I can single-handedly decide to give all the money to her kids?"

"Yes."

"Oh." That took a load off my chest. "Well, okay. I need to find out when she was in the hospital before. What happened with that surgery she won't talk about. I need to get her to talk to me."

"Think you can?"

"I have to try. She was real defensive before, but maybe if I approach things differently, she'll actually talk. The doctor kind of put her on the spot."

"If you think you can get her to talk-"

"Do you see another option?"

"Look in her medical records?"

"No, see, the doctor said it wasn't in there. It must've been from when she was in the US."

"Oh, right."

"And I don't suppose there's any way I can get her US medical records?"

"I wouldn't even know where to look. Her childhood doctor died ages ago and then where did she move? Provo? Can't really call every practice in Provo about records that old. And you'd have to fill out forms to receive them, to prove you've got a right to them, and I don't think we do in this case. We're not her doctors or lawyers or anything like that."

"Does she still have old friends who would've known her back when it happened?"

"Good question. I have no idea. Problem is, there aren't any near family members of her to ask. They've all passed on."

"Yeah, so I need to get her to talk to me."

"You sure you're up to this?"

"No, but I have to try, right?"

"If you need me, I'll be there in twenty-four hours."

"Thanks, but actually, if you can just leave your phone on, that'll work for me."

"You've got it. Call any time, day or night."

"I love you, Dad."

"Love you too, honey."

I carefully packed the painting of Nora and Paul in the park and carried it the eight blocks to St. John's. I found Nora not in her bed, but in the chair, gazing out the window at the garden, where on sunny days, other patients limped around for exercise.

At the sound of my entry, she turned, and I saw her cheeks were striped with tearstains.

"Hi," I said.

"Honey, I'm sorry."

"It's fine. I'm sorry if you felt like we ganged up on you." I took out the painting and handed it to her.

She grasped it on the edges and stared. "This is gorgeous."

"Thanks. It came together pretty well."

"I'm sorry I insulted your art."

"Huh? When?"

"When I said there was nothing you could paint that would make a difference. Everything you paint makes a difference. A huge difference."

"Well, thanks. I wasn't insulted."

"I miss Paul so much."

"I know."

"Especially right now. If he were here, he'd take control and put everything right, but he's not. I feel so lost without him."

A dozen replies came to mind and I discarded them all. There was no point saying he'd want her to get her scans. That was just plain manipulative. I sat in silence instead.

"I feel like an idiot. Here I am in an oncology center and I won't even let the oncologist talk to me. I'm taking up valuable bed space."

"Listen," I said, "you and me are like war survivors. We've lost everyone. Real soldiers develop post traumatic stress. I don't see why we'd be any different."

"I suppose you've got a point there."

"How can I help you?"

Fresh tears spilled down her cheeks. "I don't know."

"Do you want to just go home? It's your choice. I won't criticize you."

"I don't want to die."

"Good. I am so relieved to hear that."

"But I have to get scans, don't I?"

"That'd be the next step."

"How extensive?"

"I don't know. Look, do you not like the machine? I can ask if maybe you can... I don't know, be sedated or something? I want to work with you here. Your happiness is what I care about."

She looked at the painting. "I wish you could paint every moment we had together. I wish you could bring him all the way back to me."

"If I could, I would." Since I'd made little progress on convincing her to get scans, I let her change the subject. It seemed like it'd keep her talking and keep her opening up to me, which might get me what I wanted in the end. "Just tell me what to paint next, and we'll get started."

"I can't hijack your life like that."

"What about when he proposed to you. What was that like?"

Much to my surprise, she laughed. "It was awful. One of the worst days of my life."

"Really?"

"Thanks to that family of his."

"What were his parents like?"

"I barely ever met them. Guess I should just tell the story from the beginning, huh?"

I nodded and helped her from the chair back into her cot. Then I sat in the chair and listened.

The Proposal

Paul was a fixture in my life by Trinity Term – that's the third trimester of the academic year, you know? He walked with me wherever I went. He sat near me while I studied. I rarely had to go looking for him, he was always right there, or if he wasn't, he'd have told me when I'd see him next.

But it was Trinity Term, which meant that in eight weeks, I'd be back home in Utah, and I knew things would end. I couldn't afford to stay in the UK, and Paul never said anything about going to the US.

One day I was in my boarding house, trying to concentrate on the most boring Anglo-Saxon translation imaginable. All the syllables just sort of jumbled themselves together and made even less sense than normal. The boarding house had a day room that just had some beat up old couches, a scuffed coffee table, and windows that looked out onto the side street on which it was located. No one else was in that day, and it was raining. Even with the door and windows closed, the rain made everything smell damp and a little musty. The air was so heavy in that room, just breathing it felt like an effort.

Someone came in the door and let in a blast of moist air and the clattering sound of rain. I didn't pay attention, and I didn't notice that they stood just inside the door for what must've been a couple of minutes. I looked up when I got the creeping feeling that someone was staring at me.

It was a youngish woman. Older than me, I guessed, because she wore a wool skirt over thick tights and what looked like a silk blouse. She'd stripped off an expensive looking raincoat and hung that on a peg by the door. I knew it was hers because no one else had one as nice as that. It looked like it was lined with satin.

All of her attention was on me, though. I looked back at her and she came to sit next to me on the couch.

"Hi," she said. "I'm Louisa Chesterton."

For a panicked moment, I thought she was his wife. I looked at her left hand and she followed my gaze with hers, then snickered.

"I'm Paul's sister."

"Oh. Hi."

"Did you know he had a sister?"

"No." I wondered how this was significant, because there was no mistaking her tone of voice. It mattered to her.

"Did you know his family is here in town?"

"What, right now?"

"Always. We live here."

"Oh. No, not really."

She looked me up and down. "How well do you know my brother?"

"Ah..."

"Or I guess I should ask, how serious are you about him?"

"Sorry?"

She frowned at me as if I were being tiresome. "We are a very wealthy family. Paul's got over a million pounds in trust-"

"I wouldn't know anything about that."

"I don't mean to make an accusation, but if that's why you've been so constantly in his presence-"

"Wait, I've never seen you before. How would you even know? Did Paul tell you?"

"I pay attention to these kinds of things."

Now that was a creepy thing to say. I wondered how she paid attention.

"So what I'm saying is, if it's the money that interests you, I'll make you an offer."

"Huh?" She made less sense to me right then than the Anglo-Saxon I'd tried to read.

"A hundred-thousand pounds for you to get on a plane and leave Britain and never come back." She looked me directly in the eye.

That gaze pinned me to my seat as effectively as a lance stabbed through my heart, the sofa, and the wall behind me. "I don't understand."

"There's nothing to understand. I'll give you the money if you go home, is all."

"Right now?"

She brushed that away. "At the end of term, of course. I know my brother is handsome, and it appears he's been kind to you, but I suggest you let him go. For your own good."

"What will you do if I don't?"

She smirked at me. "Oh, I think you wouldn't want to end up related to me. I can be quite difficult to get along with. Just think on my offer. Here's where you can reach me." She took a slip of paper out of her breast pocket and put it down on the couch cushion. Then she got up and left.

I was so shaken I couldn't see straight. I mean, what would you do after a visit like that? I wanted to find Paul, but he was at a tutorial and I didn't remember which or where. I put on my raincoat and ran to Balliol, to his room, which was empty right then. I felt so lost and confused, and then I began to wonder if Louisa might have followed me.

I didn't know where to go next, or what to do. I haunted the staircase for the rest of that day. Balliol houses students in vertical staircases, you know? Students have upstairs and downstairs neighbors. If they want to see whomever lives to their left or right, they have to go downstairs, outside, and in the next door over, to the next staircase.

But I'm rambling. Back to the point. I just stayed there until mid-afternoon, when Paul burst in downstairs and ran up to the landing. At the sight of me he froze. "You're here," he said.

"Yes. I didn't know where else to go. Your sister came by-"

"Oh I know." His hands were balled into fists. *"I know."*

"She wants me to leave-"

"I know. She needs to mind her own business."

"I didn't know you had family in town."

"Mmm." He paced as he answered me. His distant gaze let me know that the bulk of his attention wasn't on what he said. *"We have a house here, yes. Dad lives in the South of France these days, and Louisa was away in Scotland all last term."*

"Well, I won't take her money," I said. *"I mean, I'm going home anyway, so there was no need to bribe me-"*

"Don't remind me."

"Sorry. It's just, I don't know why she thought she had to-"

Paul stopped and grasped his hands together for a long moment. *"Because she doesn't know how to mind her own business. She's got her own ideas about the family and thinks my personal business is her business."*

"She told me I didn't want her for a sister-in-law." The words were out before I even thought about it. *"I mean, not that... you know. It's what she said."*

Paul's attention was still directed inward, though. He leaned against the wall and slid down it until he could rest his head against his knees. For a long moment he stayed like that, breathing hard. *"I'm sorry about her."*

"It's not your fault."

"I don't like thinking about you leaving."

"Really?" He had a string of female admirers. I knew I'd be quite easy to replace.

"Of course not. I don't want you to leave."

"Well... thanks."

"So don't."

"I have to. My visa will run out and I don't have money."

He nodded. *"Then we'll get married."*

The very idea made my heart feel like it was light as a feather. I was so full of joy I could burst. *"You want to get married?"*

"If it's that or losing you, then there is no choice, is there?" He got up, unlocked his door, and we went in his room. He was

distracted though. Still upset about his sister. We didn't celebrate, call anyone, or anything like that. He spent the evening in a funk and I wondered if he felt like he's made a mistake.

It's not the ideal proposal, is it?

"But he meant it, right? You did get married?"

"Oh yes. He never took it back. A few days later we went ring shopping, and that was fun. He smiled then and told me I could have any ring I wanted. He took me to his house, and I was just bowled over by it. I used the phone to call my family, who weren't happy at all. Your mother was the only one who bothered to be nice about it. She called me, at considerable expense, to congratulate me and apologize that she wouldn't make it to the wedding. You would've been about six back then."

"And Mom would've just had her first cancer diagnosis."

"That happened a little while after, but yes, that put a damper on things as well."

"So you never went back to the US?"

"No. No one there seemed to want to see me."

I remembered the family reunion and my heart ached with sympathy for her. "I can't imagine how that must've felt."

"Lonely, in a word."

"What did Louisa do?"

"She and Paul exchanged words. I never knew the details, but she disappeared for a good long while, and when she surfaced again, she made an effort to be nice to me, but she was nosy. Everything was her business. Her brother was hers, the house was hers, the family name was hers. That's why, like I said, I got the locks on the house changed. She eventually married a guy in the neighborhood, and has scowled at the house every time she's walked past for over a decade now."

"So when did you and Paul get married?"

"Well, that turned out to be a little complicated. It turns out you can't just go to the registrar's office if you're not British, so he did take me to France for the day so that I could get a tourist visa when I came back to England, and we managed to get it all worked out and get married July 17. A simple wedding in the registrar's office. None of our family attended. The next time I even saw my family was at that reunion, when no one other than you would speak to me."

"Yeah, I remember that. I guess I thought that was about you leaving the Church."

"Oh, that too, I guess. But I'd never been terribly faithful. I didn't even bother to look up where church was when I got to Oxford, and I never missed going. When Paul made me tea to drink, I never thought twice about it. I only ever went to church because it was what my family did." She shrugged. "Not everyone in the family is all that devout, you know. My mother only went to church when family was in town. My brother was inactive last I knew. I don't think he baptized his children."

"Yeah, I don't think so either."

"Your mother stayed active."

"Very."

"And I guess it rubbed off on you."

"Well..." I chose my next words carefully. "People have a lot of cynical views about religion, but I can honestly say that my life is better, thanks to it."

"You were always very tolerant, though. You never pressured me to go to church with you."

"Well, no."

"You sure you're life's been better? Look at all the awful things that have happened in our family."

"Yeah well, faith hardly ever saves anyone from that kind of stuff."

"I don't think you'd give a second thought to turning thirty-one if it weren't for the Church."

"About that. Can I share something with you?"

"Of course."

"Spiritual?"

"You can tell me anything, honey."

"Right before I came out here, literally right after your phone call and before I could pack, my home teachers came by and gave me a blessing. It was the shortest blessing I've ever had, but in it they told me that God had an important lesson for me to learn."

My aunt kept her expression neutral. She might not have been religious, but she did have a childhood's worth of experience relating to religious people.

"When I came out here and bribed you with paintings, you told me about your love story, and you reminded me that it's not about time limits or what other people think. It's about finding the one person who's right for you, and that can happen anytime. It hasn't happened to me yet, and I need to remember that the right guy is worth the wait."

"You really think that's the lesson God wanted you to learn?"

"Yeah. I mean, okay, dismiss it as hindsight bias or coincidence or whatever. I'm not trying to convince *you* of the fact. But that is what I believe."

She patted me on the hand. "Think you can pray me out of this situation?"

"If I could, I would, believe it."

"I still don't want those scans, honey."

"Okay, no one's thrown you out yet. Sleep on it and we'll worry about it tomorrow. Let's end this day on a good memory of some kind. So your proposal wasn't the best moment, what was? Your wedding day? Did you have a moment at or around the time of your ceremony that sticks out in your mind?"

"Not a moment, just a feeling. A feeling that no matter what, I was the one woman Paul wanted to marry. Despite everything else, that whole mess, he chose me and stood by me."

"That a good thought to fall asleep with?"

"Yes."

"Okay. I'll see you in the morning." I got up to leave. I still didn't have the answers I wanted, but at least now I had a lead. I needed to find Louisa.

Twenty

Old Demons

Louisa made it easy for me. She was standing at the end of the driveway when I arrived. I slowed my steps and watched her. She walked up the driveway and out of my line of sight.

I hurried over to peer through the trees so that I didn't lose her. She marched up to the front door, and to my horror, pulled her keys out of her purse. I watched her try to fit the key in the lock. She turned it over and tried again. Then she selected another key and repeated the process.

Adrenalin shot through my veins. I wanted to run out and confront her, but I wasn't that brave. Instead I waited until she gave up and headed off before I dashed for the front door, went in, threw the deadbolt, and then stood, panting.

Well, I hadn't confronted her, but I still felt like I had the answers I needed. I thought of her large, hulking husband and cursed myself for ever eating her tuna casserole. I was lucky it hadn't been poisoned. I went back to the computer with the half formed intention to call my dad, but found an email from Hattie in my inbox. It read:

Eliza,

You were so right about Mike. I finally told him I didn't like my birthday present, and that he'd really let me down, and guess what? He gave me a pearl bracelet! Or, actually, he took me to the mall and asked me to pick out what I wanted. It is the most gorgeous bracelet and it goes with everything. He even took me out to dinner after! Thank you SO MUCH for your advice. I feel like I'm in a real relationship now.

Of course my brother had to ruin it. He's going to get "married" to his boyfriend and my family says that if I don't come, they'll never speak to me again. It's not like my brother would come to my wedding, so I don't know what his problem is...

That ellipsis ending was her deciding not to launch into one of her rants about the liberal conspiracy that had robbed her of her family. I felt for her, though I was jealous too. She had a real boyfriend to comfort her through the pain, or was her brother someone she was so ashamed of that she wouldn't tell Mike about him?

I sat for a moment, massaging my forehead. I didn't know what to say to her. She probably felt like no one did, which was why she ranted on about the subject.

But I did know what it was like to lose family. Unlike her, I couldn't reach mine again with a simple phone call. Maybe that was worse, having them just out of reach. I took out my sketchbook and began to doodle.

I drew a little family of mice, the littlest one stood apart with her back to the others. She had a bow in her hair, her hands clasped together primly, and a little halo of light around her. The rest of the family was huddled together, unsure of how to approach her. They whispered behind their paws and cast timid looks in her direction.

One skinny mouse looked down at his feet, which he scuffed against the ground. He was a very sad mouse who didn't understand why his sister was so aloof. Why was she so happy without him when he missed her so much?

I spent extra time on their long, sad mousy faces, drooping whiskers and all. Then sat back, looked at it, and rolled my eyes. What a dumb sketch. Not exactly subtle. Forget subtext, this was the equivalent of writing in block letters, "DON'T HURT YOUR BROTHER'S FEELINGS. YOU MAKE HIM SAD."

Still, I tucked it into the scanner, attached it to an email, and sent it to her. It was the best response I could think of.

The next morning I arrived at Nora's bedside and found a note from Colin, that read:

Eliza-
Sorry I haven't called. You interested in punting this Saturday?
-Colin

I tucked the paper in my purse. He'd be asleep now, if he'd worked all last night. My aunt looked so peaceful that I felt bad waking her. Still, we had a delicate conversation that I wanted to finish as fast as possible.

Her eyes fluttered open. "Hmm?"
"I am so sorry, but can we talk?"
"Mmm?"
"Your surgery, was it for something someone did to you? Someone beat you up?"

Her eyes widened.

Bullseye.

"Louisa's husband?" I asked.

She just stared at me, eyes wide and chin trembling.

"I figured it out. Every scan and x-ray has revealed something extra. An old break, some former surgery, and you've always wanted to keep the scope of the scans as small as possible. You're hiding old injuries, aren't you? Ones you left the country to get treated?"

"Honey..."

"Okay, so I get it. Louisa's angry because you have the family house and money and all that and she won't inherit. Somehow she found out. She bribed your old attorney, maybe." More pieces fell in place. "Ms. Grayson wouldn't take you as a client because she got scared off."

Still, my aunt said nothing.

"Are you afraid they'll hurt you more if anyone finds out?"

She shook her head.

"What is it, then?"

Her chin really trembled now and her eyes flooded with tears.

I grasped both of her hands. "You can tell me. I promise I won't say anything to anyone else."

"You... you always tell me how strong you think I am. Other people have said the same thing."

"Do you really believe I'd think less of you if I knew someone had bullied you?"

"Well..."

"Aunt Nora, there is no way any reasonable person would blame you. You're the victim."

"But I never told anyone. I never went to the police. I didn't even want to admit to them this was going on."

"Okay, look, we'll take this one step at a time. First let's get you the scans you need. No one can see your medical records but you, the doctors, and me."

"Honey, I don't want to see it. I don't want you to see it. Even if you have some warning-"

"I want to get you treatment for your cancer, all right? That's priority number one. I don't care about anything else at the moment. Will you please let them do scans? I won't even look at them if you don't want."

Her gaze moved down to her hands and she took another deep breath. In this moment she was so much younger than her forty-five years. I could see the twenty-something she'd been when she first came to the UK. "All right."

"Okay. And I'll paint you anything you want."

She smiled at that. "Deal."

"I'm going to go tell the nurse."

My aunt was booked for more scans a couple of days later. Once she'd had them, it was a long wait to see Dr. Singh. We didn't meet with him until after supper time. He looked tired and drawn as he ushered us into his office. A nurse pushed Nora in a wheelchair and then left once she was parked. I slipped into the chair next to her.

"I haven't had a chance to look at these yet," the oncologist said. "Give me a moment." He brought them up on the screen and looked them over. He took off his glasses, cleaned them on a tissue, and put them back on.

"Well?" I said.

Nora looked down at her clasped hands.

"Right... is this a cracked femur I see?"

"Never mind that," I said. "What do you see with respect to her cancer?"

He took off his glasses again, rubbed the side of his nose with the heel of his hand, and put them back on. "I see someone with an extremely high threshold of pain."

I stifled the urge to raise my voice. "Okaaay-"

"The cancer has metastasized throughout the body, and more to the point, I'm seeing it in the bones. You've had symptoms for a very long time and ignored them." He turned to my aunt. "Care to explain that?"

She just looked down at her hands.

"So this'll take multiple surgeries?" I asked.

"I wouldn't recommend surgery."

"Chemo, then? Radia-"

"Hospice care," said Dr. Singh. "At this point, trying to kill the cancer would require killing the patient ten times over. Why didn't you say anything before? And why aren't all of these fractures in your medical history? That one can't be more than ten years old."

"Never mind that," I said.

"Never mind? Do you know how much force-"

I looked him straight in the eye. "I am aware. That is a personal matter that yes, I am aware of. We're here for your oncology expertise, not your personal judgments."

He gave me an uneasy look. "I'm sorry," he said. "All I can do is prescribe painkillers and give you a list of facilities to look after her."

"How long?" I asked.

"One month? At most. In truth, I'm rather surprised you are still here." He looked over his frames at my aunt.

I put my hand on hers.

"I can send the scans on for a second opinion?" said Dr. Singh.

I nodded. "Please."

"Right, let's at least get you comfortable for the night. The pharmacy will be closed, but on site we've got some painkillers. He clicked away on the computer. "If you'll see your aunt back to her room, I'll send someone over shortly."

I got up, pulled the door open, and leaned out. Colin stood at the nurses' station. At the sight of me he began to

Paint Me True

smile, but when he saw my expression, he stopped himself. "Hi," he said.

"Hi, can you help wheel my aunt?"

"Of course." He slathered sanitizer on his hands and came to wheel her out. "You okay?" the question was directed at me.

"How late are visitors allowed?"

"It's past visiting hours, but if you really need to stay-"

"Honey, it's all right," said Nora. "Go on home."

"It's not all right. Listen, this is totally and completely selfish of me, but can I ask for one thing?"

"What's that?" She looked back over her shoulder at me.

"Can I find some priesthood holders to give you a blessing?"

Her eye popped wider with surprise, but only surprise. No horror or anger. "If you like," was all she said.

I turned to Colin. We'd arrived at Nora's room, so I waited for him to get her settled on her bed. "So, what's this?" he asked me.

"I'd like to bring two men here to give her a blessing. It's a Mormon thing." As I'd told Nora, faith hardly ever saved us from earthly pain, but maybe, just maybe, God would cut me a break. After everything I'd endured, maybe this once He'd intervene.

"All right."

"Thank you." I dug the ward list and my cellphone out of my purse. Since I didn't know names, I just started at the top.

The Abbotts were a single mother with small children. No ordained priests.

The Ansells didn't answer their phone.

The Babcocks did. "Hello?" said a voice deep enough to be an ordained priest.

"Hi," I said. "I'm, um..."

"Is this Eliza? The American visiting the ward?"

165

"Yes, yes, that's me."

"What do you need?"

"I need someone to give a blessing to my aunt."

"Your aunt?"

"She's not in the ward. I mean... she's not active, but-"

"Doesn't matter one bit. Of course I can give her a blessing."

"Okay, I'll try to get another-"

"Oh, I can do that. I'll get a companion. Where do we need to go?"

I gave him the address.

"Shouldn't take us more than fifteen minutes."

"Thank you," I said.

"It's an honor." He sounded like he meant that.

I pressed my palms together in gratitude. At least something had been easy today.

"So," Colin broke into my reverie, "Saturday not good to go out, because-"

"Oh no," said my aunt. "Saturday is perfect. Take her out for the whole day."

"Um, right." I laughed. "Guess that's a yes for punting on Saturday."

"Punting? How lovely," said Nora

"Do you want to come?" Colin asked her.

"Not on your life." She winked at me.

My face was so hot I feared it would burst into flames.

Colin smiled at me as he strode out the door.

Nora wore an expression of pure smugness.

I shook my finger at her. This little back and forth was much preferable to the difficult conversation we'd eventually have to have. I needed to find her children, and who knew what kind of can of worms that would open? Since I didn't know how to bring up that topic, I just sat in silence while my aunt lay with her eyes closed, though there was a tension in her expression that belied the pain she felt.

"Right," came a male voice from the doorway ten minutes later. It was same voice I'd spoken to on the phone. "Here we are."

I spun around and almost screamed. Stupid, stupid me hadn't checked addresses on the ward list. I'd called Louisa's husband!

Twenty-One

Another Blessing

Brother Babcock ambled in and behind him came the Bishop. I turned to Nora, ready to apologize and beg forgiveness. She and Brother Babcock exchanged a rueful look. I got the sense that the large man smiled at her. She didn't look terrified.

I dashed out into the hall. Louisa had to be with him. She'd never stay home with such a prime opportunity to snoop in Nora's business. But the hallway was empty, save for the nurses. Colin gave me a curious look.

"Did anyone come in with them?" I asked.

The other nurse, a short woman with ebony skin and neat rows of braids, only shook her head.

"Everything all right?" Colin asked.

"Um... I don't know." I turned and went back into the room.

Brother Babcock hung back while the Bishop perched himself on the edge of Nora's bed and spoke to her in low tones. "You comfortable here?" I heard him ask as I drew closer.

"I've got Eliza. She makes me comfortable anywhere."

"So would you like to share anything with us?" he asked. "It isn't necessary, of course. We can do the blessing regardless. But if there's anything at all you need, you let us know."

She smiled a thin, tight lipped smile. "Mainly, I'm tired."

"Shall we just say our blessing and then leave you?"

"That'd be nice, thank you."

Brother Babcock came over and adjusted her bed and pillows so that she sat up enough for them to place their hands on her head. She didn't flinch at his touch. If anything, she seemed relieved to see him.

"Do you want me to leave?" I asked.

Nora shook her head.

The two men stood on either side of the cot, and the Bishop produced a small metal vial of oil. I folded my arms, shut my eyes, and bowed my head.

Brother Babcock began by invoking his priesthood authority and pronouncing a blessing of healing. It was the same standard phrases I knew well. My father had uttered them over my head whenever I'd been hurt or sick as a child.

Only this time, I heard them clearer than ever. They took on a power that penetrated my heart as if written in fire on my flesh. He kept his eyes shut as he spoke, oblivious to the witnessing that shone real, illuminating light into my mind. This man, I knew, was a good man. He was worthy of the priesthood, and the Lord was pleased with him.

Then it was the Bishop's turn to seal the blessing. The witnessing faded. This, I perceived, was not because the Lord was any less pleased with the Bishop, but because what He had said what He wanted to say to me. The Bishop's soft voice paused. He'd reached the point in the ordinance when he was to say any personal words that he felt inspired to say. For a long, long moment he was silent. I kept my head bowed, my eyes shut.

I heard him swallow a few times.

Finally, he began to speak. "Sister Nora, the Lord would have you be at peace. Now is the time in your life to find joy, grant forgiveness, and seek your Father in Heaven. You have not always walked an easy path, but now..."

The silence stretched so long this time that I cracked open an eye. My aunt was asleep, or so it appeared, and the Bishop was overcome with emotion. He sniffled, wiped his nose with a handkerchief, and for another long moment, struggled to speak.

"But now, know that the Christ will take your burdens upon Himself as He always has. Allow Him to help you on your way and prepare for whatever is to come." He closed this in the names of the Godhead and all of us said, "Amen," except for Nora. Her head tipped to one side and she gave a soft snore.

I hadn't seen her sleep that deeply since I'd arrived in the UK. She always seemed so restless and easy to wake.

The Bishop wiped his eyes and nose again and turned to me. "Thank you for calling us."

I noticed, out of the corner of my eye, Brother Babcock retreated. He went to stand just outside the door, out of earshot. He knew his protocol. If I wanted to talk to the Bishop in confidence, he made that possible.

"And how are you?" the Bishop asked.

"Been better." I smiled as I said this though.

"Glad to hear it."

He had a point there. If this was a happy moment in my life, that pointed to an awful life. "Thanks for coming out," I said.

"Of course, and if you need anything else, let me know. Right now, let me give you a ride home." He put his hand on my arm and led me out.

In the hallway, Brother Babcock fell into step next to us. "Louisa didn't come?" I asked him.

He chuckled. "She didn't know where I was going. She didn't overhear our phone conversation, because as you can

171

guess, she'd have a hard time keeping her nose out of the situation."

The Bishop shook his head.

"I don't tell her whom I give blessings to, though." Brother Babcock winked at me.

Which, now that I thought about it, was typical. I never knew whom my dad went out to tend to at odd hours of the night. It wasn't my business.

I felt no discomfort or fear as I stepped out into the darkening parking lot with these two men. They saw me safely to Nora's empty house and a very lonely little Pip.

Twenty-Two

Up The River

That night I dug through all of Nora's legal file to see if there was any contact information for my cousins. I found their names and birthdates, and I remembered that Nora said one lived in Bristol and one in Leeds, but Chesterton was a common enough last name that this didn't narrow it down enough.

They needed to know about their mother.

I dug through the utility drawer and searched around for Nora's address book. I found nothing. Her computer didn't have any lists saved on it where I could find them, and I didn't know how to get into her email.

A quick call to my dad reaffirmed what I already knew. He had no idea. I didn't tell him the news, because it felt wrong for him to know before my cousins did, but I'm sure he guessed. He didn't warn me against contacting them this time.

Finally, at midnight, I gave up and went to sleep on it.

The next morning I got up early and got to work. My dad put up with five phone calls from me in what were the wee hours of the morning for him, and he brushed off my profuse apologies each time. Together we decided that home hospice care made the most sense for Nora. I had access to her checking account, thanks to the debit card she'd given me, and it more than covered the fees even if her insurance didn't.

I spoke to two private home hospice nursing firms and chose the one that answered my nosy questions without pause. Then I got on the phone with St. John's and organized transportation to get Nora home.

By late afternoon the next day, she was back in her own bed with an IV drip and prescription strength painkillers. I thanked the nurse who'd set everything up and she told me she'd be back in a few hours. I let her out the front door, then went back upstairs to perch myself on Nora's bed.

"Okay, not sure how to broach the subject," I said, "but I guess I should just do it?"

Her eyebrows went up. I'd piqued her interest.

"I want to contact your children."

At that she wilted. Her expression went from exhausted to despair, and then a notch beyond. "Best leave them be," she said.

"They're going to want to know about this."

"No, honey, they won't."

"You're their mother."

She shook her head like a stubborn two year old refusing to eat her peas. "Please, honey, leave it. My children and I parted ways a long time ago."

"You're sure you can't-"

"I'm sure. Just leave it." She lay down and rolled so that her back was to me.

I wondered if she was in denial about how sick she was, or how much her children would regret not knowing. I wished my mind would drop the subject as easily and completely as she had. My stomach lining was getting thin.

The next morning I woke with a start. It was Saturday. I'd promised Colin I'd go punting with him, but that felt all wrong. He knew how bad Nora's condition was. He'd understand.

I got up and went to peer into Nora's room. She was awake, and looked me up and down. "I thought you had a date this morning."

"I did, but-"

"You're going, aren't you?"

"Aunt Nora-"

"Listen to me. If you don't accept life's invitations, you'll never get anywhere interesting. Thank you for caring about me, honey, but I'll be fine for a few hours. You, on the other hand, have an invitation from life that I expect you to honor."

I remained in the doorway, unsure whether to ignore or obey her.

"In other words," she said, "get lost. I don't want to see you until after your date."

It felt wrong, turning away. I'd never left my mother or my sisters during their last days. I'd absorbed every last memory I could with them and learned them by heart so a part of them could be with me for the rest of my life. Then again, I looked back on those days and felt I gazed into a bottomless pit of despair. How much of life had I set aside to follow each of them into death?

"You're still here," said Nora.

"Well, you're disrupting my routine."

"Good. I'd hate to be remembered as agreeable and passive. It's those last memories that stay with a person, you know?"

"That's morbid."

"It's the truth. Begone. Now." Her eyes had their old sparkle.

"I'll be back this afternoon."

"Not too early." She shooed me again.

I went to take a shower, and then got to work on my makeup. I had to be waterproof, and I didn't care if Colin had seen me as my normal self at the hospital. This was a potentially serious date. This could lead to kissing. I had to treat it appropriately.

But the magic that had suffused my paintings recently did not affect my cosmetics routine. My lips looked too pink for my taste and my eyes just a bit overdone. I finally gave up out of frustration, got dressed, and got myself out the door.

Colin was already at the Cherwell Boathouse. The day was so sunny that it was impossible not to squint. There were a lot of people milling around, and the slightly dank smell of the river permeated everything.

"Sorry I'm late," I said.

He shrugged. "You're not. Sorry I'm so tired. Tried to sleep last night, but used to being awake and on duty."

"You want sugar?" I asked. "Or caffeine?" I patted the picnic basket I toted under one arm. I'd packed a couple of Cokes in it along with some pasta and bean salad that I'd bought on the way. I'd also brought a big bottle of water. I wasn't sure how long we'd be out.

"Nah, I'm all right." He spoke this barely above a whisper, just a soft rumble in his throat. I indulged in the excuse to lean close to hear him. "Our punt's this way." We walked past the two dozen or so at the dock and got into the one that Colin pointed to. It was a long, flat boat, not much wider than a rowboat. I stepped carefully to the seat in the center and held my skirt as I sat down.

Colin stayed at the end of the craft and pushed it away from the shore with a long pole. I watched as he expertly hauled the pole up, dropped it straight down to the river bottom below, and then leaned against it to push the boat forward. As the pole drifted astern, he hauled it up again. Our boat nosed its way free of the others it had been docked with and soon we were sliding along against the current. Sunlight glinted off the water and mallard ducks and the occasional swan slipped past, their necks arched and serene while their feet paddled away below. Several came up to the boat, no doubt expecting treats, but I didn't have any to toss at them, so they moved on quickly.

Dozens of other boats were out on the river. The punters coming the opposite way would gesture to Colin as they figured out who would go right and who would go left. It was a bit more crowded than I'd imagined, but the sky was endless and blue above, the chuckle of the river current was soothing, accompanied by the rhythmic slosh of Colin's punting. Together those sounds washed every care out of my mind.

"So," said Colin, "how've you been?"

"All right, considering. You?"

"Overworked." He laughed. "Not that you want to hear me complain."

"Go ahead."

"Um no. Not to you of all people. Look, I'm sorry about your aunt."

"Thanks."

He went silent after that and kept punting.

I hooked my sketchbook out of my bag, flipped it open, and did a quick sketch of a duck that had stuck its bill over the edge of the punt, hoping for food. The bird was too short, and the side of the punt too high, for the bird to lean in, so the gesture had been plaintive. If it hadn't looked plenty well fed, I might have felt sorry for it.

"Amazing how you just do that," he said. "I'd make a right mess of it if I tried."

"Well, imagine what would happen if I had to put in an IV. It'd be gruesome."

"Naw. You can learn that in an afternoon. What you're doing, I think takes longer."

I shrugged. "Started out as a hobby."

"Do you want to try this?" he asked, holding up the pole.

I squinted up at him. "I don't know, do I?"

He beckoned to me. "It isn't hard."

I got up and made my unsteady way to the end of the boat. Colin moved down towards the middle and directed me from there. I'd half hoped he'd put his arms around me, but he kept his distance, though the warm smile on his face softened that rebuke.

The pole was heavy, which meant it was easy to drop down to the river bottom. I leaned against it and pushed the boat forward. So far, so good.

"Don't push down too hard on the pole," he said. "You'll sink it into the muck and it won't come up again."

I pulled the pole up with a jerk, relieved that it came. I dropped it again and pushed. Again the punt moved forward. It was exhausting, but in a good way.

The fourth time I tried to lift the pole, it wouldn't come. I gave it an extra jerk and the next thing I knew, the punt had slid out from under my feet and I was in the frigid water, hanging onto the pole for dear life. Only then did it come loose from the bottom of the river, and for a second I feared its weight would pull me down. The river closed over my head and I held my breath. With a flail and a splash I got the pole upright and stuck it in the mud at the bottom of the river again, then lifted my head back up into the air, spat filthy water out of my mouth, and looked around for the punt.

Colin had burst out laughing. "Here, hurry," he said. The river current had slowed the punt to a stop, and as I watched, it began to drift the other way, towards me. "Hold out your hand. Get ready."

My waterlogged shoes threatened to fall off if I kicked my legs. I wore simple flats, so I clenched my toes, let my body drift downstream, and held out my hand as the punt closed in. From this angle it seemed impossibly high. I didn't see how I'd pull myself up and over the side.

But as the edge came near enough, I grabbed it with one hand.

"I'll get the pole. Let go," said Colin.

I grabbed the edge of the boat with the other hand and with a twist and a kick propelled myself up out of the water and over the edge. The whole boat rocked as I hauled my drenched body aboard. My skirt clung to my legs and my blouse to my chest. I gave a brief prayer of thanks that I hadn't worn white.

Colin stumbled and stepped over me as he wrestled the pole loose from the bottom of the river, then fell when it came loose. I tried to catch him and he twisted so he wouldn't fall on me, and he almost went over the edge. For a moment the world was chaos, and the next he lay across my feet, the pole in his fist, and both of us laughing.

"Yeah," I said. "That was graceful of me."

He rolled over and got up. "Everyone does that at least once. Just you watch. I'll do it before long. You okay, though?"

"Only thing bruised is my pride." I shivered as the breeze wicked the water off my skin. Despite the warm sun, goosebumps stood out along my arms. And I felt ridiculous to be so sopping wet. I didn't want to see my makeup or hair.

Colin was a perfect gentleman, though. He helped me sit up and handed me a little hand towel to dab my face dry with. There were a couple of them in the bottom of the punt, but it looked like I'd soaked the others.

I lifted my sodden hair off the back of my neck, wrung it out over the river, and then twisted it into a bun. This was why I always wore a hair tie around my wrist. For emergencies. My skirt wanted to ride up every time I moved, so I peeled it off my legs and did my best to wring it out too.

Colin had moved back to the end of the punt and was poling us upriver again.

I looked down and saw that I'd soaked my sketchbook.

"Oh no," said Colin, noticing at the same time I did.

"It's fine. Just pencil sketches. It'll dry out."

"All that work."

"Shouldn't erase anything." I tugged my shirt loose from my upper body and clenched my teeth to keep them from chattering. I felt like Pip had looked when I'd first found him, all wet and miserable.

The punt lurched slightly and I looked up. Colin had run us into the riverbank and stepped over me to jump off on dry land. "Let's eat lunch here," he said. "You can get sorted."

The stretch of riverbank he'd chosen was an open, grassy field with only a couple of other people set up for picnics. I clambered out of the punt with the picnic basket and we set up. This was not Nora's second painting, revisited. This was me looking like something the cat dragged in, sitting across from Colin, who was all but falling asleep.

"Sorry," he kept saying, through yawn after yawn.

I set out the lunch items I'd brought. He nibbled at some salad and downed the Coke in a couple of gulps. That woke him up a little. He sat up and stretched his toned arms. I couldn't help but notice that even half asleep, he managed to look all put together and very attractive.

I looked down at myself with chagrin.

"So, Eliza," he said. "Can I ask you something?"

"Mmm?"

"Mormon.org. Is that your church?"

He'd looked up my church? I tried not to jump to any conclusions, but if he cared enough to know my church, he must have felt something for me. "Yeah. That's kind of the information site for it, for people who aren't members."

"I just-" he yawned "-after the blessing your aunt got, I was curious, so I did some digging."

"Well, you have to be careful on the internet. There's a lot of garbage on there."

"I went and peeked at the whole ordinance thing those blokes did the other night. And..."

I didn't press him. If he'd been touched by the Spirit, it might take him a few tries to express how it felt.

"You take that all quite seriously, don't you?"

"Hmm?"

"The whole laying on of hands thing." He frowned at me, clearly wanting the answer to be "no".

But I couldn't deny my faith. I couldn't even hedge the way I had when religion had come up on our last date. There was only one answer to such a direct question, so I kept it short. "Yeah." I even made myself look him in the eye.

"And you think that's a way that God talks to you, through ordinances like that?"

"Sometimes." And during that blessing, He had. Though I knew Colin would scoff at the idea.

"It's not just cultural for you, is it? You're not just bowing to tradition."

"No."

"That's... a little odd. I mean, don't take this the wrong way, but a hundred years ago your church was practicing polygamy-"

I winced. "We don't do that-"

"Anymore, right. But you believe the *Book of Mormon* was translated by a bloke with some seer stones? In upstate New York?"

"Yes, but I understand that that one's a little hard to swallow. I don't expect you to read that and think, 'hey, this must be true!'"

"But you think it is?"

I felt like I was in college again, facing some sneering out of state student who liked to pick on "those crazy

Mormons." There was little that I could say in the face of their criticism other than what I told Colin now. "Yes, I do."

His eyebrows shot up at that.

I resisted the urge to explain myself. It wouldn't talk him out of his misgivings. Though I did wonder if a lie might make him like me more.

"Have you been to one of those temple things?"

Now we were on thin ice. "Yes," was all I said in a tone that I hoped would shut that line of inquiry down. I'd received my temple endowment when I was twenty-one, young for a woman with no plans to go on a mission or get married. I'd gone because the temple was one place where the living did ordinances for the dead, which meant the veil between our world and the spirit world was thinner there. I went whenever I wanted to feel my mother's arm around my shoulders, or hear Rachel's braying laugh, or sense Lindsay's constant irritation with me. I never saw them, but I felt they were there. It was like I was in my living room as a child, with them bustling around the house. Out of sight, but making their presences known. There was no way I could share that with Colin without making him even more skeptical.

"Did you go on a mission?" he asked.

"No, but my brother and one of my sisters did."

"Do you *really* believe all that stuff I read on that website?"

"Okay, I haven't really searched mormon.org, but the answer is probably yes. I just say probably because if there's any part where people are giving their own personal views... sometimes those can get odd."

"You mean odder than what I read in the main part of the site?"

"Right."

He looked distinctly uncomfortable.

And I felt even more absurd than before. I was still disheveled and damp. I'd dabbed my face with the towel, but probably managed to smear my makeup regardless. I must've looked like a clown who'd been dragged behind a cart in a rainstorm. So much for this opportunity Nora had given me to live life. I was just making a fool of myself.

"Can I ask you something?" said Colin.

"Hmm?"

"Have you ever had a friend who's a guy?"

"What?"

"A friend? Just a friend? Who has a Y chromosome?"

"Um... no."

"Me neither. I've never had a female friend. I could really use one sometimes, you know?"

He couldn't have been plainer. This was an olive branch he held out, a way to convert this date turned disaster into something positive. "Yeah," I said, tentatively.

"I don't get birds, you know?"

"Birds?"

"Women."

"You call us birds?"

"It's like bloke. What? It's not derogatory. It's like, I dunno. 'Chicks'."

"Well, I don't normally talk to any guys about 'chicks'. If my brother used that word, I'd think he was being strange."

"Women, then."

I shrugged. "I'm not sure there's anything to get, you know? I mean, I think the only secret is, we don't know what we're doing either."

He raised his eyebrows at that again, then chuckled, then laughed.

"What?"

"Just- I don't know. It's not what I expected you to say."

"It's called honesty."

"Right. Now you're going to want the same from me I suppose. How terrifying."

"I don't have any deep and meaningful questions for you."

"I'm fine with shallow. I'm good at shallow."

"I don't have shallow ones either. I don't really have much of a social life."

"Really? I would have thought you were popular."

"I work alone and spend a lot of time in hospitals."

"That's true. And here you have to do it again. There's no one else to be here with your aunt?"

"I want to track down the rest of her family."

"What do you mean, track down?"

"It's a long story."

"Blimey. So she's got family other than you?"

"Yeah."

"I'm sorry. Is there any way I can help?"

"Know of any other way to search for people other than on the internet?"

"Not really, no."

"Then no, but thank you." I ate some bean salad and looked down at the still damp hemline of my skirt. At least it was drying without many wrinkles.

"Eliza?"

"Hmm?"

"I meant what I said, you know, about being friends."

"Thanks. Me too."

"I may not have any answers to deep universal questions, but I do know cancer. Anything you need, let me know."

"Thanks. I just need to find her family and I owe her one last picture."

"I saw the one you brought in the other day. Just smashing."

"It came together all right. I'm hoping I can get the same effect with this last one."

He glanced at his watch. "Shall we get back?"

"Yeah," I agreed.

Paint Me True

When I rounded the corner of Charlbury Road, there stood Louisa, *again,* in front of the house. This time, I knew I couldn't afford to hide from her. I had too many questions and too little time.

Twenty-Three

Family Secrets

I made myself square my shoulders and march toward her. She didn't notice me at first, just stared at the house. When she did turn, she didn't jump with surprise, just tilted her head to one side and smiled. Pretty nervy for someone who'd tried to break into the house.

"Hello," she chirped. "I just wondered if there's anything I can do to help."

"Why are you here?" Inwardly I cringed, but I hoped that didn't show. I just didn't do confrontation well.

I had the impression that Louisa did. She didn't give anything away, just said, "Pardon?"

"I saw you try to get into the house the other day."

"Oh, well, right. I don't have the right key."

"Why would you have *any* key?"

"I was given a copy."

"By?"

"It's not something I care to reveal."

"Excuse me? You have a key to my aunt's house and you don't care to tell me how you got it?"

"You changed the locks. I can't get in anymore."

"You had no business trying to go in the other day."

"I know, but you two won't tell me anything. I was trying to get information."

"What information?"

"About Nora. How she's doing."

"What business is it of yours?"

"Well it wasn't for me."

I was not in the mood for this. I was tired and wrung out and overstretched and all of these emotions together ignited into a flash of blinding anger. My inhibitions blasted to smithereens and I whipped the picnic basket off my shoulder and slammed it to the ground between us. Then I stood there, trembling with fury. I curled my fingers and wished I could wrap them around her neck. "Listen to me, I saw the scans, okay? I saw all of the old broken bones and the surgery, all of it. You are not welcome here."

"I understand. Really." She didn't look like she was mocking me.

"You *understand?* Oh gee, you just beat a woman within an inch of her life-"

"Me? *Me?* Oh no, no, no." She burst out laughing.

I folded my arms across my chest.

"Do I look like someone who could do that kind of damage? I mean, look at how small I am."

"Who did it, then?"

She took off her sunglasses and rested them on the top of her head. Her gray eyes searched my face. "You really don't know?"

"Just answer my question."

"Paul, honey."

"That is a lie. He was the perfect husband. She loved him more than anything."

"I believe the second part. She did love him more than made sense."

"You can't possibly think I'll believe that he beat her."

"Well, let's be logical about this. I couldn't have done it. Look at how small I am, and she and I haven't had much contact over the years. My brother, now, was an alcoholic temperamental little boy, just like our father."

"Or... or... you could have gotten someone else or..."

Louisa dug into her pocket and produced her keys. She separated one from the rest and held it up. "Johnny gave me this. Had the copy made with money from his allowance and had me promise him I'd always have it on me. If he ever needed anything, he'd shine a torch out his window on a little mirror that would reflect it at our house."

A torch was a flashlight. I remembered the flashlight on the windowsill. "John, my cousin, John?"

"Yes." She looked me straight in the eye.

Louisa's gaze was steady. She saw the change in my features, but she didn't gloat over it.

"Do you know how to reach him? Or his sister?"

"Why don't you and I go for some tea? I know a place nearby."

"I... dunno..."

She gestured at the nurse's car in the driveway. "Nora's being cared for. I assume they have your number?"

I nodded.

"It doesn't need to be a long chat. Come with me."

The place Louisa knew was a little bed and breakfast with a cafe that served cream tea. I felt out of place with my barely dry clothing and hair still up in a makeshift bun, but Louisa moved with confidence and soon had us seated on two comfy chairs with a small table between us. The elderly woman who brought us our tea seemed to know her well, because she didn't utter a word, just set down the pot.

"Thank you," said Louisa.

"Scones?"

"Please."

I looked at the teapot dubiously.

"It's red tea, dear," said Louisa. "Not real tea. Though if you'd like something else, we can order that."

"No, it's fine."

"I miss tea. This is the closest I can get." She poured the deep mahogany colored liquid into my teacup. "So, right. About your cousins. Yes, of course I can get in touch with them. What would you like me to tell them?"

"I just need to talk to them. It's important."

"Suit yourself." She got out her cellphone and pressed a key. Only one, I noticed. She had the number on speed-dial.

I heard the other person's jubilant, "Auntie Lou!" A man's voice.

"Hello, dear... Yes? Well I'll check my email when I get home. Are these new pictures or the ones with the twins eating potato salad? Right... Listen, I've got someone here who wants to speak to you very badly. Her name's Eliza and she's your cousin, from America... Yes, that Eliza. Sweetie, just let her speak to you. She'll keep it short." She passed the phone over to me and folded her hands primly on the edge of the table.

I put the phone against my ear as if it were made of spun sugar and liable to disintegrate if I squeezed too hard. "Hello?" I said.

"Hello." The man's voice was guarded.

"Listen... there's no easy way to say this."

"Just say it, then."

"You need to come visit your mother."

"Why is that?"

"She's dying."

Louisa clapped her hand over her mouth, her eyes wide with horror.

I turned to one side and did my best to keep my voice steady. "I'm so sorry. She wouldn't go in for any tests or anything and I-I finally got her to, but it was too late. Way too late."

"What's wrong with her?"

"Cancer. You know, the family curse?"

"Sorry?" He genuinely didn't know.

"Look, can you come immediately? She doesn't have much time left."

"Let me have the phone," said Louisa.

I passed it back.

"Listen, dear, I'll book you all a train. Tell me when you can leave and I'll book it... Don't start with me. Tell me when you can leave... Right, call me when you've done that. I'm putting more money on your phone. Go talk to Bea. Hurry now. I love you." She hung up.

I tried to piece together what I'd heard. "You're paying his train fare and for his phone?"

"I help however I can. He's got *no* money. Works as a binman and lives on a council estate."

It took me a moment to translate that. He worked as a garbage man and lived in government housing. "What? Why?"

"Because his mother cut him off is why."

"My aunt-"

"Is proud as a peacock. But who am I to judge? I never understood much about her. See, I thought it was a religious dispute, but then you show up at our ward and scupper that whole idea."

"Excuse me?"

"I thought Nora didn't like Mormons."

"Is John a Mormon?"

"Of course he is."

"Wait, what?"

She blinked at me owlishly. "Right, I suppose you wouldn't have a clue. Yes, Johnny's a Mormon. He was just ordained a high priest, and Keeley's thinking over whether or not to put papers in for another mission. She served in Haiti last time and found it such a growing experience. But first she's going to finish her masters."

"Her masters?"

"I think I'd best decide on how to tell this story and just tell it, or else it'll come out in jumbled bits and make no sense at all. Right... so do you believe me that Paul was a monster who beat his wife?"

I didn't want to answer that.

"Fine, well, he was. And one day when he and Nora were having a monstrous row, two men knocked on the front door. Johnny was the only one who heard it and when he answered, the men explained that they were Nora's home teachers, and they asked if they could help him with anything. He asked if they'd take him home with them.

"I lived out a ways back then, so you can imagine my surprise when I came home to find Bruce Babcock on my front stoop. I didn't know him at the time, but he explained he was a counselor in the bishopric of the ward and he asked if I'd be willing to tell him a few things about the family. We sat out in my front garden and I told him what there is to tell, how there's been drink and violence going as far back as I knew, how my dad beat my mum so bad she committed suicide-"

"What?"

"My dear, I am not of goodly parents. No one in our family is. It's why I never dared have children of my own."

"So what did the Church do for my cousins?"

"I wouldn't know the full extent of it. I imagine they talked to Nora and my brother. They got the children some sessions with a counselor, maybe the parents too, I don't know. The ward put together a rota of babysitters, willing to look after the children at a moment's notice without asking questions, provided there was never a mark on them, and there never was. Nora managed to keep them safe in that respect.

"And I went to visit my niece and nephew when they were being babysat by ward members. It was sneaky of me, I know, but I was afraid that if I contacted Nora, she wouldn't want me around them. We bonded at once, those children and

I. People began to bring them to church every week and I went too, just to see them at first, but then I saw so many other things. Take Johnny, for example. He's from a long line of abusive, alcoholic men. It's not just Paul and our father. His father wasn't much better. Things like that become a matter of course in a family and it seems like it'll never end. I ended it by not having children, but Johnny did one better. He's got a lovely family. One generation and look at what he's done."

"Yeah," I said. "It doesn't always work out, but people can do it."

"Your family have a story like that?" She perked up.

I shook my head. "My dad's been a Bishop and is now a Stake President. People came to us sometimes, when I was a kid, to thank him. I heard a lot of stories like what you describe with John."

"Oh, well, I'd just thought that if your family was like that, perhaps I could understand Nora, but I fear she only was ever interested in the money and the house and all that."

"I don't know," I said. "I think these things tend to be more complicated. But that's why you tried to buy her off so that she wouldn't marry Paul?"

"I tried to save her life and she was horrid to me. She's still horrid to me, even after all I've done for her."

"I thought you two didn't talk."

"Not usually, no, but whose front door did she drag herself to when Paul beat her so bad she couldn't even walk? Mine. That was after Bruce and I were married, so it was just 'round the corner. And who helped her get on a plane back to America right then and there? Me. We got her to A&E to get her stabilized and then off she went to New York. She didn't want to go to Utah, but she hinted that she would after she got more treatment. I couldn't believe it when she was back with Paul six months later."

"How many times did you help her get out of the country for medical treatment?"

"Well, just the once, really. The next time I told her she had to help herself, and she cursed me for it. She wasn't beaten as bad. She turned her children over to another ward member and left for a few weeks. The children hadn't been out of their home five minutes before they came and asked to stay with me. My house was where they always ran when they were scared. I love those two darlings as if they were my own. I never thought I could have a family like that - I know they aren't mine. They're Nora's, but I thought that any child I had would end up like my father or my brother."

"And John gave you a housekey?"

"Right, yes. He gave it to me so that he could feel safe. We rigged up a mirror on the back garden fence so that he could signal us any time. We promised we'd come get him, no matter what. I didn't spend a single night away from my house for ten years, just in case that little one needed me."

"So did you pick up the mail and feed Pip a few weeks ago?"

"Yes, that was me. I found Nora unconscious on the floor and called the paramedics too."

"And let them in?"

"Right, yes."

"How did you know?"

"Well, the usual way. I always peek into the house when I walk past. It's an old habit, even though Paul and the little ones are gone. That night, her little dog scratched at the window when he saw me and barked and barked. He was so upset, I knew something was wrong. But tell me now, do you believe me? I wouldn't hurt your aunt, difficult as she is."

Her account fit all the facts. The only discrepancy was that it required me to believe that Nora had lied to me about Paul. "So how is Keeley these days?" I asked. "Her brother's got no education but she's doing a masters degree?"

"She applied for scholarships and bursaries and got them. Johnny's not done well with all that. He married young and has his children, whom he loves. I support them as best I can. Keeley is doing quite well, though she's very guarded in her personal life. Doesn't like to date. But she and I get on like old chums."

"And she and John don't talk to Nora?"

"Unfortunately, no. It's not how I would have things, but Nora doesn't believe that. Thinks I stole her children from her. I fear she doesn't talk to them because she thinks she'd also have to talk to me, not that I make a habit of forcing myself on her-"

"Except when you go in the house uninvited – not that I'm angry about the first time. You helped get her to the hospital. But trying to break in a couple of days ago? Not cool."

"Right, fine. Perhaps I do pry a bit more than necessary, but no one tells me anything. What is this about Nora dying from cancer?"

"She's past the stage when it'd be treatable. It took me a couple weeks to get her to have the scans she needed. She refused them because she didn't want anyone to see her old scars from all the years of abuse."

Louisa pressed her mouth into a thin line. She picked up a scone off a plate that had arrived sometime during our conversation – I'd been too preoccupied to notice when – split it in half and put it in front of me. "So he finally did it," she said.

"Pardon?"

"My brother. I thought when he got killed in a car accident that his reign of terror would be over, but no, even dead he managed to kill Nora."

"I guess so."

She looked across at me. "I am very, very sorry."

"Can we call Keeley?"

"Right, yes."

Again she hit just one key on her cellphone, and again I heard an, "Auntie Lou!"

"Hello dearest... well, I'm going to have your cousin tell you that... Eliza, from Amer- yes her... Just let her talk to you, sweet. I'm going to pass you over."

Again I took the phone in my hand and pressed it to my ear. "Hello?"

"What is it, then?"

This was most definitely a female relative of mine. She didn't beat around the bush. "Your mother's got cancer. You need to come see her before it's too late."

"My mother?"

"Yes."

"Right..."

"Listen, have you ever been tested for the BRCA mutation?"

"What's this?"

"Something we need to discuss. It's killed a lot of women in our family, so I speak from experience. No matter how you feel about your mother, you need to see her one last time. You'll regret it if you don't."

In the silence that followed, I wondered what my cousin looked like on the other end of the line. All the pictures I'd ever seen of her were from when she was a child with her light brown pigtails and gap toothed grin.

"Please come," I said.

"Put Lou back on."

I passed the phone back and again Louisa told my cousin that she would pay for train fare.

As she hung up the phone, I said, "Nora made me her sole heir."

She nodded, brusquely.

"So I guess it falls to me to decide who gets what. I need your help. I mean, I assume John should get the house, since he has children, but I don't even know how much money there is or anything like that."

Louisa did not look at me as she said, "You're not obligated to give them anything."

"It's not really mine to give. Nora... you know how she is. She must've had a fit of pique a few years ago, but what she did was a mistake and you know it. So help me."

"Well, I suppose we'll need to look into matters, yes. But now eat your scone, dear. I know you wanted to get back to Nora." She put the little tubs of butter, jam, and clotted cream by my plate. She was as meddling and bossy as ever, but now I could see the love that motivated her.

"Look," I said, "now that I've found my cousins, can you help me with a few things?"

"Of course, of course."

So much had changed in the course of a day that when I finally got home and went upstairs to see my aunt, I was shocked at how she looked the same. She was thin and frail and sleepy, but she still smiled when I walked in. She didn't know that I'd dug into her secrets. I was still the one who painted her beautiful pictures of Paul.

I'd obsessed about this moment and now it was here. I reminded myself that I'd weathered an awkward conversation with Louisa just a few hours ago. I could do this.

"Hello, dear," she said.

"Hi. Are you comfortable?"

"I am. Did you have a good date?"

"Um, you know? Yes. It went really well."

"What have you got there?" She nodded at the large bag I toted under one arm.

I unslung it from my shoulder and set it on the floor. "I got four," I said as I dug in with a crackle of plastic and came up with a large teddy bear. I didn't bother to add that Louisa had come shopping with me. "Found the Toys R Us. It's got microfiber fur. Feel." I passed it to her and she took it in her hands and caressed the plush fur.

"Four of these-"

"All the same, of course. Nothing for them to fight over. They're for John's kids."

"You're sending these to John?"

"Well, that'd be doing it the hard way. He'll be here tomorrow, midmorning."

She dropped the teddy bear and gave me a startled look as if I'd just fired a gun into the ceiling of her bedroom. "John's coming?"

"And his kids, and Keeley. Yes."

"They're coming? Here?" She cast about, as if looking for a place to run and hide. Then she looked up at me, a thousand questions in her eyes. How had I found them? What had they said? What did I think of her as a result? If I'd found her children, I had access to what they'd say about her and their father.

And now the moment had arrived. The moment when she realized I knew the truth and then what? Would she fly into a rage and throw me out? Burst into tears? Curl up into a ball and not respond when I tried to talk to her?

I picked up the teddy bear and stuffed it back into the bag. "Anyway, I'll get started on that third painting of Paul as soon as possible, but I wanted to get the house ready first. I've got beds to make and all that stuff."

Her gaze turned quizzical.

I kissed her on the cheek. "I love you. Call me if you need anything."

I was up so late getting the house ready that it was a struggle to stay awake in church. Brother Babcock had me sit next to him. Louisa, he explained, was going to meet John and Keeley at the station and bring them to the house. He patted my shoulder sympathetically as I yawned my way through

Sacrament meeting. He then gave me a ride home and we arrived at the house just as Louisa pulled into the driveway from the other direction. The nurse's car was also in the driveway, so it was a tight squeeze.

I got out and stood with my hand shielding my eyes as my two cousins, whom I'd never seen outside of anonymous photographs on the walls, emerged. John was so tall he unfolded from the car to stand up straight, then leaned back in to extract one baby and a woman I took to be his wife – given she was shorter, rounder, and had much redder hair than the Keeley I'd seen in pictures – extracted another. Two other children with the big eyes of toddlers clambered out and looked at me as if I were their new headmistress and they weren't sure what they thought of me yet.

The passenger side door opened and out stepped a woman with light brown hair, a very slender frame, and freckles over her nose. At the sight of me she gave a hesitant smile, then turned to get her luggage.

Brother Babcock waded into the fray to get suitcases and when I tried to follow, I found there were none left for me. Keeley turned around and found herself in the same situation. It was then that our eyes really met.

"Hi," I said.

Her mouth twitched, and it wasn't because she suppressed a smile.

"I tried to get in touch with you sooner," I said, "but I didn't know how. I mistakenly thought Louisa was evil. Didn't occur to me to ask her."

At that Keeley did chuckle. "She's not too evil."

"Not excessively," agreed Louisa.

I dug in my purse and produced two house keys. I handed one to Keeley and one to John. Louisa looked at me expectantly. "There are only those two extras right now," I lied. There was no way I was going to give her another key to the house. She might have apologized for trying to go in uninvited, but I suspected she wouldn't be able to resist the temptation to do it again if she had the chance.

She gave me a tight lipped nod, then picked up one of the two toddlers and carried her towards the house. "This is your grandma's house," she explained.

John came to stand beside me. He didn't say anything, just looked me over.

"Your mother's in her room," I said. "She'll have regular visits and care from nurses."

"For how long?"

"Until the end." I shrugged.

"Right."

He looked a bit like my other cousins on that side of the family. The same angular jaw and hesitant stance when he found himself out of his depth.

Since I didn't know what to say next, I followed Louisa inside. As everyone filed in, I could feel the house change from the lonesome, empty place it had been every time I'd visited, to a home full of chatter and running feet and giggles upstairs. Pip raced around and shot up the staircase, tags jangling and tail wagging frantically.

"Best not to let her know I'm here," said Louisa in a low voice. "I'll go see if there's anything for lunch in the kitchen."

John's wife, Bea, followed her and when I looked in the sitting room I saw Brother Babcock with an arm around Keeley. She smiled up at him while they caught up with each other.

John's voice called out upstairs, "Put your bags next to your beds. Here, like so." His voice got softer as he moved away.

I climbed the stairs to Nora's room, knocked, and entered when the nurse opened the door. My aunt was propped up on pillows, looking thin and drawn. I went over to hold her hand and her gaze darted to me with the quick, jerky movements of a bird. "I'm guessing you know they're here," I said.

The nurse slipped silently out.

"Yes."

"You ready?"

"No." That came out as a whisper.

Heavy footsteps sounded in the corridor and there came a sharp knock.

Nora grasped my hands tight. "Eliza, I-"

"Come in!" I said.

The door opened and John peered around it.

Nora grasped my hand so tight I felt the bones give. I gently pried to loosen it, but she didn't even notice.

"Mum," he said.

The door opened wider and his daughter peered around as well, her brown eyes wide.

"Leah, this is your grandmum. Mum, this is Leah Nora Chesterton."

Nora dropped my hand and moved to sit up.

"Hello, Grandma. Thank you for the stuffed teddy bear."

I could tell Nora was about to cry. I moved quietly around the bed and slipped out. This was their moment.

I went downstairs to check my email. There I found a message from Hattie.

> Hey,
> So... okay. I thought it over and decided you were right. I called my brother and he wasn't too horrible. I didn't talk about the Church and he didn't either. I'm going to the "wedding". No idea what to get for a gift.
> Things are better, though, so thank you.
> -H

I blinked and read that over again. She'd reconciled with her brother? My cartoon had convinced her? I'd spent my entire career living from one thin compliment to the next. I got a lot of, "That's beautiful"s and "Perfect"s, but this was the first time anyone had told me something I'd drawn had made them change the way they lived their life.

This was *Hattie*, who believed the Democrats, Satan, and Hollywood were part of a cabal bent on stealing her family and making her miserable. *She* had offered reconciliation?

I felt like I'd been away from home for a very long time.

Twenty-Four

Paint Me True

As the evening wore on, I felt more and more like a fifth wheel. The Babcocks and my cousins had a lot of catching up to do. The children got over their initial shyness quickly and staged a teddy bear wrestling match in the sitting room. I found myself pushed to the corner time and again. I sketched the children silly pictures of mice eating off toadstools and frogs playing piano, which they cut out and spread on the floor to make up stories. I found myself being served food for dinner and unable to elbow my way in to help with dishes. Then after dinner there was a frenzy to get the children ready for bed.

I slipped upstairs to the studio to get a moment to myself. I'd promised Nora that third painting, but how could I paint it given all I now knew? Especially with her children and sister-in-law in the house?

I had to paint something, though. My hands were itching. After a moment's fiddling, I got the lamps on and positioned how I wanted. Paul's proposal and Nora's disappointment surfaced up in my mind. She'd known then that there was something out of kilter in her fairytale. She had a feud with the in-laws before she was even married. That proposal wasn't a moment that she wanted to capture, but could I paint an idealized picture of a proposal or ring shopping? Some subjects just couldn't be made pretty with any kind of artistic tricks. Some truths were inherently ugly.

The real question was, did I want to knowingly paint a lie? What would my cousins and Louisa think? I had to find something positive I could say about Nora and Paul. There had to be good things, even if they'd been fleeting. I didn't bother with preliminary sketches this time. This one would be rough, but that was okay. I was painting for Nora, who had mere weeks left to live, if that. I took a deep breath and cast about for a memory of a good spontaneous romantic moment from my own love life.

Needless to say, Len hadn't given me any. He didn't do spontaneity. Whenever he had called up out of the blue, it was because he'd worked long hours all week and hadn't paused long enough to call me earlier. Rather than take control of the situation, he'd open with an apology and pause, as if to see whether I'd tell him to get lost. Then he'd make his tentative offer.

"So... you want to go to the movies?" was a common one.

"You... want to watch a DVD?" was another.

Occasionally he mixed up a little. Once he said, "You want to go to the park and fly a kite?"

"Do you have a kite?" I asked.

"No, but I have instructions I downloaded from the internet on how to make one out of balsa wood and tissue paper."

"Do you have balsa wood and tissue paper?"

"I have the wood. We can go get the paper."

"I have tissue paper." I'd been playing around with it after one of my nieces posted a link to the *Hungry, Hungry Caterpillar* fanpage on Facebook. Eric Carle had done such beautiful illustrations with tissue paper and glue.

"Oh yeah? You have some that we can use?"

"As long as you're okay with only using the ugly colors," I said.

"I'm not gonna know what those are, so as long as you're the one to pick them out, I think we're good."

"Yeah."

"Thank you for not making the obvious joke."

"Which is?"

"That if I don't know what colors are ugly, how do I always pick them out to wear? Well, that's what my mom would say, at least."

"Can you not compare me to your mother?"

"Sorry. I'll come by in half an hour?"

"Okay."

At the park we lasted about twenty minutes before I wanted to throttle him. "Look, you have balsa wood lying around your house, that means you know how to build models, explain to me why you can't glue two pieces together and keep them straight?"

It was a gray day with a steady wind, ideal for kite flying, though it had a damp chill to it that foretold rain. The sky above was still light, though, despite the horizon to horizon cloud cover. Around us were a crowd of kids celebrating someone's birthday, dozens of people walking their dogs, and the usual scattering of couples on picnic blankets, all of whom were packing up to leave before any drops fell. In the distance, a few kites danced in the sky.

"Not even my sisters would put balsa wood and models together." The wind blew his too long hair into his eyes so he had to have one hand on the top of his head at all times to hold it back. That did not improve his kite building skills.

"Will you stop comparing me to your female relatives?"

"My mom would. Probably."

"*Len.*"

"It's a favorable comparison. Look, why don't you glue it. You've done sculpture before, right? You ever done balsa wood and tissue paper?"

I snatched the crooked kite frame from him and knelt over it as I straightened it out, held it while the glue set, and then set about wrapping the tissue paper over the frame. Len looked at me as if I were a swimsuit model making calf eyes at him. Only a true nerd would go goggle eyed at a woman performing a minor act of engineering. I scowled at him.

"Okay, you're doing the technical part there, maybe I could do the aesthetics? Can I draw on it with marker?"

"No."

"Aw..."

"Only if you don't draw teeth on it, and shark gills."

"Aw, maaan. Can I do eyes at least?"

"No!"

He laughed. "Okay, gimme the marker."

I raised an eyebrow and handed it over. He pinned the kite gently with one knee and drew a smiley face.

"That's just great," I said.

"You are harsh, you know that? Keep this up and I'm gonna make a picture of this kite your screensaver."

"I know how to change my screensaver."

"Well... I'll... think of something." He shook a fist at me as he got up and held the kite out. The wind grabbed it immediately and tugged at it like a puppy worrying a rag. Len tossed it up in the air with a practiced motion and let the string slide through his fingers as the wind carried it up and up. For a moment it danced on the end of the line, its multi-colored tail of tissue paper streamers swirling in its wake. Then the string broke and it dropped, nose first and broke up into a pile of wood pieces and torn tissue paper that began to blow away along the ground. Len and I had to chase after it.

"Well," he said, as we stuffed the remains of the kite into a garbage can while the first drops of rain began to fall. "You want to go watch a DVD?"

I painted on and on into the night, until my arm had a cramp in it and the scent of the paint gave me a headache, until my eyes were so tired from focusing on details that I carried on with them out of focus, until I caught myself jerking awake after falling asleep on my feet, brush still going. I had a hazy idea that I was painting a fictional proposal, Paul on bended knee before Nora, who turned her face away from him and towards the viewer, tears on her cheeks. It was in the archway Colin and I had walked through in Balliol College, the one that led to the larger quad full of sun and green grass and trees. I supposed that was supposed to be symbolic of Nora and Paul's relationship going from modest beginnings to bigger things? I was too tired to dwell on how poor and unsuitable that metaphor was. I was just grasping at whatever memories came to hand, since I'd done zero research for this, not even looking at the staircase where Paul had his room and had done his actual proposal.

When the clock struck one, I couldn't keep painting. I dropped my arms, rubbed my neck, and did my best to clean my brush. The house was dead silent. Everyone else had gone to bed.

I stumbled down the stairs to get a drink from the kitchen. The water was cool right from the tap. I downed two glasses full, then opened the dishwasher, rolled out the top rack with a rattle, and nestled my glass in among the other dirty dishes.

As I reached the foot of the stairs, I saw that I'd left the lights on in the studio. Their bright white glow looked garish and inappropriate in the dark hallway. When I climbed the stairs, though, I found Nora was awake, and even more surprising, out of bed. She stood in the doorway of the studio. Her back was to me, so I couldn't see her expression.

I winced and wished I'd covered the painting up. It was a rough draft, at best. Something slapped down in a few hours with no preplanning and a heart full of bitterness. Nora was still as a statue, her slim hands grasping the doorframe.

"Hey," I said softly.

She inhaled sharply and I heard her sniffle. "Oh, honey."

Unsure if those were tears of pain or joy, I went to stand next to her and forced myself to look at that painting.

It wasn't half bad. In fact, it was better than I would have thought possible, given how it was put together. When I looked sidelong at my aunt, I saw that her eyes glowed with happiness. "It's perfect," she said.

"It's how things should have gone," I told her.

"Thank you."

"You okay? Hungry or thirsty or anything?"

"I'm fine." She turned to me and held out her arms.

I pressed her frail, skeletal body to mine and tried not to notice how her bones jutted out at harsh angles. "I love you," she said.

"Love you too. You want to stay up for a while or-"

"I'm exhausted. Can you help me back to bed?"

I did, letting her lean against me. She was lighter than she'd been a few weeks ago. I lifted her into her bed and tucked the covers around her. She lost consciousness before I straightened up to ask her if she needed anything else.

It was way past time for me to get to sleep. I went to turn out the studio lights and shut the door, and then I think I was out before my head hit the pillow.

When I opened my eyes again, it was to the sound of a sharp knock on the door. "Eliza?"

I rolled over. The light outside my window was gray, which meant it was still very early. My neck was still sore and when I held up my hands, I noted I still had paint in the grooves around my fingernails.

"Eliza?" the voice repeated.

"Yes?" I sat up.

The door opened and Keeley peered around the edge, her eyes solemn.

I leapt out of bed. "What happened?"

"She's gone."

It took a long moment for that to sink in. "What?"

"She's... she's gone." My cousin began to cry in earnest.

Instinct took over and I went to put my arms around her. Much to my surprise, she hugged back.

Beyond her, in the corridor, John stepped out of his mother's room. His eyes were red too. At the sight of me, he gave a friendly nod, then wandered off towards the stairs as if he wasn't entirely sure where he was going. I knew that feeling. It was what happened when someone you were bound to left the world. Once the connection unraveled, you felt like you were adrift. There were days I still felt like that, as if Mom's death had been just hours ago.

I stroked Keeley's hair. "I'm sorry I didn't find you sooner. I wanted to call you and tell you about your mother-"

"No, no. It's best this way. If I'd been here longer, I'm sure Mum and I would've gotten into a row." She half laughed, half cried as she spoke. I knew that feeling too, when life was too sad for one heart to contain it all. When humor got wrapped around the tragedy, because that was the only way it was survivable.

John's footsteps in the hall let me know he was coming back. Keeley heard him too because she let go of me and turned to him. They clung to each other, there in the hallway.

I slipped back into my room, shut the door and only then did I let myself cry. It would be hard enough for my cousins to have their complicated relationship with their mother over before they could ever hope to set it right.

Me, I'd lost my best friend, my second mother, the woman who through her praise, generosity, and insight had made me an artist. Once again I had a hole ripped in my life that no one else would ever fill. It was like every death took a little piece of me with it, or in this case, a big piece.

I emerged only after I heard everyone else leave the house. Louisa stuffed a note under my door to let me know they were going to "get things sorted". She jotted her cell number down so I could get in touch.

I started in surprise when the nurse padded up the stairs. "Sorry," I said, "I didn't hear you arrive this morning."

"I stayed here all night. She seemed poorly. I just need to gather some things and then I'll be off."

I wondered how I'd missed her, or if my last memory of Nora was just a dream. I went over to the studio and opened the door. The painting was still there, looking just as I'd remembered it. It had been the easiest painting I'd ever painted, which made no sense to me. Paul looked like the hero of an action adventure movie with that direct gaze of his and muscled physique.

I went all the way in and shut the door. The photograph of Paul I'd first used to sketch his likeness was leaning against the wall on the far side of the room. I went to retrieve it and saw that it was a picture of a man in his thirties, better looking than average, but with a rather blank, uninteresting expression. He gazed off into the distance at nothing much, as if he were thinking about nothing much. He was the sort of person I'd pass on the street, the sort of person I most certainly did pass on the street every day. There was nothing remarkable about him.

The photograph didn't employ any of the artistic tricks I'd used to make him more interesting. He didn't gaze directly at the viewer with a penetrating stare. His eyes weren't shaded in a way to make them seem deep and intense. His hair wasn't crafted to look tousled in a scruffy, sexy kind of way, and his mouth didn't half smile with the promise of hidden secrets.

Nora hadn't been the only liar in this. I'd supported her lies with my art, drawing the man she wanted Paul to be, rather than the man he was. I'd always thought of art as a window into truth, but I spent a lot of time orchestrating "truths" while these lies came easily. These lies all made good use of my hard earned tricks of the trade.

Paul's eyes, for example. I looked at the picture again and squinted. They weren't even the same shape, or the right distance apart. I held up my hands to mask the rest of Paul's face in the painting, leaving only the eyes.

Realization hit like a bolt of lightning. I knew those eyes, only they weren't gray as I'd painted them. They were pale blue.

I let my hands drop. The mouth, with the hint of a smile. The angle of the shoulders as he put his full attention on Nora. I knew all of these features, and none of them belonged to Paul. That's because when I had channeled my ideal of a perfect boyfriend, I hadn't channeled Paul.

I'd channeled Len.

Twenty-Five

Regrets

It was obvious, now that I'd noticed it. These pictures had almost nothing to do with Nora's stories. For one thing, they were backwards. Nora had talked about her infatuation with Paul. How unattainable he seemed and how she would do anything for him. These pictures showed Paul infatuated with her. She was the unattainable one. She was the object of desire. No wonder she'd loved them so much. It's what she'd wanted so badly.

And it was what I'd had, until a few weeks ago. Even the proposal with tears now took on a new meaning to me. I got down on the floor and rested my forehead in my palms. Chris's blessing surfaced up.

Your Heavenly Father would have you know that He has a very special lesson for you to learn.

As was often the case when the Lord had something to say, it was more complicated than it appeared at first blush. I thought Nora had taught me about true love, and maybe she had, just not in the way I'd thought. All of my paintings had made her a cipher. Her back was usually to the viewer, leaving it unclear how she felt about "Paul's" attentions. I'd put

Nora in my place in my last relationship. My subconscious thought it was the perfect relationship, evidently, or did I just think Len seemed appropriately infatuated? I had to admit, once I gave him a virtual makeover, he was gorgeous. If I changed the hair color, eye color, and shape of the face to match the real Len, the figure in the paintings would be even more gorgeous.

Had I really just looked at Len's scruffy wardrobe and no deeper? Had I ignored the attentions of a guy even more attractive than any of my previous boyfriends because he barely ever spent money on himself? I was an artist. I was supposed to see past the surface.

Right then, I realized that I missed Len. I couldn't go a day without thinking about him, and whenever I painted from the heart, it was while I went over memories of him. Now that I put two and two together, I felt a sharp, physical pain in the center of my chest that made it hard to breathe.

I missed his hugs. He didn't give them often, but he gave them like he meant them. First he'd wrap his arms around me, then he'd take my hand in his, look me in the eye, and ask me how I was. There, in the safety of our embrace, I could say anything and those eyes would stay fixed on mine for as long as I spoke.

And his kisses. He did pure, chaste kisses that would have fit at the end of a Disney movie, only he had a way of lingering over them - his eyelashes brushing my cheekbones, his fingertips stroking the nape of my neck - that made me crazy for him. And when the kisses were over, the hugs would carry on, and I'd pour my heart out. Or I'd lean my head against his chest and just listen to the whisper of his breathing. Times like that he'd say, "I love you," in that heartbreaking way of his. He said it like it hurt him, because he knew he wouldn't hear it back, but he said it anyway because it was the truth.

I folded my arms, bowed my head, and fought against the tears burning in my eyes for the second time that day.

Please, Lord, I thought. Please don't let it be too late. Please can I have a second chance with him?

Well, as my father always said, it was all well and good to pray like it all depended on God, but then the next step was to get on your feet and work like it all depended on you. I went downstairs to the computer and logged in to my gmail account.

My inbox loaded and I glanced at the lefthand column, at the contacts who were logged in. Len's name was at the top. I blinked and looked again. It was his name, all right, and next to it was a little green circle that let me know that he wasn't just logged in, he was active. He was sitting at his computer working. I breathed a prayer of gratitude and double clicked his name. A chat window came up, but I clicked the little phone icon.

"Hello?" It was his voice!

"Hi."

"Yeah... hi." I could hear the sound of him typing, each keystroke a hard clack, and given the speed he typed, they rattled on like a machine gun.

I glanced at the clock. It was three a.m. where he was. "You're up late."

"I'm at work. Stupid interaction issues with our anti-malware software and something else, which I still can't find."

"I'm sorry."

"Eh."

"Listen, do you have a minute?"

"Why? You need something."

"I need to apologize."

"Well, whatever."

"No, I'm serious."

"Okay, hang on a minute."

The typing stopped and I heard the sound of a door closing in the background.

Then he was back and the typing resumed. "You sure you're okay?"

"I'm in England-"

"Yeah, I know. My cousin told me. How's the new guy you're dating?"

"I'm not dating any new guy. I'm not interested in any new guy. I was... hoping that maybe you and I could... maybe try again?"

The clacking noise of keys tapping stopped again. "Did you talk to Hattie?"

"Huh?"

"Or Jenna?"

"What?"

"Or go on Facebook or something?"

"I don't know what you're talking about."

"Listen, you've got to be kidding me. You can't be this shallow."

"I was shallow but-"

"I cannot believe you'd call me, now of all times."

"Why is now a problem?"

"Just, don't even."

"No, I really don't know. What are you talking about?"

"I'm hanging up now."

"Do you have a new girlfriend or something?"

"Yeah, sure. Let's go with that. Obviously I'd have to, huh?"

"Wait, what? Len!"

The channel cut out. Len had never, ever done that to me, even when I'd deserved it and had insulted him every other sentence while I moaned about my problems. "I love you," I said to the now silent computer.

Twenty-Six

Funeral

Louisa and the rest of the ward got a funeral planned and executed in a matter of days. I wish I could say it was touching and moving, but I hate funerals. I've been to too many in my lifetime. I've gotten to the point that I don't participate. I was offered the chance to give a eulogy, but passed on it. I stood at the back and tried not to be too weird about it all. My aunt's bright, vivid life had been distilled down to this room full of people who barely knew her.

When my first aunt died, I'd been too young to really understand what had happened.

When my mother died, I'd sobbed through the service.

When my first sister died, I'd given a long eulogy about how she used to pick on me and how I wanted her around anyway, even if she never stopped picking on me. People had laughed.

When my second aunt died, I felt like a veteran. I knew funerals forwards and backwards. I recognized the flower arrangements that decorated the hall.

When my second sister died, I didn't have the heart to do this anymore. I'd given a short speech and spent the rest of the time feeling numb and shell-shocked.

Now I was hyper-aware of people's glances. They were looking to me to see how they should feel about Nora's passing. I was the one who'd been closest to her. I felt like the room was running out of oxygen again. We were in the LDS chapel, even if Nora would not have a full LDS burial. She didn't wear the funeral clothes, but she did lie in state at the chapel and we would probably be eating potatoes au gratin in the cultural hall afterward. Those were so much the tradition that Saints often called them "funeral potatoes".

I was dwelling on the food, that's how messed up I was over all this. I wished that once, just once, I could get a big miracle that would make this easy. I reminded myself that I'd get small ones, plenty of them, I just had to be ready to receive them.

The chapel doors swung open and in stepped Colin in a suit. His arrival was like a ray of sunshine. He panned his gaze until he found me and came over. "Hey."

"Hey. Thanks for coming."

"Of course. Hope it's not an imposition. I heard what happened and called the house and someone invited me here."

"Definitely not an imposition."

"So how are you?"

"Really sick and tired of burying people."

"You must be."

"I'm now the oldest woman in my family, not counting in-laws."

"You're joking."

I shook my head.

He held out his arms and hugged me, and that felt amazing. Louisa gave hugs, but even though I liked her more now, she was bony and had a way of digging her fingers into my shoulders that wasn't comfortable. My father had offered to fly over, but he barely knew Nora and I knew that was quite an expense for him. I'd planned on getting through this without a good hug.

He even kept his arm around me, which summoned Louisa over like a moth to a candle.

"This is Colin," I told her. "A friend of mine and one of the nurses who looked after Nora."

"Oh right."

Colin shook her hand and gave me a knowing look as she bustled back into the crowd.

"Totally not a fair request, but can I just lean on you through this?" I asked.

"Of course. It's good to feel useful for that much, at least." He gave my shoulders a squeeze and I shut my eyes as the organ began to play. I let myself zone out.

Afterward there was a potluck, complete with funeral potatoes. Colin and I took our paper plates to the far end of the hall. "So you're all right?" he asked.

"Yeah."

"You going back to the States now?"

"Eventually. There's still stuff with her Will to deal with. How've you been?"

"Eh, all right, I guess."

"Just all right?"

"Haven't lost any relatives."

"How terribly normal of you."

He laughed. "Got the cold shoulder from a bird the other night. I think I offended her."

"Oh? Was this on a date?"

"No. Was just at the pub."

"Were you making a pass at her?"

"Not at all. Just answered her question and she got rather huffy about it."

"Well, was she with another guy or something?"

"Not that I saw."

"When you went up to her-"

"Ahem, she came up to me, if you must know. Came over and was typing on her phone, then looked at me and said, 'What?', and I told her I hadn't said anything and she said, "Oh, I thought you said my name, which is Angie', and-"

"Oh..." I stifled a giggle. "She was making a pass at you, and you didn't respond."

"I don't think she was making a pass."

"You can't possibly think that isn't a pass."

"Oh what? You weren't even there," he said.

"I'm female, and an artist. Can't you sense my deep intuition?"

"Really? You think she was making a pass?"

"Yes."

"I can't see it."

"I guess that's better than assuming that every woman who talks to you is making a pass at you. But she was."

"Surely you can think of a better way to make a pass at a fella?"

"Probably not, but I wouldn't know."

"You've never done it?"

"I'm really bad at that kind of thing."

"Probably haven't needed to do it."

I picked at my potatoes as I thought back to all my dateless months recently. I had just waited for guys to hit on me, which was just a little self centered.

"Sorry," said Colin, "did I hit a nerve?"

"I tried to get back together with my ex and he shut me down."

"Ouch."

"Thing is, I deserved it."

"Naw, don't say that about yourself."

"I wasn't very good to him."

"So apologize."

"I did... But, I was really not good to him."

"Hard for me to believe. How bad could you have been?"

I fumbled in my purse for The List that Hattie had written out for me. It was down at the bottom, scrunched but legible. I smoothed it against my thigh and handed it across the table. "Would you want to date someone who thought like this?"

"Rule One, he has to ask you out three times. What's wrong with that?"

"That means he keeps asking after being rejected twice."

"Ah, right. Give good gifts. How much is fifty dollars in pounds? That's what? Thirty pounds on flowers?"

"Something like that."

"That a gift he has to offer before the first date?"

"Ideally."

"Bit steep for a girl you barely know."

"Yep."

"A date is like a job interview. No pressure, fellas!"

"Yeah."

He handed me the slip of paper. "Doesn't really seem like you."

"Good. Maybe I've changed, then."

"So tell me about this bloke of yours."

"He's just a really great person. Nice to everyone, funny, makes the world seem like a funnier place. Always made me laugh. He treated me so well. Whenever I needed him for anything, he was there and totally devoted, you know, provided I was nice to him. I wasn't always, and he'd let me know that hurt him."

"Good kisser?"

"You've got no idea."

"Guess you didn't do much more than kiss, though."

"Mind your own business."

"Do you ever think about–"

"Hey, getting personal here."

"Right. Sorry. Was he nice about the break up, at least?"

"Total gentleman. Took me out for steak. Thanked me for the relationship and apologized for letting me go, but he knew I didn't love him. Even let me cry. Booked a private table in the restaurant so no one else saw-"

"Well, at least you cried."

"I cried because it hurt my ego to get dumped by a nerd. I ordered prime rib after that."

Colin frowned at me as if I had a giant boil dripping puss right in the center of my forehead.

"Yeah, I know," I said. "Like I told you, I was a bad person."

"How long did he date you?"

"Six months."

"And he broke it off?"

"Yeah. I only kept dating him because I wanted to date someone. What he did was fair. More than fair."

"Did he tell you he loved you?"

I shrank from that question. "Yeah," I said in a small voice.

Colin rolled his eyes.

I didn't bother to say, "I know," again. Instead I just stared down at my plate. "I just want to make things right."

"What do you mean, make things right?"

"I told him I loved him and groveled for another chance. I'd never treat him the way I did before. I've seen the light."

"Let me guess. He said no?"

I nodded. "I thought maybe-"

"You thought wrong. What are you, insane?"

"I cried."

"So?"

"Thanks." I slouched my shoulders, like a kid who didn't want to be called on in class. I wished I could just disappear.

"It's not like you don't know how to get him back."

"Huh?"

"Oh please."

"What?"

He looked at me as if skeptical. "Really? You don't see it?"

"Don't see what?"

"Blimey, I'm neither a woman nor an artist, but I can see it. It's obvious."

"What's obvious?"

He pointed at the list. "You want him back, you better pass your own stupid test."

I looked down at it. "Really? Would that work?"

Colin burst out laughing.

"What?"

"Sorry, it's just... are you serious? You would do this?"

"Yes," I said. "Definitely. Only... I don't think flowers are his kind of thing."

"You'd have to modify," he said. "You also can't keep asking him out. Not sure if it's the same in the States, but over here that'd be acting desperate, which isn't attractive."

"So what do I do instead?"

"Oh, I don't know. I'd have to think about it."

"Will you? Please?"

"Seriously?"

"Yes."

He humphed and ate more potatoes. "Right, well, you can't ask him out three times, but you can make it clear that you'd like to go out with him and just leave it at that. Be friendly in a non-creepy sort of way. I mean, you follow him around and he'll just run, but if you act casual and nice to him, he'd have to be a real jerk to shut you down. Especially if you do it in public."

I almost choked on my potatoes. "In public?"

"Of course. It's the best way to go. Why, you too chicken?"

"Yeah, but I guess I have to change that."

Colin looked at me appraisingly, as if looking at an x-ray as he decided whether or not he though the patient needed more treatment. "Right, well, sure. Why not? If you want help winning your fella back, count me in."

"Seriously?"

"Yeah, sure."

I grinned. *"Thank* you."

He just chuckled.

Twenty-Seven

Last Details and Goodbyes

The following day, when I checked my email, Len was on. My heart lifted. He hadn't blocked me, and I knew better than to think that might have been an oversight. This was Len. It wasn't like he didn't know how to block me. He'd given me a chance. Now I just had to not blow it.

I took a deep breath and pulled up a text window to send him a chat. I had to sound nice and not desperate.

Edunmar: Thanks for talking to me the other day.

I stared at that line. Too much? Too little? If I made a mistake, it was better that it be writing too little. That I could adjust as I went along. If I said too much, he'd block me. I hit the button to send the text.

And then I turned away. Only, the moment I did, plink as a response came in. I turned back around.

Hodgehog: I heard your aunt died. I'm really sorry about that.

I looked at the clock. It was ten in the morning, which meant it was two where he was. I debated whether or not to reply at all. I wanted to, but I had to be careful. No gushing.

Edunmar: Yeah, not a good day.

I deleted that. Wrong tone.

Edunmar: Thanks.

That was better. I sent that one.

Hodgehog: How long you staying in England?

Hope ignited in my chest. He wanted to know when I'd be home?

Edunmar: I'll be home next week.
Hodgehog: Well, have a good trip.

Now was the tricky part. I took a deep breath.

Edunmar: I would really like to see you again.

When he didn't reply for a moment, I forged ahead.

Edunmar: But it's up to you, of course. I'll see you at church, at least. I'm signing off. Have a good day.

There, I thought. Not too desperate, was it?

Hodgehog: Have a good night.

I turned away from the computer and found Louisa standing in the doorway of the office with a sheaf of papers on her hand.

"Right," she said, "I've got Nora's Will here."

I didn't bother to ask her how she found it. Louisa, I'd decided, was like a force of nature. Opposing her or trying to contain her would just wear me out.

"And I talked to my solicitor. It's quite clear that Nora intended you to be her sole heir."

"But can I change the distribution of the estate?"

"Theoretically-"

"If I just refuse to inherit, will my cousins automatically inherit everything?"

She lifted an eyebrow. "I don't know, but you will need a solicitor to sort all of this out."

"Fine, can yours do it?"

"Do you know how much is at stake here?"

"I don't care."

"Thirty million pounds."

"Mmm." I shrugged.

I heard the front door open and Johnny's kids come tumbling in. He herded them on through the kitchen and out into the backyard, where they hollered and shrieked and ran around. Keeley, Johnny, and Bea's voices all stayed in the kitchen. The sound of chairs scraping let me know they'd sat around the table.

"You want tea?" Keeley called out to us.

"Herbal tea," said Johnny.

"Thanks. Sure." I got up. "It's better if they don't even know."

"Not possible. The Will's a public document."

"Well, fine. Whatever. Tell me what I have to sign and let's be done with it." I moved past her and went to join my cousins in the kitchen.

"So I wanted to ask you," said Keeley, when I walked in, "about this gene I should be tested for."

"Yes, would it affect my girls?" Johnny asked.

"Everyone should get tested," I told them. I launched into my lecture about what the BRCA mutation was and how bad the family cancer legacy was. I told them about how many relatives I'd lost and how unusual Nora had been, living as long as she did.

My cousins listened, asked questions, and in the end thanked me for explaining it to them. Louisa sneaked into the room and took her seat at the end of the table.

"So," said Keeley, "you're an artist?"

I nodded.

"Nora's got a lot of paintings. Did you help her choose them?" asked Johnny.

I gestured at the walls. "If you mean these, I painted all of them."

The three of them looked around in surprise. "All of these?" said Louisa. "They're lovely!"

"Thanks."

"That," said Johnny, "would explain why Mum has so much religious art on her walls. I did wonder."

"I had no idea," said Keeley. "I've just seen you drawing those animal pictures for the kids."

"Yeah..." I shrugged. "I've just been letting myself go lately and drawn whatever's really inside. Turns out it's a bunch of talking animals and cartoon stuff. So much for artistic greatness."

The four of them laughed.

"These paintings here are all yours now, unless you want me to take any of them. I don't mind if they're not your thing."

"We might need you to provide extra copies of the ones we both want," said Johnny, and his sister nodded in agreement.

"Okay, speaking of paintings, I've got some that I don't know what to do with. Hang on." I went upstairs and got the three paintings of Paul. I kept them against my chest as I went downstairs so that the others couldn't see what they were of. "Sooo, to make your mother get treatment, I bribed her and... I didn't know. She wanted so badly to remember her marriage as the perfect love story, I helped her create those memories. I didn't realize she was working to believe something that wasn't quite that way." I laid the three paintings on the table.

Johnny put his head to one side.

Keeley frowned.

Louisa leaned in and looked them over. "I'd quite like one of these," she said.

"Yes, me too," said Keeley.

"Really?" I said.

"It's how I'd prefer to remember my father," said Johnny. "You've made him look so handsome."

"But still like himself," said Keeley. "When I look at these, I think of how he did love us, and that's what I want to remember about him."

"Well," I said, "they're yours. I hope you'll let me come visit sometimes and paint pictures of the kids and all that-"

"Oh *would* you?" Bea's voice startled me a little. She sat so quietly, I'd forgotten she was there.

"Would you really?" said Johnny.

"Yeah, of course. It's what I do."

"That would be lovely," said Keeley. "I'm so bad about getting photos, but imagine how posh I'd look with paintings of the family on my walls."

"I know, sounds like the kind of thing nobility does," agreed her brother.

"Me too," said Louisa. "Can you make prints?"

"Of course."

"That is extremely generous," said Johnny.

"I'm no good at knitting them sweaters or hats or anything like that. I'm a bad Mormon auntie."

Louisa cracked up at that. "I did look up how to make casseroles after the first munch and mingle at church."

"Oh don't start," said Keeley. "I can't even cook."

A month ago, I never would have thought I'd be here, talking and laughing with my cousins. I didn't realize how much family I had on this side of the pond, or how much I'd miss them.

"So are you moving back to the States?" said Johnny. "Or are you going to live here?"

"Um, what?"

"Our last fight with Mum was when she made you her heir." Keeley said it matter of factly, like she didn't even mind anymore.

I looked at Louisa who only shrugged.

"I won't be inheriting," I said. "Louisa's going to help me get a lawyer to fix all that."

"Fix it how?" said Johnny.

"To have you guys inherit instead of me. You're her children."

"Oh, you can't just cut yourself out entirely," said Johnny.

"You're the one who looked after her all these years," said Keeley. "She adored you."

They exchanged a look, though, that made it clear they weren't against the idea of getting some of the money for themselves.

"I don't want any money – hey!" I turned to Louisa. "That's why you were asking me nosy questions about how much I make? You thought I'd talked Nora into making me her heir?"

"I didn't know you, dear. Just knew you were a gospel painter who spent rather a lot of time around her."

"How much do you make?" asked Keeley.

"It depends on the year, but seriously, it doesn't matter."

"It can't be that much," said Louisa.

"Look, I house sit for my stepmother. I don't pay rent or anything like that. I'm fine."

But my cousins exchanged a knowing look. They knew what it was like to be poor.

"You're not cutting yourself out entirely," said Johnny.

Paint Me True

"We'll go in thirds," agreed his sister.

"It's my decision," I said.

"We'll sic Auntie Lou on you if you don't agree," said Johnny.

Louisa smiled, accepting the challenge.

I looked up at the ceiling. "Do what you want." Even though I was the only person with legal rights in this situation, they'd gotten the upper hand.

In the end they did split everything three ways. Louisa got a lawyer who did all the paperwork and told me where to sign. Johnny got the house in Oxford. Keeley got the one in the south of France that I didn't even know about. Bea had a somewhat dazed expression on her face as all of this unfolded. I learned that she'd never met Nora before, nor known about Johnny's past. She'd expected to live on government benefits for the rest of her life, and now she and Johnny were looking into what private schools to send their children to.

The rest of my stay was like a whirlwind. Johnny made it clear that my room and my studio in the Oxford house would remain as they were, and I was most welcome there. It seemed like an odd prospect, now that Nora was gone, but if he wanted to put forth the effort to become close, the least I could do was reciprocate. I promised to visit again just before Christmas.

It felt odd to pack my things and close this chapter of my life. I boarded the plane for Portland with a couple of things I'd never had before: Friendships with my English cousins and financial security.

Twenty-Eight

Rule One

I arrived back in Portland in the evening and caught a cab home. Carrie's house was just as I'd left it. Hattie was an impeccable house-sitter. Everything was dusted and vacuumed and there was a fresh carton of milk in the fridge.

It also felt bigger and emptier than it had before, which surprised me. I'd thought it might feel small after Nora's mansion, but the last days I'd spent there, it had been so full of people and laughter and life. Now my little house echoed with silence. I'd already decided to ask Carrie if I could buy it from her. I knew how badly she wanted to sell it.

On the voicemail were two messages. One was from Chris asking if I was back in town and wanted him and his companion to come visit. The other was from Rachel, the Relief Society president. She wanted to know if I could teach a lesson two weeks ago, and I cringed when I heard it. I hoped she'd found someone else without too much trouble.

It was nine o'clock on Saturday night. I'd see Len at church in twelve hours. I wasn't ready. I had an image of myself bursting into tears the moment he walked into the chapel.

So, I took a deep breath and called his cellphone. Colin had coached me and I willed myself to do this right.

"Hello?" he picked up after the first ring. This was a good sign. He could see my number on his display, so it wasn't like he didn't know who it was.

"Hi," I said.

"Hey, Eliza."

"How've you been?"

"All right. I'd ask you the same, but I know you've had better months."

"It all ended pretty well, actually."

"That's good."

"So, listen, I don't want to harass you, but I do want to see you again." I bit my lip. Did saying I didn't want to harass him count as not harassing him?

"Yeah..."

"I've missed you."

"I know you've been through a lot-"

"No, listen. Yes, this month has helped me realize a few things, and no, it hasn't made me desperate to grab onto the nearest guy and never let go. It's hard to call you like this, because I know I didn't treat you very well. It's embarrassing."

"You don't owe me another date to make up for that."

"No, I think I owe it to you to leave you alone and let you move on, but I don't want that." I wanted to tell him again that I loved him, but I could just picture Colin making a cutting gesture across his throat.

"Listen... I don't know."

"Yeah, fine. I won't pester you about it. I'll just see you tomorrow, okay?"

"Yeah."

"Have a good night."

"You too."

Again I wanted to say I loved him. This was the point in the conversation when he used to say he loved me. "Bye," I said, and hung up after his response. "I love you," I whispered into the phone, once the connection was cut. Had it hurt him this much to say it to me all those times, knowing I wouldn't reply?

At church the next morning, Hattie met me in the foyer with her left hand extended. On it was a diamond ring.

"Wow," I said.

"I know!" she squeaked.

"Since when?"

"Friday." She beamed at me. "I wanted to tell you but not over the phone. You aren't mad, are you?"

Mad? I thought. Then I took a moment to consider that. A month ago I wouldn't have been *mad*, but I'd have been slighted. I'd have felt bitter that she had a fiancee and I was about to turn thirty-one without one, but my nice conversation exercises that Colin had insisted on were paying off already. I gave Hattie a hug.

She squealed right in my ear and hugged me back.

"How did he ask?" I wanted to know.

"Oh, so you saw." That was Jenna. She stood behind me, her arms folded across her chest.

"How've you been?" I asked her.

She blinked at me.

Had I really been this awful and catty? A friendly greeting was an oddity from me?

"Fine," she said.

"How's work been?"

"Been good. Had my hard look review."

"Okay, first I want to hear about the proposal-" I pointed at Hattie "-and then I want to hear about that."

"He took me to the beach," said Hattie, "and set up a table where we ate by candlelight and he got down on bended knee right before dessert."

"Nice," I said. The three of us moved into the chapel and found seats at the back.

"It was *sooo* romantic."

"She's been on and on about it," said Jenna.

"How'd your review go?" I turned my attention to her.

"They said I was the best associate they'd had in years."

"Wow! That is so great!"

"So, wait a minute," said Hattie. "Like, three weeks ago, when I talked to you, you said you were gonna date some guy? Colin?"

"Oh, yeah." I waved that away. "Didn't happen, but we're friends. He's been a great friend."

"I'm sorry," said Jenna, who never showed compassion to anyone.

"It was for the best. Look, I know you'll think I'm crazy for saying this, but I'm not over Len. I don't want to be over Len. I miss him."

"Lemme guess," said Hattie, "you decided this last week?"

"Yeah."

Jenna snickered.

"What?" I said. "What happened last week?"

"You don't know?" Jenna looked me straight in the eye as if willing me to tell the truth.

I had no secrets to hide from her. Not about this. "I have no idea what you're talking about. Really."

Motion out of the corner of my eye made me turn.

It was Len, standing in the aisle, or a guy who looked vaguely like Len, at least. He had a smartphone in his hand and a new trendy satchel slung over his shoulder. His burgundy shirt was brand new, as were his gray slacks. His hair was styled even, nothing complicated, just a little gel.

He was gorgeous now. Better looking than I'd envisioned him with all my artistic tricks. This guy wasn't the ward loser anymore. He probably had all the younger, sweeter, prettier girls scratching each other's faces over him. I wanted to die, just crawl under the nearest pew and curl up. Never had I felt older or plainer, but I made myself act sane. "Hi."

He waved as if his hand were disconnected from his brain and he didn't know he was doing it. Then he turned and walked up the aisle as if it were some winding path in the forest that he'd never been down before and he had to feel his way along.

"Yeah, he's different now," said Hattie.

"He's kinda hot," agreed Jenna.

"Since when did he... uh... So that's what happened last week?"

"He's still the same dork," said his cousin. "Reads scriptures off his iPhone."

"Has a computer voice read them when he teaches Sunday school," supplied Jenna.

"I take it he's dating someone," I said.

But Hattie shook her head.

"His sister took him shopping," said Jenna. "Or, that's the gossip at least. Someone said his work had a new dress code."

"He has been on dates with people," said Hattie, "but he's not officially dating anyone."

I stole a glance at the front row. Len was busy reading off his phone, but two girls had settled in next to him and were trying to get his attention. He smiled and glanced in their direction, but they didn't get anything more than that. Still, that was too much for me.

"I haven't got a chance with him now, do I?"

"You really didn't know? About his new look?" said Jenna.

I shook my head.

"I thought that was why you called him last week," said Hattie.

"He tell you about that?"

"Mmm. You still have a chance with him. He's still the same dork, remember?"

"If you want a chance with him," said Jenna.

I never knew how hard guys had it. I kept my shoulders square and my head up as I walked past him on my way to Relief Society. "Hi," I said, as if he were just an old friend.

He looked at me, slightly startled. "Hi." Again with the awkward wave, and then he turned down a side hallway and disappeared.

I tried to pay attention in Relief Society, but my mind kept replaying that encounter, as if I might glean some hidden meaning from it. Before I knew it, everyone was singing the closing hymn. I mumbled my way along with them, then bowed my head for a closing prayer I didn't hear, and then it was time to toughen up once more.

Hattie walked with me and gave me the occasional worried glance. I marched down the hall, off of which was the clerk's office. The door was open, and Len was inside, lounging back in the chair, tapping away at the keyboard. "Hi," I said again.

He looked with his eyes and didn't turn his head. "Hi." His fingers stopped typing.

Hattie raised an eyebrow at me and sped up, leaving me to pause in the doorway by myself. "I'd ask how you've been, but I already asked that half a day ago."

"I've been fine. You?"

I shrugged.

"Hattie and Jenna approve of you talking to me now?"

"I don't know. Didn't ask."

He swiveled to face me then, a look of genuine confusion on his face. "So, when you called up last week, you hadn't talked to them about me?"

"I don't talk to them about you. They're my friends, but they can be a little judgmental, you know?" As if I were one to talk.

But Len didn't press that point. "You thought you were still talking to the scruffy guy?"

"Mmmm-hmmm. Look, don't get me wrong, you look nice, but not *that* nice. I hear you're still the same person."

He laughed, his blue eyes sparkling.

My heart just about melted, but I hid that as best I could. "And that's what I care about. You don't think I wanted another chance just because someone took you shopping, do you?"

"Weeeell..."

"Okay, fair enough. I was that shallow. I'm sorry." Ouch did it hurt to say that, plain and clear, in public. There were still people walking down the hall, behind me.

He shrugged and waved a hand dismissively.

"Can I have another chance?" I said. I could just imagine Colin swatting me if he were there. "You promised not to pester him," he'd say.

Len's easy, relaxed posture faded. He sat up straighter, rested his elbows on his knees, and looked down at his clasped hands. "As flattering as that is, let's not go there, okay?"

Emotion built in me like a tidal wave that I had to hold back with a thin veneer of confidence. I wanted to tell him that I loved him, that I was sorry, that things would really work this time. None of that, though, would convince him I was anything other than desperate. I had to do this the right way, the hard way. "Just, let me know if you change your mind. You can call me anytime, okay?" Was that too desperate, I wondered.

He looked at me as if he wasn't sure he'd heard me right. "Um, okay."

"See you later." I took two careful steps away from the door, then dashed for the exit and my car.

Hattie stepped up beside me as I tried to unlock my door by punching the right button on my keychain. "Hey," she said.

"Hi. I know, I'm being stupid." I gave up on the keychain and collapsed against the side of the car.

"This hasn't got anything to do with me getting engaged, does it?"

I shook my head. "I called Len before I even knew about that."

"Okay, well, so... I don't know if it'll help, but I'll slip that into family gossip. My mom and his mom talk all the time."

I looked up at her.

"Yeah," she said, "my mom and I are talking again."

"Wow, really?"

"Ye-ah... I apologized for putting her down and she apologized for cutting me off and... it's not all perfect, but at least we talk. Look, can I ask you a huge favor?"

"Of course."

"Do you have your endowment?" She wanted to know if I'd been through the temple. I knew that she hadn't, but now that she was getting married, she would need to in preparation for her wedding.

"Yeah, I do." I'd never let on that I had it, because I felt like it made me seem older. Petty of me.

"So... my mom wants to be my escort." Everyone who went through the temple had an escort to help them through the ordinances, answer questions, and provide support.

"Your mom still got her temple recommend?" I asked. I didn't know the details of how her mother had left the church, but I knew it had been years ago. If she'd had a temple recommend, it would have expired.

"No," said Hattie, "but she's working on it."

"Wow."

"I know. I just wonder... if she can't get it before I need to go to the temple, would you be my escort?"

"Are you kidding?" That was a high honor. Escorts were nearly always family members.

"Please?"

"Of course. I mean, I hope your mom can do it, that is so great that she's trying, but yes, I'll be there for you no matter what you need."

She hugged me, tight.

Twenty-Nine

Rule Two

"So how did I do?" I asked Colin in my debriefing that afternoon over Skype, right before he went to work. "Did I make a fool of myself?"

"Doesn't sound like it."

"Think it'll work?"

"If he's still interested, yeah, it'll work. And given the way he's responded to you, he's either still interested or very polite."

"He is very polite. But he's had a makeover. All of these girls are after him now."

"Was anyone else trying to flirt with him after church?"

"No."

"I think you're just paranoid, then."

"I hope so. But, listen, the second thing on the list is the perfect present. Examples are shoes and flowers-"

"Flowers," Colin repeated with derision.

"Obviously he's not going to want flowers. I was thinking maybe a new case for his smartphone? A new tie to go with his new shirts-"

"Those are typical woman gifts."

"Is that bad?"

"Yes. You know what women like about flowers?"

"Um... it sounds like you have a theory about that. I would say just that they're pretty."

"They're a complete waste of money. They're expensive, and they last a few weeks at most. A guy who buys you flowers is saying, 'I'm buying you something I would never buy otherwise, just because you want it.'"

"O-kay."

"You buying him a phone case or a tie, that's something for you. You want him to wear it so that he'll look more like you want him to."

"No, I'd like him to change back into his old clothes so that no one notices him. It's not about me."

"He'll think it is."

"So I should buy him flowers?"

"You should find out what is like flowers to him, you know? What's something that you know he likes that you'd never spend money on, if you didn't really fancy him?"

"Liiiike..."

"Like tickets to a sports match or a gift certificate to his favorite pizza place or-"

"Oh," I said.

"You've got something?"

"Yeah. Okay. This'll be interesting."

The kid working behind the counter at the game store looked me up and down the moment I stepped in the door. He had a round face, glasses and hair that stuck straight up in tufts. If he weren't in the company polo shirt, I imagined he'd wear a t-shirt with 20-sided dice on it that had rolled in a way that geeks would find hilarious. "You play *World of Warcraft?*" he asked.

"Um, I don't really know what that is," I confessed.

"Oh, right. You need directions somewhere?"

"No."

"We only sell computer games here. No board games or anything like that."

"No console games?" I looked around in confusion. There was shelf after shelf with little, brightly decorated boxes, set out like videos at a rental place. I had searched the internet for the right kind of store and was sure I'd weeded out all the wrong ones, because like he said, there were a lot of different kinds of game store.

"Oh, yeah, we sell those. What are you looking for?" He gave me his full attention now.

"I want to get a gift for someone."

"Oh, right." He nodded as if the world now made perfect sense to him once again. "For your brother, or...?"

"For a guy," I said. I moved away from the door and went over to the counter. "So, it's like this, I really blew it with a guy who's into console games, and I want to tell him I'm sorry and that things'll be different if he gives me another chance."

The kid looked me up and down again as if he doubted this story. "What are his favorite games?"

"I don't know. I never paid attention. I know, it's awful."

The kid blinked, slowly and deliberately, like a lizard. "Does he not play much?"

"No, he plays all the time. It's his favorite thing to do, and I never even bothered to look at what he was playing."

"And you think that's bad?"

"Isn't it? I mean, how annoyed am I when a guy doesn't know or care about what I do?"

"Are you for real?"

"Excuse me? Look, I just... what's a game that's not as well known? That he might not have, but is still really good."

"How good?"

"Like, will make him think I deserve another chance kind of good. After I treated him like garbage for six months straight."

The kid looked at me like I'd just grown a second head. Again his gaze traveled down to the floor and then back up to my face. Boy was I getting tired of that. "Um, okay. What kind of console does he own?"

I looked past him at the consoles in their packaging behind the counter. "That one and that one. Are there any good games for those that aren't well known? Or, maybe I need to spy on him? Get his roommate to help me?"

"Listen," said the kid, "I can hook you up, but you have got to *swear* to me that you won't tell anyone."

"I don't want to steal a game."

"No stealing. Just faking some records."

"What?"

"Wait right here." He looked past me, out through the front windows, as if checking for surveillance, then darted through a door behind the counter. When he reemerged, he had a box clasped to his chest and a smug grin on his face. "Okay, this isn't officially released until next week, and I *swear* I am in such deep trouble if you tell anyone I sold it to you."

"I don't want to put your job at risk."

"Oh, I can cover my tracks. I'm the manager and I know what I'm doing. I'm doing this for the karma. I help you get your nerd, maybe the universe will send me a hot chick who is cool with my gaming."

My cheeks flushed hot. "Thank you," I said.

"Just, you understand that if anyone knows that you have this, the game company can sue me for everything I've got. Your guy trustworthy?"

"I'll make sure you don't get in trouble."

"Okay." He stuffed it in a bag and tapped some keys on the register. "The receipt is gonna show a different title."

"Right." I tugged the bills out of my wallet and passed them across the counter.

He counted out change and handed it to me along with the bag, which he placed reverently in my hand. "Good luck," he said.

"Thank you *so* much."

"Welcome."

I walked out of the store with an item I would never, ever spend money on if it weren't for the fact that Len loved games. My version of flowers.

Out in my car I laid out the wrapping paper I'd brought, wrapped the game, and tied it with a bow. Then I slipped it into a gift bag. Just a plain white one, nothing over the top. Now it was time to write the card. I spread this open in my lap and mulled over what to say.

"Just my way of saying how sorry I am," I scrawled. For a moment I debated whether to write "Love, Eliza". No, I decided, too forward. I just wrote my name, sealed the card, and stuck it in the bag.

I then drove over to Len's house and found Chris home, watching television.

"Hey," I said, when he answered the door. "Give this to Len when he gets home?"

"What is it?"

"None of your business. Just give it to him."

"Yeah, fine." He grasped it in his hand.

I held onto it and looked him straight in the eye. "You'll make sure he gets it?"

"Yeah, what? You think I'd try to steal it? What is it, even?"

"Men's cologne," I lied. "And I will notice if you wear it."

He wrinkled his nose. "I'll go put it on his bed."

"It was expensive, okay?"

"I'm not gonna touch it." He tucked it under his arm, looked at me like I was crazy, and disappeared into the house.

I left, confident that he wouldn't open it. I called Len as I got back into my car.

"Hello?"

"Hey, listen," I said. "I left something for you at your house. Talk to me when you get it?"

"What is it?"

"Nothing much."

"Wait, why did you-"

"I'll talk to you later, okay?" I hung up. Chicken of me, but it was the only thing I could think of.

Thirty

Rule Three

At six thirty that evening, right as I was putting the finishing touches on a painting of a kitten pawing at wispy clouds in a powder blue sky, my phone rang and Len's number popped up.

I answered, feeling as nervous as if I'd stepped onto a stage naked in front of an amphitheater full of people. "Hel-"

"*Where* the heck did you get this?"

"I can't tell you, and you can't tell anyone you have it. I guess the guy who sold it to me will be in big trouble if the news gets out."

"What, you got it from some pirates or something?"

"No, no, it's legit. It's real. I just got one of the copies earlier than is allowed."

"Holy cow!" came Chris's voice from the background. "That isn't cologne!"

"Huh?" said Len.

"Just, great. Can you get him to swear to secrecy too?"

"Liza, I am not keeping this."

"What, are you nuts?" said Chris.

"I can't give it back," I said. "The guy at the store already did whatever he had to do to make it look like they never had that copy."

"Could we, like, even play this or will Interpol come bust down our door?" said Chris. "If we don't register it and don't play in networked mode, will they even know? Man, come *on*. Let me see it!"

I heard a scuffle, then Chris bite back a curse as a door slammed.

"I can't believe you did this," said Len.

"I didn't mean any harm. I just wanted to get you something you'd want, and I didn't know what games you already had because I never paid attention, and I'm sorry."

"I can't accept this."

That, I realized, was another advantage of flowers. There was little point giving them back. My plan was coming apart at the seams. "I'm sorry," I said. "I didn't mean to cross any lines. I just wanted to do something nice for you."

"This is beyond nice."

"By which you mean to say, it was totally inappropriate."

"No, no... I mean... I just... uh..."

"I just meant to say I was sorry and get you something you would like. I'm sorry. I screwed up."

"No. Listen..."

I waited.

"Um, I feel like if I accept this, I should go out with you again and I just can't-"

"No," I said. "You don't. Never. I wouldn't do that."

"Well, I feel like a jerk just accepting this."

That, I recognized, was an opportunity, but one I'd have to make careful use of. I didn't want to shame him into anything he didn't want to do. "Can we just talk sometime? Meet up for hot chocolate or something?"

"I..."

"Okay, forget about it. It's fine. Really."

"Yeah, let's talk."

"When's good for you?"

"I'm so swamped with work at the moment. I just got a text from work saying I need to go back in. We got a whole new shipment of PCs that we need to integrate into the network and it should be easy, but it's not. Sorry, I'm rambling here."

"It's fine."

"I don't know, is the answer."

"Well, okay, if you're working late, I'll bring you dinner sometime."

"No, don't-"

"I think it's better that we have something to do other than just talk, you know? Less pressure, natural ending time. Seriously, let's do that."

"Well... okay. Yeah, okay." His voice got more certain. "Fair enough. That sounds good."

"What day do you think is best for you?"

"Anytime in the next week."

"Okay, well, let me get these projects done and I'll give you a call." I bit my lip. Here I was, playing my old games. I didn't have any projects due. I was painting kittens and turtles and mice having tea. I needed to get some more gospel pieces done, but not urgently.

Len, however, sounded relieved. "Sure, you do that. I'll talk to you later."

"Bye," I said.

"Bye."

I noticed that he waited for me to hang up.

"Hard to say how that went," said Colin in the next Skype session. He looked exhausted from his last shift. He wore a jacket over his scrubs still.

"Yeah," I agreed. "I didn't really do it right, did I?"

"I dunno. What do you think usually happens when a guy gives flowers? Sometimes the bird's happy, sometimes she doesn't even call, and sometimes it's just awkward. I think you did okay."

"I've decided, this dinner is going to fill the perfect date on the list. I mean, I should assume that this'll be it. Right?"

"Right."

Tears welled up in my eyes and I turned away from the webcam. "Yeah, sorry," I said. "That's what makes this awful. This is it, you know? Probably the last time I talk to him."

"Hey, it's all right. You can walk away from this situation and say that you did your best. What you need to do is make sure that you finish this without regrets."

"Which means I need to make sure not to cry or beg or do anything else embarrassing that night."

"Might want to avoid messy sauces or anything with the food."

"No, actually, I want something to focus on. If I have to worry about not messing up my clothes, I can not obsess about the conversation."

"Well, if that works for you."

I flopped back in my chair. "Thank you," I said.

"For?"

"Helping me through this. Being a friend. How are you, by the way?"

"Eh, I'm all right."

"You been on any dates lately?"

"Um, you know, after our last conversation I... well I went and bought a rose and gave it to that girl I offended."

"Oh really?"

"And we had a nice talk. We're going to the cinema next week."

"Right on. Way to go."

"Question, what should I wear? I know that sounds like a girly question..."

"When we went out for fish and chips, you looked good."

"Really? The unbuttoned shirt wasn't too much?"

"Um, no. I didn't think so. You looked very casual and relaxed and easy to talk to."

"And unbelievably hot?"

"That too."

"That's what really matters, you know?"

"Yeah, yeah, but I'm your friend. I'm not supposed to call you unbelievably hot."

"Oh, right." He smirked at me. "And you're in love with a nerd."

"Darn tootin'."

"What?" He burst out laughing. "Did you actually just say that?"

"It's not that funny."

"I didn't think anyone said stuff like that. Do it again."

"No."

"Please?"

"No."

He laughed so hard he almost fell out of his chair. I tried to be annoyed, but it was hard to keep a straight face.

"I don't swear. I need to get creative."

That made him laugh even harder. "Do you ever watch *The Simpsons*?"

"I diddily don't. Okay, I'm leaving now."

Colin collapsed on the desk in front of him and pounded his fist against the wood. The sound picked up as a loud, hollow thunk over the mic.

"Bye," I said, over the noise.

He didn't lift his head, but he did manage a wave before I cut him off. I had a menu to plan for later in the week.

As it turned out, I did find a project to occupy my time. It occurred to me to check out agents for illustrators, since I seemed to be doing a bunch of children's illustrations these days. I didn't think I had a chance. This was a seriously competitive field, but I didn't have anything to lose either. I got to work on a portfolio and was shocked to see how many silly little pictures of animals acting like people I'd done. I was never this prolific.

I was proud of the fact that the days flew by until I decided I really should take Len dinner on Thursday night. Friday he might not work late. I called him mid-afternoon, just as I put the pasta sauce on the stove to simmer, and I left it to simmer for the next several hours. As the time grew closer, I made pasta, which I tossed with the sauce and then left the two on the heat together for a minute to blend the flavors. I also did a batch of garlic bread in the oven, a green salad for a side, and decided to omit dessert. Dinner was long enough. I didn't want to look like I was dragging it out.

For the whole afternoon I was able to delude myself into rationality. We'd either have a good conversation and get back together, or not, and if not, I would walk away from the situation without guilt.

I packed everything in foil containers, with towels as hotpads, and loaded it into the front seat of the car. I arrived at Len's office highrise just as the sun was going down and called him again from the parking lot.

"Yeah." He sounded hesitant. "I'll come down and get you." His building had secured access after hours.

I hefted the food containers and carried them around to the front of the glass and steel building just as one of the elevators across the bare, gray lobby opened and Len stepped out. Since the lobby was lit inside, he couldn't see me on the other side of the glass until he strode across and opened a door. Once he did see me, he hesitated.

"Hey," I said, my voice casual. "How's work been?"

"It's been awful." He leaned back and let me in, then held out his hands to offer to carry things. I gave him the pasta and held onto the bread and salad. We got into the elevator, which was plain and gray and featureless, and rode it to the fourth floor. I didn't talk, and I didn't feel like I needed to talk. Len knew me. There was no point putting on some kind of show for him.

He did glance sidelong at me a couple of times. I could already tell that things were not going my way. He was uncomfortable.

I was determined not to let myself feel like I was out of line. I wasn't. He had to eat. I knew how to cook. I wanted to talk to him. That was all. "Are your coworkers going to want any?" I asked.

"No one else is here."

"You have to work late alone?"

"Well, the other guys have kids, so the new deal is, I keep track of all my extra time and get a comp day now and then."

"Oh, that's a nice system."

"Works for me."

The doors slid open and we stepped out. I followed him past all the dark desks with computers on standby to the little cubicle area in front of his office. He set the food down on a table and hauled it away from the wall so that we could sit opposite each other. I accepted the folding chair he passed over to me and once we were both seated, I offered to say a blessing. I kept it simple and to the point, then started to unpack the food. The garlic bread smelled heavenly when I unwrapped the foil. I handed him a paper plate and plastic fork, then took the cellophane off the bowl of salad and passed it to him.

He took it, dished out some salad, and then looked across at me, as if sizing me up yet again. "Thanks for the game," he said.

"I'm sorry about all that. I just meant to be nice."

"It was nice."

I shrugged that off and stabbed my fork through a piece of lettuce. "So, yeah," I said. "I've told you how I feel. I'd like another chance. If the answer is no, then it's no. I just wanted to make sure you understood that I'm serious."

His mouth twitched as if he'd just eaten something bitter. "Why?" he said.

"Because I realized that I really do love you. I've learned a few things the last few weeks."

"Such as?"

I had to be careful how I answered this. "Such as the fact that I can be incredibly shallow. I thought I was more mature than I was, but I had a really childish view of what makes the ideal date. When I thought about what I really want, I realized it was you. That's why I'd never really committed to anyone else. They weren't eternal companion material." I hesitated then. I'd just made it clear that I wanted to marry him, and I knew that might shut the conversation down right then and there. Though, we were Mormons. It wasn't *that* unusual of a thing to say to a potential date.

"Can I be blunt?"

"Please."

"Is your new ideal just a fiancee before you turn thirty-one?"

"That was my old ideal."

"Right."

"You know, provided he was stylish and had other girls after him and... yeah, I don't really want to think about that any more than I have to."

"So what happened over there in England?"

"Long story, but I'll try to make it short." I told him about Nora and Paul, me and Colin. I told him my realization that Nora's rosy view of Paul was her fighting regret. "And I was fighting regret over our breakup by telling myself that I didn't want to be with you, but whenever I tried to paint the ideal man, I used you as a template. I do love you. I know I never said it and I treated you badly. I don't deserve another chance, but I'd like one." I shut my mouth then.

"Because I'm a geek who can't throw a punch? I'd never hit you?"

"Um... you never really displayed any of the personality traits that go with the whole violent, possessive thing. But none of the guys I've ever dated did. This isn't about that. I'm not going to end up a battered woman if you turn me down, you know."

He looked down at his plate.

I took that as my cue to get out the pasta. I hadn't eaten my garlic bread so much as picked at it, so I only had the crust left, which I quickly bit into and ate.

Once we had our next course – our last course – in front of us, I looked over at him again. "So, anyway, that's what I wanted to say." A couple of tears threatened to fall, but I kept my spine straight and they didn't slip down my cheeks.

"Yeah... well... okay," said Len.

"You've moved on," I said.

"I guess so. It wasn't easy to get over you, okay? Me going out and getting new clothes... I just wanted to make you regret that you'd ever let me go."

"Clothes are totally beside the point," I said. "They don't change anything."

"As soon as I did it, you called, and I was so angry. I realized I'd thrown a lot of months away on you, when you thought you were doing me a favor. And then girls started to talk to me and... I guess it's not so much that I've moved on, but that I'm ready to move on. I feel like I can date now, without thinking about how things ended with you."

I nodded. "So I'm too late."

"When I dated you, that wasn't a great time for me. I mean, on one hand, I was with this woman I'd had a crush on for months, but on the other hand, I felt worthless. She clearly didn't want to be with me, she just wanted to be with someone."

"That's fair," I agreed.

"So, I shouldn't have let that situation go on as long as it did, and even after I broke up with you – don't take this the wrong way – but I was glad that you had to go to England. It gave me space to just deal and get over the hurt."

I nodded again. I felt like I could use another trip to England, to get over my hurt for real this time, but I didn't bother to say that out loud.

"You have been so nice to me since you got back."

"I care about you," I said. "So, yeah. Now you know everything I had to say. I don't expect you'll change your mind, but if you do in the near future, you know where to find me."

"Listen, lots of guys are interested in you. Since we broke up, do you have any idea how many guys have asked me about you-"

I held up a hand. "That's awful and I'm sorry that happened to you."

"Let me tell you who-"

"No. Don't. I don't care. I'm not ready to move on quite yet, and I turn thirty-one in a few weeks. I think I'll finish out my time in the singles ward single."

"Seriously, Vince Walker-"

"Len, I don't care." Vince Walker was very good looking, and had always seemed very nice to me. In a few weeks, if he was still interested, I'd consider it, but right now there was no way. I focused on my pasta instead, on getting it eaten.

Len did the same.

And then, several minutes later, that was it. Our meal was at an end. "You keep the leftovers," I told him. "And thanks for letting me come by."

"Liza, you just cooked me dinner."

"I had to cook dinner anyway."

"I should be thanking you."

"You're welcome."

"Thank you."

"It was good to see you again," I said.

"Yeah, you too."

"Can you walk me back down? Or can I get out on my own?"

"I'll take you."

Together we went back to the elevators, down to the lobby and across to the parking garage. I kept a careful distance so that I didn't give into some mad impulse to hug him. He didn't seem to know how to say goodbye, so I made it easy on him, waved, and walked over to my car without looking back.

I'd just been turned down, completely, no room for misunderstandings, but surprisingly, I didn't need to cry about it. In fact, I felt all right as I drove home, provided I didn't think about Len. I was proud of myself. I'd figured out how to be interested in a guy without playing games or freaking out. The only drawback was the fact that I was thirty and only just learning this. I'd wasted a lot of good years and hurt more than my fair share of men. It was only right that the one guy I loved turned me down. I thought about the kid at the game store and karma. I had a lot of negative karma to repay.

Thirty-One

What Came After

The following late afternoon I arrived at the post office and dumped a stack of heavy envelopes on the counter. "Hi," I said. "Do I have time to mail these today?"

The man behind the register didn't bat an eye. "Yep. Put 'em on the scale, one at a time."

I put the first on and tried not to fidget as he pecked away at the cash register. He grabbed the stamp that printed out, slapped it on the envelope and motioned for me to put the next one on the scale. "These all going to New York?" he asked.

"Most of them."

"They the same weight?"

"No. Some are, but not all of them."

He frowned in response but kept on working.

These were submissions to agents. Classmates of mine who had wanted to go into that line of work had been super-dedicated and built elaborate portfolios. They'd all had much higher grades than me too. I was being optimistic.

But what did it hurt to ask, was what I now thought. The agents would probably reject me, and then I'd know. It was worth it for the tiny chance that one might say yes.

Besides, researching agents and putting together portfolios took time and work. That kept the general sense of misery at bay and let me forget, for moments at a time, that Nora was gone and I'd have to see Len at church in two days. I knew what I had to do, just tough it out and be nice and friendly, but the very idea made me want to cry.

My heart was still rubbed raw, and two days wasn't enough time to get calluses built up. I considered going to another ward, but that felt like chickening out to me.

The cashier stuck the last stamp on the last envelope and rang up the total. I swiped my credit card, signed the receipt, thanked him, and went home. I reminded myself to keep on working. Just fill my time with painting.

When I got home I painted until I began to fall asleep in front of the easel. Only then did I go to sleep and when I got up the next morning, I went straight to the studio and carried on. I didn't eat meals, just snacked as I worked. The sun went up and then down again. I still wore my sweats and had my hair up in a bun.

The doorbell rang just as I was laying down the first strokes of a watercolor. I glanced at the clock and saw that it was seven. I wiped my hands, put on my slippers, and headed downstairs. When I opened the door, there was Len. My heart did a summersault, but I only let myself smile. Don't get your hopes up, I told myself.

"Hi."

"Yeah, hi." He wouldn't look at me. Not a good sign. He was probably just here to pick something up. "Um, look... you want to catch a movie or something?"

I flung away my years' old habit of never saying yes on the same night and nodded. "Sure. Let me get my shoes." I held open the door to let him in, but he stayed put.

Paint Me True

I dashed to the back door to get my shoes, put them on, grabbed my jacket and purse, shook out my hair from its bun, and headed out the front door. I had no makeup on. My face felt naked. At least I'd brushed my teeth and hair. Len was his usual, gentlemanly self. He held open the car door for me. I did my best to act casual. I wanted him to remember that we knew each other well, not feel like he was on a first date with a stranger.

On the drive over to the theater, though, he refused to look in my direction. I did my best to just sit and not seem fidgety. Silence didn't have to be awkward silence, after all. Besides, I had no idea what to say. Still, I was acutely aware of every one of the thirty minutes that passed on the drive. The theater wasn't that far from my house as the crow flew, but the traffic lights and intersections made it a slow journey.

The ticket line was like our first date all over again. We didn't talk to each other, just the cashier. Len wouldn't let me pay for my ticket or popcorn, but this time I felt like I was imposing. It took real effort to keep my head up and put one foot in front of the other as we went into the theater.

The movie seemed both interminable and over too soon, and I didn't really follow the plot. It was a cartoon with talking animals and I kept analyzing how they'd been anthropomorphized and what techniques had been used on the backgrounds. Len kept looking at me, though, but this time around I didn't think he was wondering why I was there. He was wondering why he was there.

Calm, I told myself. He'd already shut me down. I needed to not let myself get my hopes up just to be dashed again. Tonight he'd had a lapse, and he regretted it. The best thing for me to do was enjoy the popcorn and try not to think of my paints lying out back at home. I wasn't a fool for trying again, I kept telling myself. It could have turned out differently.

The important thing for me was to handle this like a grown up. I could curl up and cry about it later. As soon as the credits rolled, Len got up. I followed and busied myself with details like tucking my used napkins into my empty popcorn bag and getting into the short line at the garbage can. Len pulled out his phone and frowned at the screen.

"You get called back into work?" I asked.

"No, someone wants to know if I can do a blessing."

"Oh, okay. I can stay here, or whatever."

He looked up at me, meeting my eye for the first time that evening. "I'm not leaving you here at ten o'clock at night."

"Well, I don't mind. I can walk over to your house if that's better." It was only a block and a half away.

"You sure you're okay with that?"

"Uh-huh."

He considered that a moment, but I knew what his answer would be. Church duties came first with him. I wiped my hands on my scrunched napkins one last time before I dumped all my trash into the garbage can.

"Okay, this shouldn't take too long and I'm driving you. I can pick up Chris at the same time."

I nodded and followed him out of the theater.

He looked at me again. "Thanks."

I waved that away. He was being ridiculous.

Again he strode ahead to his car and opened the door for me. On the brief drive over I wondered if I'd be able to hold it together once he left me at his empty house. My ability to act like everything was okay in my world was starting to slip.

But I at least held it together as we drove to his house. Chris was stepping out the door, his eyes on his cellphone, his thumb working the keys for a text.

"Hey," Len called out, "I can go with you."

"Cool." He didn't look up.

I got out of the car and left the door open for Chris, who looked up at me and froze.

"Hi," I said.

He said nothing.

Paint Me True

"Um... is your door locked?" I pointed to the house.

"Yeah, sec." He unlocked it and handed me the keys.

"Thanks." I went inside, out of the chill air and into the stillness. The place always smelled like wood varnish. The kitchen was a mess as usual and beyond it was the living room, with one of the gaming consoles out on the floor, a game loaded and a list of saved games on the screen.

As the car pulled out of the driveway, its headlights stretching across the back wall, I cast about for a copy of scriptures or something to keep me busy. There weren't any books out in the front room. I sat down on the couch, knees together, like I was waiting to be called up for a difficult job interview. I tapped my toes and drummed my fingers on my knees.

I thought about trying to watch television, but I did not understand the six remote controls laid out on the coffee table. I didn't know how to turn off the gaming console, so I was just stuck staring at a screen that said "New Game" and "Load Saved Game". I wondered if it was the game I'd bought Len. I hadn't looked all that closely at the package because I didn't want to get caught holding it.

As the minutes crept past, I let myself stare at the "New Game" option. There was nothing else for me to do, unless I wanted to wash dishes, which I didn't. If I tried a new game and didn't mess with any of their saved games, I wouldn't disrupt anything.

I slid down onto the floor and picked up a controller. It was like a weapon designed by aliens. I hefted it then turned it over to look at the buttons. I figured out which one to press to start a new game, and much to my relief, I saw that it offered a tutorial on how to use the controls. I loaded that.

The screen popped up a diagram of how to hold the controller, which I copied. Now it felt more natural in my hand, its curve cupped in my palm and buttons and toggles at my fingertips. The next screen had me traveling down a hallway, the view bobbing as if I were running. When I obeyed the instructions to hit buttons and push toggles, different weapons would appear at the bottom of the screen and I'd see my character's hands arm them, by snapping a clip into a gun or yanking a pin out of a grenade or working the slide on a shotgun.

I had no idea how to shoot or throw a grenade. The game showed me, but I was terrible at it. I'd shoot a line of holes in the wall behind the bad guys and chuck grenades too wide, so that at best, they knocked the baddies over.

And then the tutorial was over. I was playing the game. Great, I thought. I was in another dark hallway. I pivoted around to see my options, but the door behind me was closed, so there was only one way to go. I made it three steps before a baddie jumped out and shot at me. I tried to shoot back but forgot to select a weapon, so I just saw my character's fists make punching motions while red splashes of blood spurted up from all the gunshot wounds I was getting. The little display of my body armor showed it was compromised. I finally managed to load a grenade and throw it, and for once I hit the target and got to watch dismembered limbs go flying as it detonated.

Gross.

O-kay, I thought. I advanced down the hall and armed myself with a gun. The next time a baddie came after me, I turned down a side hall and ran as fast as I could. More bad guys jumped out of doors and dropped from hatches above me. I just ran until all of my armor was red and then my healthbar went down, and then I died.

So much for that. I looked down at the controller in my hands and admired how quickly I'd gotten used to it. It was well designed. The game asked me if I wanted to try again. I did not, so I put the controller down, brushed my hands off against my sweatpants, and turned around to get up.

Len and Chris were standing behind the couch. I just about jumped out of my skin. "Oh, hi," I said. "That was fast."

"Um... no it wasn't," said Chris. "It's been forty minutes."

I looked at my watch and blinked. Forty minutes really had gone by, but how? I'd only done the tutorial and made one pathetic attempt to play the game. Now I understood how Len could do three hour marathons and not think it was excessive.

"Though, to be honest," said Len, "we've been standing here for the last ten minutes."

"Why, so you can laugh at me?"

"Hey, did you hear us laugh?" said Chris.

"I didn't hear you come in, so how do I know?" I got to my feet and folded my arms across my chest, daring them to mock me. I could take it.

Chris just chuckled and headed back to his room. Len smirked. "Did you have fun?"

"Yes, blowing people up and getting gunned down as I run for my life are how I'd choose to spend my time if I get the chance. I find it spiritually uplifting. Perfect way to spend hours and hours on the Sabbath."

"I don't normally get gunned down that fast," said Len.

"And you probably kill more people. Even better."

He chuckled at that. "Okay... fair enough."

I shook my head. "I wasn't actually trying to get you to stop gaming on Sundays-"

But Len had already stepped around the couch and knelt in front of the gaming console. As I watched, he popped out the game and put in another one. Plinky cartoon music played over the speakers and he tossed me the controller again. "See how you do with this one."

"Is this the one I got you?"

"No." He took the other controller and sat on the floor beside me.

"Did I get you the shooter one?"

"No." He laughed. "But they're very similar to each other, so I can see how you'd get them confused."

"I risked people's jobs to get you that game. I didn't stand around gazing at it. I wrapped it fast."

"Really, *really* fast. Before you could see the big dragon on the front."

"Yep."

He laughed again and hit some buttons on his controller.

This, I soon realized, was a racing game, only I didn't have the option of a racecar. Rather I was to choose from a bunch of vehicles that looked like they were made to sell ice cream and hot dogs on the street, but before I could make my choice, Len grabbed my controller and selected a little round pink car that looked like something Minnie Mouse would drive.

"Hey," I said.

He chose something that looked like a Hummer.

"Oh please."

"Get ready," he said.

Our cars were parked on the starting line and the lights were flashing from red to yellow to green. The road ahead was straight out of a cartoon. It lifted up off the ground and did loopty loops in the distance. As soon as the lights were green and we gunned our cars, a menagerie of fanciful animals broke loose in our path, some running, some wandering, some standing in the road. It wasn't easy to maneuver around them and I got taken out by a purple cow within seconds.

Len laughed at me.

I settled my grip on the controller, waited for my car to get put on the road again, and then I chased after him, swerving to avoid animals. Len, I saw, hit a button and jumped his car over them.

Well, that would've been nice to know. I followed suit and jumped over a blue dragon as I tried to catch up with him.

"Eat my dust," he said.

"Dream on." I was in sight of his car when we did the first loopty loop. The landscape spun around crazily as I kept my car in the middle of the road. Then a canyon opened up in front of me and I hit the button to jump. "Ha!" I said. I was closing in on his car.

"You won't be able to pass me," he said. He started to swerve back and forth.

I aimed straight for his car and hit the accelerator. The two vehicles collided with a crash and a gratifying puff of smoke, out of which bounced wheels and pieces of the car bodies.

"Hey!" he said. "What was that for?"

"For giving me a stupid pink car."

"Oh come on. It's the prettiest car."

"I want the Hummer." I reached for his controller.

"No way." He held it out of my reach.

"You scared of driving a pink car? You not secure enough in your manhood?"

"What?" He spluttered a laugh.

I made another grab for his controller and he stretched to keep it from me. His other arm went around my waist and I squirmed, assuming that was him trying to hold me back.

He kissed me.

I was so surprised that I dropped my controller. He dropped his and stroked my hair back from my cheek as he kissed me again. I shut my eyes, savoring the touch of his lips on mine. He leaned in for a third, but I pulled back. "If this is just you trying to win the game, you are the biggest jerk on the planet."

He laughed, but not as readily. "No," he said. His hand was still on my cheek.

I opened my eyes. "So, is this you just feeling confused, or is this me getting a second chance?" I had to have that answer before I'd surrender to another kiss.

Those pale blue eyes of his searched mine. The seconds ticked by.

He let out a sigh and leaned his forehead against mine. "I'm still not over you."

"Do you want to be?"

"I don't know." He buried his face in my hair.

"Well, decide, okay? Because I'm not over you and if you're going to go back and forth, I can't take it." I tried to get out of his embrace.

His arm tightened around me. "Please," he said. "I'm sorry. I did this all wrong. Yeah I want to try things again. Of course I do."

I stopped struggling. "Really?"

He nodded, his cheek brushing against mine. "I'm trying to believe that you're not just desperate to date the nearest loser-"

"You are not a loser."

His arm still held me tight, tight enough that I was starting to get a cramp in my side. "I love you," I whispered.

That made him relax. I settled myself more comfortably, stroked his hair and kissed the nape of his neck.

He inhaled a jerky breath, like a sob.

"I'm sorry," I told him. "I screwed up and I love you." I settled him against me and breathed in the musky scent of his skin. His shorter hair felt scratchy against my cheek. "I've missed you so much. You've got no idea."

Footsteps in the hallway let me know Chris had emerged again. I ignored them. He'd already seen me make a fool of myself trying to play a first person shooter, and that was infinitely worse than being seen holding the man I loved.

But Len lifted his head. "Get lost," he hollered.

"O*kay*." The footsteps retreated.

"Sorry," said Len.

I just shrugged and leaned in to kiss him. He slipped his hand in mine and he kissed my lips, only this kiss wasn't like his usual ones. It was deeper and went on far longer. When I broke it off to breathe, he moved on to my neck. "'Kay," I said. "This could get compromising."

He paused, his warm breath tickling across my throat. "Really?" There was a note of surprise in his voice.

"Um, yeah."

He let go of my hand and we just held each other.

Things weren't completely resolved with him on the drive home. He still glanced at me nervously, but I managed to catch his gaze and exchange a smile a couple of times. When he walked me to the door I took his hands in mine and stood on tiptoe for a kiss. "I'll see you tomorrow," I said.

"'Kay."

"Save me a seat?"

He chuckled. "Yeah, okay."

"And tell those other girls that if they don't keep their distance, I will scratch their faces."

"Be nice."

"Sorry. I love you." We kissed again and I went inside.

Ten minutes later, as I was washing my face, I got a text from him. "I love you, too." I slept with my phone under my pillow. It was like being eighteen all over again.

Thirty-Two

A New Beginning

  The next morning in church, I walked up to the front row and sat down next to Len. This time I didn't feel like I was eighteen all over again. I didn't gaze at him adoringly or bait him to put his arm around me so that the whole chapel would see he was mine. Couples like that got on my nerves and his. Rather than sit down like we'd had our first date last night, which in a way we had, I sat down like his longtime girlfriend, taking her customary seat. I didn't make eyes at him, just smiled and turned to dig out my scriptures. Nothing in my bearing dared other women to laugh at me, and wonder of wonders, no one did. No one even pointed. We got a lot of curious stares.

  Len leaned back in his seat and angled his body towards mine and I crossed my legs towards him. He had his smartphone in his hand and was tapping away at the screen with his fingertips, and I opened my scriptures and set them out on my knee.

  Occasionally I felt his gaze, like a warm hand laid against my skin. I'd look up and smile and watch his mouth twitch up at the corners in response. He still wasn't entirely comfortable, but months of problems didn't resolve in one evening. Over the course of the morning, I felt as much as saw him relax, notching down his stress like a rope being unwound a turn at a time.

A week later, he was asleep on my couch again, snoring, as a movie started up on the DVD player. I switched off the movie, rolled him onto his side, and when the snoring didn't stop, I tucked a blanket around his throat. That didn't work either, so I just resolved to ignore it and read next week's Sunday school lesson.

Though it seemed like his snores were getting louder. I did my best to focus. A particularly loud snort made me look up, and I caught him watching me with one eye, which he shut fast, but not fast enough.

Fine, I thought. Two could play this game. I got out my sketchbook and sketched my couch with a skinny hedgehog draped across it, its mouth open and eyes shut. Every time I sensed Len look at me, I turned further away.

I had my back to him when the snoring abruptly stopped and he snatched the sketchbook from me. "Hey!" I said.

"What is this?"

"It's a hodgehog."

"How is that different from a hedgehog?"

"I would think that's *obvious*."

He cracked up. His random sense of humor hadn't changed.

"Give it," I said.

He gave me a kiss instead.

Paint Me True

Later in the week, he had to work late. I tried not to pester him on chat too much, but it was so gratifying to type something and get a response immediately. I distracted myself with another doodle, this one of the hodgehog seated at a computer with a pencil behind its ear. For a background I drew an underground burrow that was a total wreck. The garbage can was overflowing with crumpled papers. There were dirty dishes on the desk and the floor. The hodgehog also had a half eaten burrito at its elbow. Once I'd finished off the shading, I scanned it and emailed it.

Hodgehog: Lol, what is this?
Edunmar: The hodgehog in its natural habitat.
Hodgehog: You think I'm a real slob, don't you?
Edunmar: Okay, hang on.

I got out another sheet of paper and sketched a female skinny hedgehog, sitting on the floor in a pile of papers, paint smudges all over her face and hands. The studio around her was packed with art supplies that looked like they'd collapse on her at any moment. I scanned that one and sent it.

Hodgehog: Cute.
Edunmar: The only way I keep my house clean is by not spending time in the rest of it.
Hodgehog: Your kitchen is clean.
Edunmar: And your console games are neatly organized.
Hodgehog: Touche- k, sorry need to go into the other room. Back in a few.

I felt lame, pestering him nonstop, but I couldn't peel myself away. I sketched another picture of the skinny girl hedgehog in front of her computer, her chin in her hands, pining. I set that aside, no point sending that one.

Hodgehog: All right.
Edunmar: What?
Hodgehog: I've got a comp day on Friday. You free?
Edunmar: Yes.
Hodgehog: You sure? Don't let me take up your work time.

I still hadn't told him about my inheritance and how I didn't really have to work anymore.

Edunmar: It's fine.
Hodgehog: Okay, I need to go work in one of the other offices. I'll talk to you later. Love you.
Edunmar: Love you too.

Five minutes later I sent him the cartoon of the pining hedgehog.

"So," said Len on Friday as he lounged on his couch, "guys in my office are looking up hedgehog comics online."

I was sitting on the floor, sketching a picture of the hodgehog with legions of female hedgehogs making eyes at him at church - in an underground burrow of course. I looked up. "Why?"

"Because they don't believe me when I say the pictures on the wall are by my girlfriend."

"You have them on your wall?"

"Yeah, of course I do."

My face flushed hot. "They must think I'm a stalker or something." I looked down at the sketch I was doing.

"No, they don't believe that you just do that, with pen and pencil. Or that someone that talented would be giving me free art."

I shaded in the back of the burrow. "I can do real art. I mean, if you ever want a painting or anything."

"That is real art. I already have a couple of your prints. I just haven't put them up because I'm a sloppy hodgehog."

"Don't buy those. I can give them to you for free."

He shook his head. "Of course I bought them. Don't be stupid."

I tore the finished sketch out of my sketchbook and handed it to him. "Sorry, I should move on to another theme, shouldn't I?"

"I assumed you were being ironic."

"No. I guess this is just how I deal with life, by drawing stuff. Obsessively."

Len slid off the couch to sit next to me on the floor. He traced my cheekbone with his thumb. "Works for me."

I turned to a clean page and began to draw two skinny hedgehogs flying a kite. Once Len caught on to what it was, he laughed. "Worst. Date. Ever."

"I dunno. It was kinda funny."

"Well, that's what I thought, but I got the impression you felt differently." He smirked at me.

I drew a crooked, ugly smiley face on the kite.

He cracked up.

A couple of weeks later as we walked back to his house after a matinee, he handed me a folded up piece of paper. I gave him a questioning look and unfolded it. It was a drawing of two stick figures, one on bended knee in front of the other. "This what I think it is?" I asked.

"So, I do have reservations at the steakhouse tonight, but yeah. I was afraid I'd lose my nerve."

"Really? You're really asking me?"

"I am, yeah. The ring's at my house."

"Really?!"

He stopped walking. "Yeah. Is that a yes?"

"Yes!"

"It's not a great ring. Just a cheap one until you pick out one you like better. I put money aside for a real one... okay, now what's wrong?"

I'd winced. "I kind of forgot to tell you something."

"What's that?"

I took the picture and drew a dollar bill in my stick figure's hand. On it I wrote the amount of my inheritance and handed the picture back to him.

He blanched. "What?"

"I kind of inherited some money."

"This a joke?"

"No."

"Oh..."

"I love you."

"You're *serious*?"

"Yeah. You can get that new Xbox you've been wanting." I took the paper back from him, folded it, and stuck it in my shirt. "I'm keeping this."

He didn't even protest or try to take it back, just looked shell-shocked all the way home.

Epilogue

"Hello?" I answered my cellphone as Carrie loaded my dress into the car and my dad pulled out an envelope with my temple recommend and live ordinance recommend in it.

"Hello, is this Eliza Dunmar?"

"Yes." For the next two hours, I added in my mind.

"This is Jessica Finlay. I'm an agent?"

"Yes, right."

"I've got your portfolio here and I love it. I'd like to offer you representation."

"Really? That's great!"

"I'm sure you have questions."

"I should but... I'm kinda... yeah. Overwhelmed. My wedding is in two hours."

"Oh?" She laughed. "Why don't you call me back in a few weeks then? You have my number?"

"Yes."

"Congratulations."

"Thank you!"

After she hung up I copied her number out of my phone onto the back of the card Colin had sent me that said,

"Congratulations for getting married you crazy religious weirdo."

My parents both waited in the car for me, so I dashed out the door to join them.

We arrived at the temple as Len was getting out of his car and he waved to me as Carrie pulled around into a parking space.

"Eliza, can I have a moment?" my dad asked.

Carrie got out of the car and shut the door.

I turned to him and leaned my chin on the back of the front seat. "Yeah?"

"I'm not gonna make it through this without crying," he said.

"Don't you start."

"Honey, you and I have lost a lot of people in our lives."

I nodded.

"And I know losing your mother is devastating, but I think it's even worse to lose a child."

Again, I nodded.

"You have no idea how many nightmares I've had about losing you."

"Me?"

"Of course, you're the only daughter I have left." He reached over the back of the seat and patted my knee. "I'll try to hold it together, here-"

"Dad, as rough as it is to lose my mother, I can't imagine losing a child. Or two children."

"Yeah." He nodded curtly.

And there was a chance it might happen to me. Even on this, one of the happiest days of my life, the shadow of the family curse cast its usual pall.

He patted my knee again. "I really like the guy you chose. He's one in a million."

"I know."

"*Almost* good enough for you." He winked and then turned to get out.

I took my wedding dress down from the hook and slung it over my shoulder as I clambered out my door. Len came to take it from me and kissed my forehead. "You sure about this?" he asked.

"No backing out now," I warned him.

He grinned. We walked hand in hand to the door of the temple, where Keeley, Hattie, and Louisa (who could not be kept out of anything) all stood waiting. They gathered around with excited shrieks and hugs and Louisa snatched the dress from Len. Keeley flashed me a knowing smile and we both hunched our shoulders with silent laughter.

Len and I exchanged one last grin before stepping into the temple, and the rest of eternity together.

Author's Note

Thanks so much for reading. My next book has the working title, *Castles on the Sand,* and will be out in late summer, 2012. For other upcoming book releases or more information about me, please visit my website at www.emtippetts.com.

If you enjoyed this book, please consider posting a review on Amazon or Barnes and Noble. A book's fate depends entirely on its ratings.

Other books by me are:

Time and Eternity
Someone Else's Fairytale (a preview of which is at the end of this book)

Each is a stand alone and not part of a series.

I have also sold several science fiction and fantasy short stories under the name, Emily Mah. To get information on them and to find out more about that side of me, please visit www.emilymah.com.

Acknowledgments

I've been blessed with a lot of supportive friends in my life. First thanks always goes to Char Peery, who reads everything I write, and I mean everything. Multiple times even. Other readers include: Michael Bateman (an author and EMT who helped with the medical details - all mistakes are my own entirely), Eliza Nevin (who edited a much earlier version of this manuscript years ago, when it was under contract with Covenant Communications), Kate Seagrave (fellow Oxford graduate and real, live British person - not to mention a lifelong friend), and Melanie Goldmund (who found a typo missed by all others and was kind enough to send me a glowingly supportive email the morning before I began transferring this book into Kindle format). The cover was designed by the multitalented Jenn Reese of Tiger Bright Studios (check out her new books coming out next year from Candlewick). People who helped me choose which cover include: Melinda Snodgrass, Victor Milan, Terry England, Ian Tregillis, S.M. Stirling, Mary Mah, Polly Tucknott, and Stephanie Spier. Thanks guys, for everything.

Excerpt from:

A NOVEL

E.M. TIPPETTS

One

That Day

I stepped out our front door into the frigid, Albuquerque night. The crisp air, tinged with the scent of woodsmoke, flushed through my lungs, and the stars winked distantly in the deep cobalt sky. It was three thirty a.m., way too early to be awake.

A truck turned the corner and rumbled its way over to our house. I watched it parallel park, then go silent as the lights switched off. The driver's side door opened, and my best friend, Matthew, stepped down. His cowboy boots thudded against the asphalt, then crunched across the gravel that covered our front yard. "Howdy," he said.

I stifled a laugh. He was the walking stereotype of a Texan, with his muscular build, tight jeans, and flannel shirt. His hazel eyes were smiling, though. Like me, he was a senior at UNM, and he was a source of sanity, something I needed to counterbalance my housemate, Lori, who just then skipped out the front door, jumped down onto the gravel, and struck an action pose, both hands up, ready to karate chop whatever imaginary adversary might be lurking under the giant cottonwood that dominated our front yard. She wasn't wearing any nylons with her skirt.

"Aren't you cold?" Matthew asked.

"Yep, but I don't think this is a cold weather scene we're in."

"We're extras," I said, for what felt like the millionth time. "Nobody's going to notice what we're wearing."

"How did she talk you into this?" Matthew asked me. The three of us started towards campus, on foot. We'd been told not to drive because there was limited parking.

"I don't know," I said.

"Come on, just picture it." Lori waved a hand, setting the scene "-we're on the set, and Jason Vanderholt walks by."

I rolled my eyes.

"I tell him how hot he was in the *New Light* movies-"

"Because I'm sure he never hears that," I said. The *New Light* franchise was a trilogy of gladiator movies that I'd managed to avoid seeing, despite the fact that Jason Vanderholt's long haired, shirtless figure had been plastered on every vertical surface for three years straight while they came out.

"Sarcasm," chided Matthew.

"You should ask him why his character was named 'sword'," I said.

"Gladius," Lori corrected me.

"Right. That's Latin for, 'sword'."

"It was his *nick*name. But you're ruining my narrative here."

We stepped off the curb to cross the street. Given the hour, there was no traffic, though in the still night air, we could hear voices of other groups who, like us, were headed towards campus on foot.

"He stops to talk to us," said Lori.

"Then what?" said Matthew.

"That's it. He stops to talk to us."

"That's it?"

"A girl can dream."

"Apparently not. That the best you can do?"

"Shut up okay?" Lori stuck her tongue out at him. "I'm a math major."

"At least come up with something to talk to him about."

"Ooooh! You know what? I should totally ask him if he remembers Vicki Baca! Remember, she said she had a locker next to him in high school?"

Aside from being the star of the multi-bazillion dollar *New Light* franchise, Vanderholt was also a local, or he had been before he'd hit it big with a show on the Disney Channel back in his teens. I cleared my throat. "I know about thirty people who claim to have had the locker next to him in high school, which makes me wonder how they do the lockers at La Cueva."

"I so hope we get to meeeeeet him." Lori turned a pirouette.

Matthew shook his head. "You're gonna catch a cold."

I sneaked in a smile the next time he glanced my way. He chuckled, his shoulders moving silently.

The film set was barely controlled chaos. "Just line up here!" a woman was shouting when we walked up. "We're still getting the catering area set up for you. Line up here!" She gestured at the walkway that led up to the UNM anthropology building, a wide strip of concrete that bisected the lawn. The pre-dawn light washed the color out of everything, making the world look like a faded photograph. The rounded, stucco walls of the building seemed old and historic.

Matthew, Lori and I found a place in line and stood with our paper cups of hot chocolate that we'd bought from The Frontier on the way. I sidled up to Matthew. "Okay," I said, "I get why Lori's doing this. Why are you?" I noticed that he'd combed his light brown curls with water, and a couple of them had frozen.

He smiled. "It's once in a lifetime, you know?"

"Don't tell me you're a closet Jason Vanderholt fan?"

"Sarcasm?"

"Oh, and you were being serious just now?"

"Ohmi*gosh!*" Lori shrieked so loud that I had to cover my ears. Not easy with a cup of hot chocolate in one hand.

"Lor-" I said.

But I was cut off by more shrieking up and down the line. I turned and saw that the girls on the other side of us had collapsed. One of them sobbed. The other just shook. "I love you!" someone shouted.

Lori dropped to her knees.

"Uh," said Matthew. He knelt down next to her. "You all right?"

Tears streamed down her cheeks and she shook like a leaf in a windstorm.

"Yes, hi," said a deep, male voice behind me. "Hello. Yep, sure. How do you spell that?"

"Ohmi*gosh!*" shrieked Lori again.

"You really gotta stop that," said Matthew.

I turned around, and found myself face to face with Jason

Vanderholt. He was just like his publicity shots, blue eyes, tanned skin, toned physique. He looked at me, one eyebrow slightly raised. Around him were several guys with cellphones out. An entourage.

"Yeah, hi," I said.

"Hey. How are you?" He was wearing a t-shirt and holding a paper cup in one hand, which he raised to his lips. I watched him shake something into his mouth, which he then crunched between his teeth. "It's ice," he said, with his mouth full.

The sun wasn't up yet and it felt like we were standing in a giant refrigerator. This guy was crazier than Lori.

He gave me a wry smile. "You want some?"

"Aren't you cold?"

"Freezing. Gotta do this between scenes so my breath doesn't steam when I say lines. See?" He was right. His breath did not steam as he spoke.

"Fascinating," I said.

He chuckled. "You look really familiar."

"Never met you in my life."

"What's your name?"

"Chloe."

"Chloe what?"

"Winters."

His eyes popped wide with recognition. "Like Chris and Beth! Okay, okay, now I know why I recognize you. You're... what? Their cousin? You gotta be related."

My pulse edged up a notch and I wrapped my jacket more tightly around myself, as if its insulated fabric were an invisibility cloak. "You know Chris Winters?"

"Heck yeah. He was in my class in high school. His dad was my dentist."

"He was?" My pulse edged up another notch. I felt stupid. I'd gotten after so many other people for making up tenuous connections to this guy that I'd overlooked the fact that he really was from town. Had grown up here and known people.

"Yeah. When I was a kid... Something wrong?"

"No." I said it too fast. "No, it's just, I don't really know him, his family. I'm not a close relative."

"Really? But you look so much like Beth."

I shrugged. "I'll take your word for it."

"But-"

One of his team of guys put a hand on his arm and said something into his ear. "Okay," he replied. "Chloe, right?"

I nodded.

He held out a hand. "Jason. Vanderholt."

"Yeah, I know."

He grinned as if that was a clever, witty reply. We shook. His hand was like ice, his skin dry. I let go and he moved on down the line.

As soon as he turned his back, I sank down to the ground and gulped the rest of my hot chocolate, which was now almost cold. Lori stared at me with wide eyes. "He knows you?"

"No."

"Who's Chris Winters?" said Matthew.

I looked at him, then at Lori, then at him again. "I don't want to talk about it. I'm sorry. My family's a little messed up and-"

"Say no more," said Matthew.

"Thanks."

"Just, tell me you didn't fall for that Mr. Charming act he pulled?" He nodded in the direction of the actor's retreating figure.

"Was he charming? I guess he knows how to work a crowd."

Lori cursed. "I didn't get his autograph! Ohmigosh! I can't believe it."

"What do you want his autograph for?" said Matthew. "What would you get him to sign anyway?"

"He coulda signed this." She held up her cup. "And what do you mean? It'd be a souvenir."

"It'd be a dirty cup with writing on it."

I loved how literal Matthew was.

"What?" Lori snapped.

But by now the line was moving. The woman who'd yelled at us to line up, was now yelling at us to move into the anthropology building. "We've got food set out for you in the first room on the left," she announced.

Lori pulled out her compact and checked her makeup.

I drained the last dregs of my hot chocolate and tossed the cup into the nearest trash can.

This is what I did for my big film debut. I stood around in

short sleeves at five in the morning with a bunch of other people next to the anthropology building. And I did that for over an hour. Every little while someone would shout, "Quiet on the set!" and several minutes later, "Cut!"

We could start talking after every "Cut!" and at least they didn't make us chew ice. Goosebumps stood out all along my arms and I wished I hadn't had my hair cut the week before. I could've used more warmth on the back of my neck.

The camera and crew were a good thirty yards away, as were the actors in the scene. I wasn't near the front of the crowd, so I couldn't really see what the actors were doing, or who they even were. Besides Jason Vanderholt, the film starred Corey Cassidy, a blond, former model turned actress. Supposedly the two were a hot couple, involved in real life. Lori had told me this. I didn't read tabloids.

"I really feel like I'm growing, artistically," I said to Matthew.

He smirked at me. "Working on your irony?"

"How do you know I'm not serious?"

"This is so cool," said Lori.

"If you say so," I said.

"Quiet on the set!"

I looked over at Matthew again, who was smiling down at me. He didn't look cold. He'd had the foresight to wear long sleeves.

"Cut. That's a wrap!" someone shouted.

"Okay, okay, okay!" yelled the woman who'd been herding us all morning. "Everyone I've asked to stay, please stay. The rest of you are free to go."

I tromped with the rest of the crowd back inside. "That was really glamorous," I said. I glanced at my watch. It wasn't even seven yet.

Standing at the doorway of the catering area was a guy with spiky blond hair and all dark clothing. At the sight of me he said, "Chloe Winters?"

"Yeah."

"Come with me."

I glanced around. The yelling woman had made it crystal clear that we weren't allowed to wander.

"It's okay," the guy said. "Just come with me."

Lori and Matthew and I exchanged glances. Matthew

frowned at the guy, but didn't say anything.

I stepped away from the crowd and followed Mr. Spiky Blond Hair back out of the building. "I'm Dave," he said.

"Hi."

"So did you have fun this morning?"

"Sure."

"You been an extra before?"

"Nope."

"Dave!" Someone called out.

We both turned, to see a guy standing at the far corner of the building, but Dave pointed at me and the guy put up both hands and turned away, as if amused. "He need you?" I asked.

"No, it's fine. Come on."

We cut across the lawn in the direction of the parking lot, where row upon row of trailers were parked. The sun was just over the horizon, washing the campus in pale, gold light. The stucco walls of all the surrounding buildings glowed as if lit from inside.

"It is a pretty town," Dave agreed. He'd seen my wistful gaze.

Another woman in a headset stepped out from between the trailers, saw me and Dave, and smirked, as if to herself. When she caught me looking at her, she shook her head and kept walking.

Dave and I stepped into the shadow of the trailers and walked around the first one to the door. "Go on in," he said.

I looked askance at him.

"It's fine." He pulled it open.

I stepped up the stairs and inside, seated on a couch with his feet up, was Jason Vanderholt, reading a magazine. "Hey," he said. "Come on in."

I looked around again. He'd just summoned me here? Alone? Dave hadn't come in with me and I had the feeling he'd shut the door behind me once I took another step forward. The amused looks from the other crew now took on a new context.

"No thanks," I said. I turned to leave.

But a crowd of men cut off my path and boxed me in by the stairs. It was Vanderholt's entourage from this morning. They made a wall of black t-shirts and muscle that stood between me and freedom. "Let me go, please," I said. I tried to elbow through, but one of them grabbed my arm in a grip like a vise.

Someone Else's Fairytale
is available now in ebook and print format
through Amazon.

Made in the USA
Charleston, SC
29 March 2012